Sin Killer

Also by Larry McMurtry
in Large Print:

Texasville
Duane's Depressed
Comanche Moon
Walter Benjamin at the Dairy Queen
The Last Picture Show
Crazy Horse
Boone's Lick
Roads

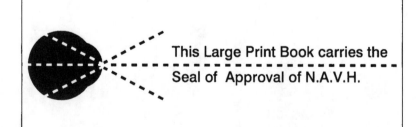

This Large Print Book carries the
Seal of Approval of N.A.V.H.

LARRY MCMURTRY

Sin Killer

The Berrybender Narratives, Book 1

Published in 2002 by arrangement with Simon & Schuster, Inc.

Wheeler Large Print Hardcover Series.

The text of this Large Print edition is unabridged.
Other aspects of the book may vary from the original edition.

Set in 16 pt. Plantin by Al Chase.

Printed in the United States on permanent paper.

Library of Congress Cataloging-in-Publication Data

McMurtry, Larry.
    Sin killer / Larry McMurtry.
        p. cm. — (The Berrybender narratives ; bk. 1)
    ISBN 1-58724-301-6 (lg. print : hc : alk. paper)
    1. British — West (U.S.) — Fiction.   2. Eccentrics and eccentricities — Fiction.   3. Missouri River Valley —Fiction.
    4. Women immigrants — Fiction.   5. Young women — Fiction.
    6. Large type books.   I. Title.
    PS3563.A319 S56 2002
    813'.54—dc21   2002068977

The Berrybender Narratives *are dedicated to the secondhand booksellers of the Western world, who have done so much, over a fifty-year stretch, to help me to an education.*

The Berrybender Narratives are to be a tetralogy, or four-decker, in which we follow the adventures of a great English sporting family, the Berrybenders, as they make their way through the American West, in the years 1832–36. The four novels which make up the tetralogy are set on or beside the four great rivers along which the Berrybenders travel, these being the Missouri, the Yellowstone, the Rio Grande, and the Brazos.

Various people who had lives in history wander through these fictions — their fates in this story are entirely invented.

Contents

Characters

Berrybenders
Lord Albany Berrybender
Lady Constance Berrybender
Tasmin
Bess (Buffum)
Bobbety
Mary
Brother Seven
Sister Ten (*later,* Kate)

Tintamarre, *Tasmin's staghound*
Prince Talleyrand, *parrot*

Staff
Gladwyn, *valet, gun bearer*
Fraulein Pfretzskaner, *tutor*
Master Jeremy Thaw, *tutor*
Mademoiselle Pellenc, femme de chambre
Cook
Eliza, *kitchen maid*
Millicent, *laundress*
Señor Yanez, *gunsmith*
Signor Claricia, *carriage maker*
Venetia Kennet, *cellist*
Old Gorska, *hunter*
Gorska Minor, *his son*
Piet Van Wely, *naturalist*
Holger Sten, *painter*

Tim, *stable boy*

Captain George Aitken
Charlie Hodges, *boatman*
Mery-Michaud, engagé
George Catlin, *American painter*
Toussaint Charbonneau, *interpreter-guide*
Coal, *Charbonneau's Hidatsa wife*

Jim Snow (The Raven Brave; Sin Killer)
Dan Drew, *prairie hunter*
Maelgwyn Evans, *trapper, Knife River*
Master Tobias Stiles, *deceased*
Father Geoffrin, *Jesuit*

Indians
Big White, *Mandan*
The Hairy Horn, *Oglala Sioux*
Blue Thunder, *Piegan Blackfoot*
Nemba, *Oto*
Pit-ta-sa, *Teton Sioux*
Blue Blanket, *Teton Sioux*
Neighing Horses, *Teton Sioux*
White Hawk, *Sans Arc*
Three Geese, *Sans Arc*
Grasshopper, *Sans Arc*
Cat Head, *Sans Arc*
Big Stealer, *Sans Arc*
Little Stealer, *Sans Arc*
Step Toe, *Mandan*
Rabbit Skin, *Mandan*
Draga, *Aleut-Russian*

The Bad Eye, *Gros Ventre*

French
Georges Guillaume, *trader*
Simon Le Page, *Hudson's Bay Company agent*
Malboeuf, *his assistant*

John Skraeling, *trader*
Malgres, *Mexican/Apache*

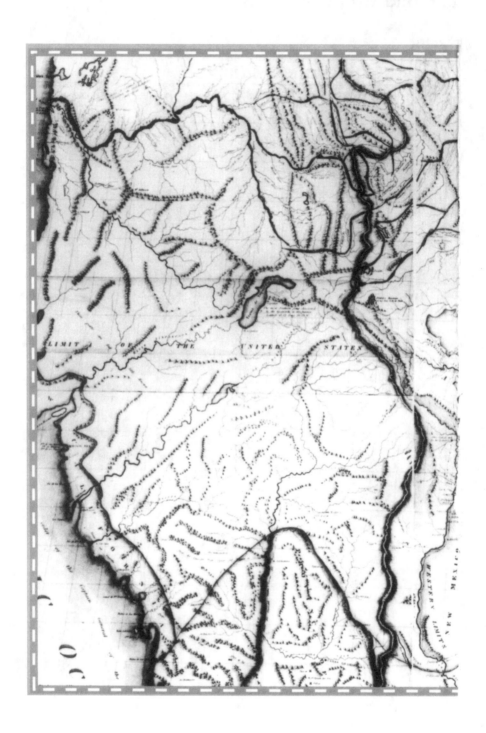

14

I ate between battles, I slept among murderers, I was careless in loving and I looked upon nature without patience. Thus the time passed which was given me on earth.

BRECHT

1

In the darkness beyond the great Missouri's shore . . .

In the darkness beyond the great Missouri's shore
at last lay the West, toward which Tasmin and her
family, the numerous Berrybenders, had so long
been tending. The Kaw, an unimpressive stream,
had been passed that afternoon — Tasmin,
Bobbety, Bess, and Mary had come ashore in the
pirogue to see the prairies that were said to stretch
west for a thousand miles; but in fact they could
hardly see anything, having arrived just at dusk.
The stars were coming out — bright, high stars
that didn't light the emptiness much, as a full
moon might have done. Bess, called Buffum by
the family, insisted that she had heard a buffalo
cough, while Bobbety claimed to have seen a great
fish leap at dusk, some great fish of the Missouri.
The three older Berrybenders tramped for a time
along the muddy shore, trailed, as usual, by the
sinister and uncompromising Mary, aged twelve,
whom none of them had invited on the tour. In
the last light they all stared at the gray grass and
the brown slosh of water; but the great fish of the
Missouri did not leap again. Disappointed, the
agile Bobbety at once caught a slimy green frog,
which he foolishly tried to force down Mary's

dress, the predictable result of his actions being that the frog squirmed away while Mary, never one to be trifled with, bit Bobbety's forefinger to the bone, causing him to blubber loudly, to Buffum's great annoyance and Tasmin's quiet contempt. Though Bobbety attempted to give his sister a sharp slap, Mary, like the frog, squirmed away and, for a time, was seen no more.

"It is said that there are no schools anywhere in the American West, in this year of our Lord 1832," Bess declaimed, in her characteristically pompous way. The three of them were attempting to row the pirogue back to the big boat, but in fact their small craft was solidly grounded on the Missouri mud. Bobbety, muttering about lockjaw and gangrene, dropped the only paddle, which floated away.

"Do get it, Tasmin . . . I'm bleeding . . . I fear the piranhas will inevitably attack," Bobbety whined; his knowledge of natural history was of the slightest. Tasmin might readily have given him a succinct lecture on the normally benign nature of the piranha, in any case a fish of the Amazon, not the Missouri, but she decided to postpone the lecture and catch the paddle, a thing soon accomplished, the Missouri being distressingly shallow at that point of its long drainage. Tasmin got wet only to her knees.

In her large family, the ancient, multifarious Berrybenders, Tasmin was invariably the one who recovered paddles, righted boats, posted letters, bound up wounds, corrected lessons, dried tears, cuffed the tardy, reproved the wicked, and lectured the ignorant, study having been her passion from her earliest days.

Far out in the center of the broad stream, the steamer *Rocky Mount* seemed to be as immovable as their humble pirogue — mired, perhaps, like themselves, in the clinging Missouri mud. Sounds of the evening's carouse were just then wafting across the waves.

2

Occasionally she caught a note of Haydn . . .

"No schools at all, how liberating!" Bess repeated in her exasperating way; she seemed not to have considered that even if Oxford itself had been transported to the banks of the Kaw, their father, Lord Albany Berrybender, would never have spent a cent to educate any of his girls.

"Yes, that is why it has been necessary to bring Fraulein Pfretzskaner and Master Jeremy Thaw, to tutor you and Bobbety and Mary and, of course, our brother Seven and our sister Ten," Tasmin said.

There were, in the Berrybenders' great house in Northamptonshire, a block of offspring known collectively as the Ten, all born during a period when Lord Berrybender decided he preferred numbering to naming — the latter required a degree of attention he was ever more reluctant to grant, where his offspring were concerned. Only two of the Ten had been allowed to come to America: the boy Seven, possessed of a cleft palate but otherwise physically unobjectionable, and the girl Ten, a wild brat so clever at hiding herself under tables and in closets that she could seldom be easily located — not that

20

anyone had reason to seek her with any frequency.

Mary Berrybender, born just before the onslaught of the Ten, remained, as she had begun, sui generis, neither one of the older children nor one of the Ten. No less an expert than Piet Van Wely, the Dutch botanist, whose duties, never well defined, required him to deal with whatever flora or fauna the company might encounter, had been the first to remark on the fact that Mary fit no system and conformed to no category, being quite clearly in possession of special powers.

"She can sniff out roots, edible roots, Jerusalem artichokes, tubers, onions," Piet confided to Tasmin, not long after they left Saint Louis. "She has already sniffed out a small edible potato quite unknown to science. Should we find ourselves in a famine the little one can be quite useful, if she cares to be."

That, in Tasmin's view, was a considerable "if," Mary having so far not evinced even a trace of sentiment for any member of the household, though, to be fair, she was rather fond of Tintamarre, Tasmin's great red staghound, who had bounded off a bit earlier and now came splashing back to the pirogue, where the affectionate beast proceeded to lick Tasmin's face.

Fraulein Pfretzskaner and Master Jeremy Thaw (the tutors), Señor Yanez (the gunsmith), Signor Claricia (the carriage maker), Holger Sten (the painter, a dank Dane), the aforementioned Piet Van Wely (the botanist), Old Gorska (their hunter, assisted by Gorska Minor, his son), Mademoiselle Pellenc (the *femme de chambre*), Miss Venetia Kennet (singer, cellist, and, at present, Lord Berrybender's acknowledged mistress), Gladwyn (the Welsh valet, butler, and gun bearer), Tim (the stable boy), and, of course, Cook and her two helpers, Millicent (the laundress) and Eliza (the kitchen girl), comprised only a small part of the eventual Berrybender entourage; it was, though, the part with whom the Berrybenders sailed from Portsmouth to Baltimore, where, after a rather lengthy stay on what had once been Lord Baltimore's plantation, they made their way by wagon and carriage over the deplorably ill-kept roads to Pittsburgh, where they acquired their various boats and set forth down the placid Ohio.

At Saint Louis the famous Captain William Clark himself, then commissioner of Indian Affairs, lent them his interpreter, Monsieur Toussaint Charbonneau, a man said to be fluent in the languages of the many native tribes they expected to meet. Captain Clark also helped them secure the services of a dozen or so *engagés*, small, smelly Frenchmen from the northlands, who were to help with the boats. But even Captain Clark's vigilance on their behalf could not prevent the last-minute arrival of the painter George Catlin, a balding, finical man of — in Tasmin's opinion — a decidedly cranky nature;

Mr. Catlin leapt aboard just as the steamer, virtually surrounded by the Berrybenders' flotilla of pirogues and keelboats, set forth from the village of Saint Charles, a small community but a few miles from the confluence of the Missouri with the Mississippi.

Mr. Catlin, who could hardly be called reticent, at once made plain his feeling about the Missouri, the river that was to carry them some two thousand miles into the mysterious reaches of the West.

"I call it the river Sticks," he said, emitting his characteristic dry, nervous cackle, "for as you will soon learn it is filled along much of its length with dead trees, many of them hidden just beneath the surface.

"I'm punning on 'Styx'," he added, assuming, incorrectly, that none of the Berrybenders would know their Homer. "That's the river the dead must cross to get to Hades . . . and many of us *will* be dead, unless we're exceptionally lucky."

"Oh, do hush about the dead, sir!" Lady Constance Berrybender pleaded — she had turned quite white beneath her copious rouge. Lady Constance had never been fond of the subject of death. Fortunately her husband, Lord Albany Berrybender, was just sober enough to draw Mr. Catlin off the unwelcome problem of mortality by a timely mention of Mr. John James Audubon, the bird painter, whom the Berrybenders had recently encountered in Baltimore.

"Why, Lord Berrybender, I've seen my share

of birds and they do *not* look like that man's birds," Mr. Catlin protested, at once forgetting his bias against the Missouri River. "I fear the fellow's altogether a humbug — I believe he's a Creole of some kind — don't know what the fellow's thinking, drawing birds that don't look at all like the birds *I* see — and I *do* see birds."

John James Audubon, in Tasmin's view, had seemed queerly birdlike himself, a reflection that did not help her much as she caught the floating paddle and returned to the pirogue, in hope of rowing it out to the steamer *Rocky Mount*. The pirogue was still quite firmly settled into the Missouri mud, though in fact it was no worse off than the steamer, grounded for the night on what the river men called a riffle, or sandbar. Mr. Catlin, though mildly ridiculous, had not been wrong to call the Missouri a plain of mud. The Berrybender family, with all its get and chattels, was, for the moment, stalled.

"What shall we do, Tasmin?" Bobbety asked, as usual referring all questions of procedure to his older sister.

"Let's examine the matter from the point of view of logic," Tasmin said. Her beloved mama and papa — Lord and Lady Berrybender, that is to say — were, of all the great race of human beings, the least likely to accept the severities of logic. Whim alone was their lodestar and their guide — whim it was that caused them to pack up and leave their great house in Northamptonshire; whim had brought them through America to their present resting place on a sandbar in the Missouri River — and only so that Lord Berrybender could shoot different animals from those he shot at home.

"This pirogue won't move, but our legs will," Tasmin pointed out.

She was going to suggest that they wade back to the ship and join the evening's carouse when little Mary walked out of the dusk holding an immense, vicious turtle above her head, a creature half at least her own weight, which she promptly flung amidst them, into the pirogue — no boat was ever emptied of its human occupants more quickly. Tintamarre, Tasmin's gallant hound, set up a violent braying and attempted a lunge or two at the turtle, of course to little avail. The Berrybenders were in the water, and the turtle was in the boat.

"It's entirely your fault, Bobbety," Buffum said. "Why *will* boys attempt to thrust frogs down little girls' dresses?"

Bobbety made no reply — he was sucking his bitten finger, so that no drop of his noble blood would drip into the Missouri to tempt the piranhas from their watery homes.

There seemed nothing for it but to swim back to the steamer, leaving the outraged turtle in possession of the pirogue. The water proved so shallow that no swimming was required, though Mary, perhaps amphibian by nature, dove and bobbed like a dolphin. Tintamarre floundered off after a mud hen, which eluded him.

The fact that the four of them, muddy as muskrats, arrived in the midst of dinner and rushed to their seats at the great groaning table aroused no comment at all; the group, as usual, was going at one another hammer and tongs: Lord Berrybender was profane with Gladwyn, who had dribbled the claret; Master Jeremy Thaw, entirely overcome with drink, was slumped amid the salads, snoring loudly; Mr. George Catlin was attempting to make it up with Lady Constance by explaining the Hindu doctrine of reincarnation. The fat Fraulein Pfretzskaner and the skinny Mademoiselle Pellenc were shrieking at each other: the two despised everything that their respective nations stood for. The dank Dane, Holger Sten, annoyed to find that another painter had presented himself on board, was staring daggers at Mr. Catlin, while the two Mediterraneans, Señor Yanez and Signor Claricia, having drunk far too much of Lord Berrybender's excellent claret, were directing looks of frank concupiscence at Miss Venetia Kennet, who sat with her cello at the ready, waiting for the din to subside before favoring the group with a little Haydn. Piet Van Wely, aroused by Mademoiselle Pellenc's fiery rages, puffed rapidly at his foul pipe; and of course, there was Lady Berrybender's ancient, raggedy parrot, Prince Talleyrand, who was allowed the freedom of the table and was liable to pluck tidbits virtually off the tongues of inattentive diners.

Lady Berrybender's brow was furrowed, always a sign of intense and unaccustomed mental effort.

"I don't think I should wish to come back as an eel, if I must come back at all," she was saying, rather querulously. Late in the day Lady Constance was apt to grow careless with her dress; one of her great dugs was at the moment almost fully exposed, a fact not lost on the Mediterraneans, or even the normally monkish Holger Sten.

"Madam, the eel is only one of many possibilities reincarnation offers," Mr. Catlin said, rather stiffly.

"I will endeavor to come back as a mosquito and bite Mary and give her malaria and cause her to foam at the mouth," Bobbety announced, failing, as he often did, to correctly match his symptoms with his disease.

Tasmin had never lacked appetite. The goose was excellent — Cook had even been rather clever with some sweetbreads. Delicacy was the last thing wanted at the Berrybender table; Tasmin shoved, grabbed, elbowed, ate her fill, and then got up and left. A restlessness seized her — though she had nothing much against Venetia Kennet, she felt like avoiding Haydn for once and so went out on the upper deck, to take the rather humid air.

Below her on the underdeck was the rabble who would be expected to do most of the work on the Berrybenders' grand expedition: the smelly *engagés* in their greasy pants; Tim, the randy stable boy; Old Gorska and Gorska Minor, the former quite drunk; the shambling Monsieur Charbonneau, taller than the *engagés* but no less smelly; and a few scowling boatmen, all of them swabbing up pork gravy and hominy, belching, expectorating, breaking wind.

Though Tasmin had been raised amid a mob, and was now traveling with a mob, her nature, her spirit, was solitary. She possessed, of course, a level of social assurance appropriate to a young woman of her station, but she had always liked her own company best. Walking out after dinner, she was seized by such a powerful inclination to be alone that she was at once over the side, wading back through the sluggish, coolish waters toward the unseen Missouri shore. By the time she found the pirogue the turtle had fortunately gone its way. The pirogue was, of course, a little muddy, but Tasmin had never been finical about such trifles: in most respects the small boat made a perfect bed, a bed in which she was soon happily stretched out. Occasionally she caught a note of Haydn; occasionally the wild coyotes yipped. Happy in her solitude, Tasmin yawned, she sighed, she slept.

3

. . . wafted, though she didn't know it, on the gentle current of a summer river . . .

Tasmin slept deeply, wafted, though she didn't know it, on the gentle current of a summer river: the Missouri rose during the night, just enough to ease the pirogue off its muddy base and send it a mile or two downstream, where it gently deposited the little craft against a weedy bank. Tasmin opened her eyes to a dawn of such brilliance that it seemed the planet itself was being reborn. She was a young woman very seldom awed, experience having already shown her the shallowness of most sensation; but when the great molten sun swelled up from the horizon and cast its first light over the vastness of the prairies, Tasmin felt a joy stronger and more pure than any she had yet known. With the huge sky drawing her eyes upward toward infinity, she felt at one with an earthly magnificence that her tidy island upbringing had left her unprepared to imagine.

In that single moment of waking on the prairie's edge, with the sun not yet even fully broken free from the eastern horizon, Tasmin felt that she had at last shed all bonds: she was done with

Englishness, done with family; she cast off, quite literally, her muddy clothes and waded out, drenched and shivering, into the waters of the New World, determined to make her life, somehow, on the vast prairies of America, where she would never again be without the purities of that great embracing light.

No purer bolt of joy had ever hit her, and yet — Tasmin being a girl who liked a hearty breakfast — she had to face the fact that she was hungry. The very clarity of the air seemed to sharpen her appetite: thus, she reflected, does the practical ever follow sharp upon the poetical.

Of the steamer *Rocky Mount* there was no trace, anywhere on the wide brown flood. Somewhere upriver the *engagés* were no doubt hard at their ropes, straining to pull the steamer off the sandbar; perhaps by now they had succeeded and were proceeding upriver without her. Whatever she might find to breakfast on, it was not likely to be poached eggs and kidneys, her customary fare.

Not far down the bank a cheeky raccoon was washing a mussel of some sort; Tasmin would cheerfully have eaten the coon, had there been any way to kill him and cook him — but she had no weapon and no cook fire.

It was while she stood, clean but naked, in water up to her thighs that Tasmin realized she might not be the only early bather on this stretch of the river. Below her some thirty yards, beyond a little point that was especially thick with reeds and rushes and, perhaps, a few plum bushes, she distinctly heard a rustling. Fright, for a moment, threatened to overcome her. The rustling continued, but the weeds and rushes completely blocked her view. Captain Clark had warned them of the unequaled ferocity of the great bears of the West, the white bear or grizzly; he had warned them, also, of the troublesome ways of several of the savage tribes. What if a bear was producing that rustling? What if an Indian had come to the river? Either might be seeking the succulent plums, just then at an apogee of ripeness: only the day before, Cook had rendered some of them into a fine tart jam.

The pirogue seemed Tasmin's best hope of escape, so to the pirogue she crept, taking care not to splash or otherwise announce her presence; but then, when she was only a few feet from the boat, a young man naked as Adam walked into the water just beyond the reeds. Tasmin saw *him,* and at almost the same moment, he saw *her:* shock quite froze them both. The young man was bearded; his hair was as long and light as Tasmin's was long and dark. Their mutual surprise was so extreme that a long moment passed while they merely gaped at each other; then the claims of modesty asserted themselves. Tasmin reached to cover her privates — the young man did the same, before he recovered his power of movement and fairly skipped back to the shelter of the reeds.

Once the young man disappeared Tasmin shot

to the pirogue as if released by a spring — in a trice she had donned her muddy shift. A hectic rustling resumed beyond the weeds — she expected that at any moment the young man would come forth, clad, perhaps, in the homespun of the pioneer, to mumble apologies for the accident of their mutual exposure, which, after all, had done neither of them any harm. The Berrybenders, at least, had never placed modesty very high among the virtues; Lord and Lady Berrybender's lives had been little more than a riot of procreation. There were fourteen children, after all, and that handsome tally failed to include Lord Berrybender's bastards, said to number at least thirty, whose importuning had played its part in the lord's decision to leave green Albion's shores.

Tasmin herself could hardly claim to be ignorant of the rank inclinations of men, having, from her sixteenth year, been taken often and lustily by the head groom, Master Tobias Stiles, in the stall of Lord B.'s great stud Charlemagne, a dalliance that ended only when Master Stiles was killed at a jump; she had thus been led early to appreciate the energies of the well-formed male, though in fact none had appeared to tempt her since the death of Master Stiles.

What led her to hope for the prompt reappearance of the young man she had surprised at his bathing was not lust but hunger. Perhaps he possessed a biscuit or two, or even a piece of bacon.

But to her growing vexation, no young man

appeared. The prairies had assumed an almost eerie quiet, broken only by the skipping notes of a plover. Patience, like modesty, was not a virtue much prized by Berrybenders. Where was the shaggy fellow? Having inadvertently shown himself naked, why wouldn't he show himself clothed? Had the mere sight of her nakedness perhaps put him to flight — the hairy prospect and all that? Could timorousness have overcome him? Tasmin had to know — she tramped straight through the weeds and quickly burst upon the fellow, clad now in ragged buckskins, sitting on a log with his hands clasped in prayer. A long rifle lay beside him; also a bow and a quiver of arrows.

"Do pardon me, I did not mean to interrupt you at prayer," Tasmin said at once, whereupon the young man glanced briefly at the heavens, unclasped his hands, and stood up.

"Hello, then . . . ," he said, but could get no further.

Tasmin waited with what she hoped was a modest grace; but the prairie youth she had stumbled on was evidently quite lacking in talk, leaving her little choice but to direct whatever proceedings they might manage.

"I am Lady Tasmin de Bury," she said — some flash of instinct led her to give this diffident young stranger the name she had long believed to be rightfully hers. The Berrybenders were all notably blonde, whereas Tasmin, like Lord de Bury himself, had hair of a raven blackness, and Lady B., when in her cups, had been known to be careless with more than her attire. Tasmin, her firstborn, had been conceived just before Lady Constance yielded to Lord Albany and became a Berrybender — and yet the fact that she had said such a thing shocked Tasmin more than the sight of any man's nakedness. She, who had been brought up to regard with indifference, if not disdain, the opinions of the lower classes, had just exhibited a most shockingly low-bred desire to please: she had taken for herself, rightly or wrongly, a name far more ancient than that of the parvenu Berrybenders; and yet she was not at some great aristocratic soiree, where the name de Bury would have elevated her at once to the highest consideration. She was standing, instead, in a muddy shift by an American river whose banks smelled of slime and frogs and fish, speaking to a lanky son of the frontier who could hardly have known anything of English class or privilege. She might as well have claimed to be Ethelred or Athelstan — what difference could it have made to the young man who stood looking at her with mild brown eyes?

"I expect you're from that steamboat," the young man at last managed to say.

"Yes — but it seems to have left me," Tasmin said. "Might I just ask your name, sir?"

The question seemed to stump him for a moment. Tasmin waited with growing impatience — she was feeling hungrier by the moment.

"I must confess to you that I am at the moment very hungry," Tasmin said — impatience often got the better of curiosity, particularly if she happened to be hungry. "Do you know of anything that we might eat for breakfast?"

This question, delivered with more than a touch of adamancy, produced an unexpectedly winning smile.

"Know how to make a fire?" the young man asked.

He must have seen, from the expression on her face, that she was not in the habit of making fires, because he smiled again, pitched a small, soft pouch at her feet, and left, taking only his bow and quiver of arrows.

Tasmin was, as she had often asserted, the one competent Berrybender; even if she now disclaimed the family connection, she hoped to retain the competence. She had never made a fire, but she *had* read several of Mr. Cooper's novels, and supposed that, with application, she could soon master the essentials of flint and steel, the very objects contained in the young frontiersman's small deerskin pouch.

Remembering, as best she could, her Cooper, Tasmin assembled a sizable pyramid of grass and twigs, whacked away with the flint and steel, and was rewarded, after only a few minutes, with a respectable column of smoke. She was down on her knees, puffing at the pyramid, encouraged now and then by a tiny tongue of flame, when the young man came back with a dead doe over his shoulders, the arrow that had killed her still wagging from her side.

No sooner had he dropped the doe behind the log where he had been praying than he bent and with a flick or two reduced her grassy pyramid to one half its size, after which, immediately, a sturdy flame shot up.

"Too much grass," he explained. In only a few minutes he had the liver out of the deer, seared it over the blazing fire, and offered it to Tasmin on the point of his knife. A lifetime of eating amid the violent contention of the Berrybender table had long since rid her of any pretentions to lady-like etiquette when it came to food. Well used to fighting off her siblings with elbow and fist, Tasmin seized the dripping liver and ate it avidly; no meat had ever tasted better.

Her host and victualler watched in silence, then quickly butchered the little deer, which was already beginning to attract a green buzz of flies.

"Do you know that girl that sniffs out roots?" he asked, watching Tasmin closely.

"Yes, that's my sister Mary — she seems to have an unusually keen smeller," Tasmin said. "How did *you* know she could sniff out roots?"

"I seen her last night — she was talking to a snake," he said. "The snake led her to that turtle. A turtle that size could have bitten her arm off, but it didn't."

"No doubt she took it unawares," Tasmin

said, a little puzzled by the drift the conversation had taken.

"A child that talks with serpents has a powerful sin in her," the young man said. His brown eyes had suddenly turned to flint. The look was so hard that Tasmin, of a sudden, got goose bumps. Who *was* this young fellow, who looked at her so?

"I still don't know your name, sir," she pointed out, meekly, hoping that such a normal inquiry would make him mild again.

The young man shrugged, as if to suggest that a name was of little importance.

"Depends on where I am," he said. "Round here I'm mostly just Jim — Jim Snow."

Intrigued, Tasmin ventured another question.

"But Mr. Snow, who are you when you're somewhere else?" she asked, coquettishly.

"The Assiniboines call me the Raven Brave," he said — "they're way north of here. Some of the boys just call me Sin Killer. I'm hard when it comes to sin."

Tasmin could see that, just from the change in his eyes when the subject of sin came up, a subject Tasmin had never given even a moment's thought to, though growing up in a family of flagrant sinners had given her plenty of opportunity to observe the phenomenon at first hand.

"You've got no kit," Jim Snow pointed out, more mildly. "I expect you could use some help, getting back to the boat."

"Why, yes . . . if it wouldn't be too much

trouble," Tasmin said, but Jim Snow was already shifting some of the more edible portions of the butchered deer into the pirogue. His rifle, bow, and knife seemed to be his only possessions. In a moment he had settled Tasmin in the front of the pirogue and quickly moved the small craft toward the middle of the river: they were on their way to catch up with Tasmin's wandering kin.

4

As there was only one paddle, and Mr. Snow had it . . .

As there was only one paddle, and Mr. Snow had it, Tasmin could be of little assistance — she sat idly in the front of the pirogue, in a mood of indecision. Her oarsman soon demonstrated a keen eye, easily anticipating sandbars and hidden trees, obstacles he skirted with a few flicks of the paddle.

The fact was that Tasmin didn't much want to return to the steamer *Rocky Mount*, and yet, when she considered the matter from the point of view of logic, it became readily evident that she had little choice. Only two hours earlier, a naked Amazon exalted by the prairie dawn, she had resolved to cut all ties, to accept such fugitive company as the prairies might offer, to roam free and roam forever. She *liked* it that the country was so unsettled; on her native isle quite the reverse applied. *Everything* was settled, including the matrimonial futures of herself and all her sisters, all sure to be married off to such pasty lords as could afford their dowries. Lord Berrybender regarded his daughters as being little more than two-legged cattle — they were taught the little that they *were* taught so that they could more swiftly marry and mate.

Cleansed by the Missouri's water, thrilled by Western sunlight, Tasmin had for a moment supposed herself deliciously free, a notion of which Jim Snow quickly disabused her. The fact was she had *no* kit, not even shoes. Though she had scarcely covered fifty yards on shore her feet had already been stuck with burrs and stickers, her ankles scratched by stiff prairie weeds, and her calves attacked by an invisible burrowing mite which produced a most aggravating itch. The mite, Mr. Snow informed her, was called a chigger — he advised her to apply mud poultices to her itching legs, a remedy Tasmin adopted with some reluctance, since it rather cut against her vanity.

Tasmin had never before had to consider what a difference shoes made. Barefoot, she could have walked across half of England; in the rough Missouri country the same two feet would barely have taken her a mile.

Of course, with a little effort she could easily acquire kit: shoes, blankets, skillets, guns. Various servants would be only too happy to escape Lord Berrybender's incessant demands. Tim, the stable boy, whose crude embraces her sister Bess was occasionally disposed to accept, could be stolen in an instant. Vanity led Tasmin to suppose that she could easily tempt half the party; but the fact was, she didn't want *any* of the party. She wanted this New World to herself, and yet the morning's mild exercise had demonstrated only too forcefully that she lacked not merely the equipment but also the skills to master it. Though she had seen foals birthed and cattle butchered she could not easily have extracted that delicious liver from the doe; though she *did* believe she could have eventually made a fire, by working along Cooperish lines.

Her companion, Jim Snow — Sin Killer, or the Raven Brave, depending on his location or his mood — was not an easy man to make conversation with. He rowed; he didn't talk. The long silence, broken only by the occasional slap of a wave or call of a bird to break it, contributed to Tasmin's low mood. For a time she thought seriously of jumping out and swimming away: better to drown than to go back; and yet, with the water so shallow, she would probably merely have bogged, a ridiculous comeuppance to one so wedded to extremes. And thanks to the chiggers, she had quite enough mud on her legs anyway.

"How long will it take us to catch up with that wretched steamer?" she asked, finally. Jim Snow had rowed steadily, and yet the river ahead was empty as far as the eye could see.

"If they slip through the riffles we won't catch 'em today," he said. "If they stick we might."

Tasmin had not considered that their pursuit of the lost steamer might mean a night spent on the river, or the prairie, with her rescuer, Mr. Snow. That prospect did not worry her particularly; she was mainly desirous of securing a less muddy dress.

"Once they figure out you're missing I expect

they'll send a boat back for you," he said. "Some of them Frenchies are pretty good boatmen. They might show up and get you home for supper."

Tasmin doubted that any such expedient would occur. Lord Berrybender considered his oldest daughter such a marvel of self-reliance that he might consider a rescue attempt superfluous, presumptuous even.

"What, Tasmin missing? . . . Why, I expect she's only picnicking . . . Might take offense if we harass her . . . bound to show up in a day or two . . . No need to worry about Tasmin . . ."

Some such, she felt sure, would be her father's response, if the fact of her absence was conclusively determined — after which His Lordship would take a little snuff; Lady B., meanwhile, would tuck into a great beefsteak, washed down by a bottle or two of claret. The wine would soon numb whatever anxiety she might feel about Tasmin, which was not likely to be excessive, anyway: after all, Master Stiles had been *hers* until Tasmin grew up and caught his eye; the years had not yet much abated the bitterness of Lady Berrybender's jealousy.

Danger Tasmin didn't much mind — it was ennui she despised. Mr. Snow's long silences left her increasingly bored, a condition she could endure only so long without protest.

"Look here, Mr. Snow," she said, when she had had good and enough. "I fear I am taking you a dreadful distance off your route. I am quite a competent rower, when it comes to that. Why don't we put into shore? You can go your way and I'll just row along until I come up with the boat."

Tasmin's frank speech startled Jim Snow greatly. He looked at her briefly, and then turned and gave close inspection to the western shore of the river. Then, rather to Tasmin's mystification, he pointed to the sky, empty except for a great flock of birds, winging so high above them that Tasmin could but faintly hear their call — rather an odd, whistling call it was.

"It's the swans — they're coming in," he said.

"So they may be, but I don't see that it affects our situation," Tasmin told him. "You need go no farther out of your way. I'm quite sure I can get back to the steamer on my own."

"No," he said, and went on rowing, as if his mere denial was all the explanation needed, in which regard he reckoned without the notable obstinacy of the de Burys — obstinacy enough to have carried them through three Crusades.

"Explain," Tasmin demanded, speaking quite sharply.

Jim Snow frowned.

"Explain!" she repeated, even more fiercely this time.

"We're close by the Swamp of the Swans," he said, with another gesture toward the high whistling birds, whose long necks were outstretched. "When the swans come the Osage come too, and there's plenty of Osage in these parts even when the swans ain't nesting. If the Osage get you, you'd be in for worse than chiggers, I guess. They'd sell you to some slaver who'd haul you off to Mexico, if you lasted that long."

The steamer *Rocky Mount* was rife with just such rumors of rapine and kidnap. The only common ground Fraulein Pfretzskaner and Mademoiselle Pellenc had been able to find was a shared fear of abduction by red Indians. Even the haughty Venetia Kennet could be reduced to a jelly of apprehension by the mere suggestion of the ravishment she could expect to suffer should her fair form ever fall into savage hands. Lord Berrybender, though hardly wishing his daughters to adorn the harems of Comanche or Kickapoo, nonetheless saw the matter mainly in practical terms: that is, the prospect of greatly reduced dowries should rumors of these ravishments follow them all back to England.

Having come so recently to the country, Tasmin hardly knew how to assess this threat — it was a fair summer day, and except for the gliding swans, not a creature was visible on the whole huge plain to the west. Having spent one of the most restful nights of her life sleeping alone in the pirogue, she could not persuade herself that any such woeful captivity was imminent; and yet she knew that she had much to learn about this New World. Mr. Cooper's books had said nothing about grass burrs, scratchy weeds, or chiggers.

The Raven Brave, as Tasmin now liked to

think of him, was clearly knowledgeable. It had taken him only a few minutes to find a deer and kill it. Now he seemed to consider it his duty to protect her, an attitude she would have been happier to accept if she could have detected in it some tendril of fondness, of liking, of hot lust, even. She was, after all, a woman whose nakedness he had glimpsed. If he was only going to think of her as a duty, she felt she might prefer to take her chances with the Osage. A duty — a mere duty — she did not care to be.

"I don't fear the Indians, Mr. Snow," she said. "I'd prefer to put you ashore now — I've wasted enough of your time."

Jim Snow looked at her as if she had gone daft.

"You ain't got good sense — just hush about it," he said.

Tasmin found the remark peculiarly irritating, since among her own family she had long been applauded for the very quality Mr. Snow claimed she lacked: good sense.

"You are entirely wrong, sir!" Tasmin retorted hotly; but before she could refute his silly assertion a wild yodeling commenced on the near shore and a bullet whacked into the side of the pirogue, just above the waterline. The plain that only a moment before had seemed so empty now sported a host of more or less naked, vividly painted savages, all of them screaming and shrieking in their fury. Several of them rushed into the water, brandishing hatchets and knives, a development that prompted the Raven Brave to at once turn the pirogue and row as rapidly as possible toward the opposite shore. A second bullet skipped off the water just beside the boat, but was the last. Distance rapidly grew between themselves and their attackers. Several savages on horses had arrived at the western shore, but they didn't enter the water.

Mr. Snow seemed no more concerned by this little attack than if it had been a sudden gusty wind or squall of rain. Though his comment about Tasmin's lack of good sense had been immediately driven home, he himself seemed to have forgotten it. Tasmin felt, for the oddest moment, that she had stepped off the steamer *Rocky Mount* right into a Cooper novel, with Mr. Snow as Hawkeye, a man well equipped to protect her from the harsh inconveniences she would be sure to suffer if captured by the red men. He now seemed to be making for a low bluff on the eastern bank of the river; the Osage, if such they were, were now mere dots on the western shore.

"Bravo! I do believe we've eluded them," Tasmin said, when the boat reached the shallows.

"Not yet . . . there's plenty of them on this side too," Mr. Snow said. He hastily pulled the pirogue out of the water, took his rifle, bow, and haunch of deer meat, grabbed Tasmin's hand, and urged her to a breakneck run along the muddy shore, their goal, it seemed, being the little bluff she had noticed as they crossed the river.

Tasmin thought such haste to be unnecessary

until she heard a babel of shrieks just behind them and looked around to see four more savages, painted in yellows and blues, giving hot chase, hatchets in their hands.

The Raven Brave was confident of his tactics, though. They raced to the little bluff, where, quickly cupping his hands and indicating that Tasmin was to step in them, he hoisted her atop an immense boulder at the foot of the bluff, after which he turned and faced the Osage, then some hundred yards away. Tasmin expected him to shoot them, or at least loose an arrow or two, but instead, mildly amused, he pointed at the cliff above them, whereupon the Indians stopped as abruptly as if they had run into a wall. The painted faces that, a moment before, had been contorted with fury now wore looks of uncertainty, or even dejection. From being wild killers they became, in an instant, stumpy Pierrots, clowns in a show that had somehow gone wrong.

When they stopped, the Sin Killer's eyes became flint again and he hurled a great cry at his pursuers, a violent ululating cry in a language Tasmin knew not. The Osage quickly passed from dejection to terror — they immediately ran away, disappearing into the underbrush where they had been hiding before the attack began.

Tasmin made no attempt to conceal her astonishment: they had been surprised, they had been chased, and now they had been saved — she felt extreme excitement but not much fear. Her companion of the day, the Sin Killer, was evidently more than a match for the painted Osage. On this occasion he had been content to frighten the Indians away, but had it been necessary to kill one or all of them, she had no doubt he would have done just that.

His face still reflected the violence of his expression; but, once the Osage were clearly gone, his face cleared, his eyes softened, he became mild Mr. Jim Snow again — he pointed above her at a kind of drawing on a rock that extruded from the little bluff. Tasmin could just see that some crude figures had been traced on the rock face, stick men of the sort that a child might draw, except that these stick men sprouted antlers or horns from their heads. There was also a sketch of a shadowy four-legged beast of some kind, perhaps a mammoth or great mastodon — one such, Mr. Catlin claimed, had been excavated from a bed of loam not far down the river.

"The Osage won't come here — not close, anyway," Jim Snow said. "They think devils live on this hill."

"You seem to have addressed them quite positively," Tasmin said. He reached up a hand to help her climb down.

"They were so hot to take our hair they forgot about the devils," Jim said. "I reminded them."

His comment was a little startling, but Tasmin slid down the big rock anyway and followed her companion back along the muddy shore toward the pirogue, wondering what new surprises the coming night might bring.

5

The swans were whistling, high overhead.

At sunset a rain squall struck — the river threw up
a dense mist, the sun sank into it, and a little later,
a glorious rainbow arched over the river. Jim
Snow improvised a modest shelter by turning the
pirogue over and propping one end of it against a
rock. Rain blew spittings of water under the boat
and into Tasmin's face, but despite it, Jim Snow
managed to bank a fire against the same useful
rock. The raindrops fizzed into the fire, but the
fire survived; the showers ceased in time for
Tasmin to enjoy a long afterglow, as many-
colored as the rainbow, lasting until the river was
touched with starlight.

Jim Snow — or the Raven Brave — seemed
completely indifferent to the weather. The rain
did not dismay him nor the rainbow delight him.
By the time the dripping pieces of venison had
been cooked and eaten — and prairie frights had
in no way diminished Tasmin's appetite — Jim
Snow busied himself by whittling a new plug for
his powder horn. During the meal he completely
eschewed speech, as if meals and talk could not
possibly happen at the same time. He had a little
salt in a pouch — Tasmin asked if she might

share it — her request constituted the whole sum of their mealtime conversation. In the course of four months in America Tasmin had become fairly reconciled to American practicality, but she had never met as fine an example of the purely practical man as her companion, Jim Snow. Whatever was needed — of a physical nature — he did at once, with a certain grace and a fine economy of motion. He wasted no effort and contributed no words.

This young frontiersman Tasmin found herself traveling with was to her altogether a new species of male, quite unlike any she had ever known. Whether she proved to be Berrybender or de Bury, she was an English lady of noble lineage, a fact which had always produced a certain measure of diffidence in her suitors — social inferiors, many of them. Even Master Tobias Stiles, after tupping her vigorously in old Charlemagne's stall, still addressed her as "my lady" when they were finished. Such contradiction as she occasionally met with in men was usually offered cautiously — her temper had made itself respected throughout the Berrybender household. Even Lord Berrybender himself seldom challenged his spirited eldest daughter.

In their long day on the river Tasmin had offered only one or two opinions, but Jim Snow had casually disregarded even those few. He clearly felt under no obligation to respect, or even listen to, her views. He said his "no" and that was that. Frustrated, Tasmin tried her best to come up with a question she might ask that he would not resent, and after due deliberation, thought that she might just risk an inquiry about the swans.

Tasmin sat under the uptilted pirogue, Jim Snow on the other side of the fire, his face now in shadow, now in light. He was concentrated so on his task — fitting the new plug into the powder horn — that he seemed almost to have forgotten Tasmin's presence.

"Was it the swans that particularly aroused the Osage?" she ventured to ask. "I'm curious. Would they have let us pass, had there been no swans?"

Jim Snow looked up for a moment — the question, at least, seemed to interest him.

"It would depend on what band it was, and who was leading them," he reflected, his face tilted slightly to one side. It was a handsome face too, though his long irregular hair and rather scraggly beard could both have done with a trimming, Tasmin felt.

"There's a good market now for swan feathers — the white feathers, anyway," he said. "The Osage trade 'em for guns — the beaver's long been trapped out. They don't want the same to happen to the swans."

Even to Tasmin's Old World brain that made sense. A tribe that had lost their profitable beaver might be expected to be violently protective of their profitable swans.

"Was that Osage you yelled at them, this after-

51

noon?" Tasmin asked. "I confess I have never heard such a strange tongue spoken — though we are a regular tower of Babel on our boat."

"That was the Word of Jehovah," Jim Snow said.

"Goodness, are you a minister, then?" Tasmin asked, in genuine surprise. "Do you have a regular parish out here on the prairies?"

Jim Snow shook his head.

"The Word just comes out sometimes, when there's heathens that need to hear it or sinners that need to be warned," he said. "I don't preach it in church."

"Well, if that was the Word, it impressed *me*, I must say," Tasmin said. "Where did you learn your theology, Mr. Snow?"

Now that the first faint traces of conversation had been produced she hoped to encourage it — blow on it, feed it grass, anything to keep her host from lapsing back into one of his long silences.

But the word stumped him — he had evidently never heard it before.

"My what?" he asked.

"It's from the Greek *theologos,* one who studies the beliefs in the various gods," Tasmin said, hoping she was not being too inaccurate. She thought a tiny display of learning might intrigue Mr. Snow, but in this her miscalculation proved severe. In a moment the young man's face darkened, became the face of the Sin Killer, and he whipped his hand toward her and gave her such a ringing slap as she had never experienced before, at the hand of man or woman.

"You hush now — don't be talking blasphemous lies!" he said sternly. "There's only one God and Jehovah is his name."

Tasmin was so startled by the sudden slap that she could only sit in astonishment, one hand raised to her burning cheek. The slap rocked her, and yet she had instinct enough to recognize that the slap was nothing to the violence the Sin Killer might unleash if he were really in a mood to punish. Despite the sting, and the surprise, Tasmin made a mighty effort to remain calm. Her bosom may have heaved, but she did not allow herself to speak until she had sufficiently mastered her emotions to be able to address the Sin Killer in level tones.

"But Mr. Snow, I was only defining a word," she informed him. "In my country few preachers teach themselves. I only wanted to ask where you learned your doctrines."

"From Preacher Cockerell — he and his wife bought me from the Osage," Jim Snow said. "Preacher Cockerell needed someone to tend his stock."

His face had cleared — he spoke mildly again, but he didn't apologize to Tasmin for slapping her. Mention of a multiplicity of gods was evidently sufficient to merit a slap; and that was that. Now it had emerged that he had been practically raised by the Osage — how that came about Tasmin did not feel bold enough to inquire.

"We English are very forward," she said lightly. "When I meet someone I like — and I *do* like you — I cannot help wanting to know a bit more about them."

"Being nosy," Jim Snow said, with a look of amusement. "That's what I'd call it."

"Yes, that's fair, I suppose," Tasmin said. "Being nosy. I take it that you can read the Bible, since you preach."

At this he looked a trifle discomfited.

"Preacher Cockerell taught me my letters," he said. "But then he got lightning-struck and killed before I could finish my learning. When it comes to the Bible I can mostly puzzle out the verses, but I get tangled up in some of the names."

He reached into a small pouch that hung from his belt and pulled out a much-tattered and clearly incomplete Bible, bound in flaking sheepskin, which he handed to Tasmin. It seemed to please him that she took an interest in his religious calling.

"Had to tear out a few pages, when I didn't have nothing else to start a fire with," he said, evidently embarrassed by the rather riddled appearance of his book. Tasmin was moved that he would care to show her this humble article — it went some way toward making up for the slap.

"Well, there's Genesis, at least . . . and you've still got the Psalmist . . . and here's Solomon's songs," she said. Jim Snow was watching her closely; she did not want to give the impression

54

that she scorned his one treasured book.

"I don't preach out of the book — I just preach the Word that's in me," the young man said, with some intensity. "Preacher Cockerell was a fornicator — when the Lord called down the lightning bolt that killed him I was standing close enough that the bolt knocked me nearly thirty feet. I didn't wake up for three days, but when I did wake up the Word was in me. It's been in me ever since."

"What an astonishing story!" Tasmin said, and she meant it. Being riven by a lightning bolt might make a preacher of many a man.

"I mean to get a whole Bible, someday, when I've got the money," he said.

"My goodness, we have many Bibles with us," Tasmin said. "If we ever catch up with the boat I'd be happy to give you one, as a small token of gratitude for all the trouble you've taken on my behalf."

She meant it too — nothing could be easier than to make him a present of a Bible. And yet when she said it the Raven Brave drew back, as if she had made an immodest suggestion. The swans were whistling, high overhead. Without another word this strange young man whose motives so perplexed her stood up, took his rifle, and prepared to leave the camp, actions that quite distressed her.

"Oh, Mr. Snow, don't leave — it was just a thought," Tasmin said. "Am I to be allowed no generosity, where you are concerned?"

"You're too much of a talker — get some sleep," he said, before being swallowed up by the humid darkness. Tasmin was left alone, in her muddy dress, with a sputtering fire and the call of swans from the high heavens. The Raven Brave's departure was so sudden that she felt like crying — indeed, a few tears of frustration *did* fall. Tasmin, who had long been cosseted by myriad English softnesses, was now in a country where nothing was soft except the mud of the damnable river; and the least soft thing in the whole country, it seemed to her, was the young man who had just slapped her face. There were several lustful gentlemen of her acquaintance whom she could have probably driven to cuff her, had she been disposed to test their mettle; but Jim Snow's slap bespoke a hardness of an entirely different order, one so decisive that she felt quite sure she would never be moved to utter the word "theology" in his company again.

Sitting under the boat in the darkness, hearing the crackle of the fire, Tasmin felt quite alone. Her brain was racing so that she could not sleep. The night before, stretched out in the pirogue, she had been quite settled in her emotions and had slept deeply; but now her feeling surged this way and that, erratic as the Missouri's waves. Once or twice she had thought Mr. Snow was coming almost to like her, but then her tumbling speech, which she seemed unable to control, spilled out in some comment that turned his liking to distaste, if not worse.

Tasmin had rarely experienced a frustration equal to what she felt on that muddy prairie beach, and the worst of it was that this exasperating man had done the most aggravating thing that a man *could* do: he simply left. He was gone: she had no one to plead with, rail against, slap, kiss, anything. He was gone. Tasmin stared into the darkness; she listened to the whistle of the swans, to the yipping of coyotes, and to what may or may not have been the cough of a buffalo. There were rustlings in the underbrush that might have been made by snakes or raccoons, by deer or antelope, by Osage or Kickapoo — she was certainly no scholar of the sounds of a prairie night. She turned, she squirmed, she stretched, but she did not get any sleep.

6

There she sat — muddy, barefoot, with no kit . . .

It was pitch-dark, the only light being the faint glow of a few dying coals, when Tasmin gave a start and opened her eyes. The space above her had changed — where the pirogue had been was only high starlight. Mr. Snow was carrying the pirogue to the river. Tasmin's limbs were just then feeling intolerably heavy with sleep — she wanted to sleep so badly that she was almost hoping Mr. Snow would just leave her, but he didn't.

"Let's go," he said, and he led her by her hand down the slimy, slippery slope to the river. The pirogue he pushed well out into the stream before slipping into it himself and taking the oar. Tasmin yawned; now that her protector was back she felt deeply sleepy.

When she woke again the morning mist was so dense that she could only just see Mr. Snow, a ghostly form plying his paddle from the rear of the pirogue. Tasmin could gain no idea of where they stood in relation to the river's shores. Except for the very slight suck of Mr. Snow's paddle, she heard no sounds at all. No birds called, no fish leapt, no wolves howled, no buffaloes coughed. Mr. Snow somehow apprehended the angular limbs of a dead tree just ahead of them and managed to turn the pirogue so as to slip past it. Tasmin recalled Mr. Catlin's pun about the river Sticks and had to admit that it was rather apt. So indistinct were their surroundings that they might indeed be rowing to Hades, a thought she decided not to express to the Sin Killer, who might think it punishingly pagan.

They proceeded thus — silent and invisible — for perhaps an hour when the mist began to glow above them — soon sunlight filtered through, and the blue sky appeared, though colonies of mist still ranged along the distant riverbanks.

"I reckon yonder's your steamer," Jim Snow said.

He pointed, but a last line of mist drifted above the water — even when it cleared, Tasmin could not, at first, see the steamer *Rocky Mount*, at this point still several miles ahead; the best she could produce was a kind of dancing dot, far north on the water. Her blindness seemed to amuse Mr. Snow; or it may have been that the prospect of getting rid of such a talkative person had put him in a good humor — he even smiled at Tasmin.

"I guess you've just come out of the woods," he said. "Takes a while for woods folks to get to where they can see sharp on the prairies."

"There might be another reason why I refuse to see that boat — a reason that has nothing to

59

do with eyesight," Tasmin said.

Jim Snow merely looked at her — he did not inquire about what the other reason might be. The wind had come up; it sighed across the prairie grasses, and the very sighing seemed to push Tasmin's spirits down. There she sat — muddy, barefoot, with no kit — and yet the downcast feeling that filled her breast had only one cause: she did not want to go back aboard the steamer *Rocky Mount*, to the idle frivolity of the Berrybender ménage, to the vast meals, to Mr. Catlin's dry cackle, to her mother's drunkenness, or Bobbety's whining, or Buffum's gross amour with Tim, the stable boy. Every day Mademoiselle Pellenc would call Fraulein Pfretzskaner a German slut; Fraulein, in turn, would call Mademoiselle a French whore. The tutors, the gunsmith, the botanist, and the artist, the butler and the carriage maker could all sink to the bottom of the river, for all she cared.

And yet there it was, she soon saw, stuck, as usual, on a riffle, only a mile or two ahead. The moving dots she spotted were only the *engagés*, out with their ropes and poles, trying to wrestle the boat back into a navigable channel.

Very soon, like it or not, she would be back — her only hope of escape from European tedium lay with the young man paddling the pirogue. If only he had a trace of the lover in him, Tasmin reflected, he could have conquered her in a moment. He was a male, after all; she herself had seen his honest manhood in their moment of nakedness. Her own beauty had not gone entirely uncelebrated — pale but hopeful ballad makers were forever serenading her.

In less than an hour, Tasmin knew, they would come up with the boat. In that hour Tasmin coquetted as she had never coquetted before. She dipped one fair leg over the side and washed it free of mud. She knelt in the boat and bent to wash her face, exposing her young breasts almost as recklessly as Lady Berrybender exposed her great dugs at dinner. Yet her most immodest efforts completely failed. Jim Snow just kept rowing; to him she might have been a fish, a gull, a cat.

Then, at the last minute, when they were almost level with the steamer, a practical thought occurred to Tasmin — there might yet be a way to tempt the severely practical Mr. Snow.

"Will you be going to Santa Fe soon?" she asked.

"No . . . a little later . . . when it ain't so dry on the plains," he said. He seemed surprised that she had inquired.

"How much would passage cost, if one were to want to go?" she asked, a question that left him gaping.

"Passage?" he asked. "Who would be wanting to go?"

"Why, *I* would," Tasmin said. "I've always been so fond of all things Spanish — the Alhambra, you know, and the dramas of Señor

Quevedo. I'm sure I'd feel right at home in Santa Fe."

Jim Snow was so shocked by her statement that he could hardly close his mouth. Not since the moment when he had first glimpsed Tasmin's nakedness had he been so entirely deprived of speech.

"You by yourself?" he asked — but before Tasmin could answer there was a great braying from the steamer and Tasmin saw a flash of red as her hound, Tintamarre, jumped into the water and began to swim toward them.

"Why, it's my hound — what a passionate thing he is," Tasmin said.

"That big red dog is yours?" he asked. "If he's yours I'm right glad I didn't shoot him."

It was Tasmin's turn to be surprised.

"But Mr. Snow, whatever could tempt you to shoot my hound?" she asked.

Jim Snow looked at her as if she were the merest fool.

"To eat him, why else?" he said.

"Eat my dog, when there were deer aplenty?" Tasmin asked, startled.

"There ain't never deer aplenty — I hadn't seen no deer in three days, when that doe came to water," he said. "The Osage keep the deer pretty well hunted down."

Soon Tintamarre came splashing through the shallows and flung himself on Tasmin, slinging water everywhere.

"Meat's meat," Jim Snow added. "You'll

learn that soon enough, I guess."

Shock at the thought of someone eating her dog caused Tasmin's stomach to do a sudden flip. For a moment she sat uneasily in the pirogue, while Tintamarre leapt and splashed and licked her face.

7

"I know who it was — Sin Killer."

Remembering her intense hunger that first morning on the Missouri's shore, Tasmin had to reflect that hunger might indeed drive her to eat unfamiliar foods. No doubt Mr. Snow's luck in immediately providing her with a deer's liver had misled her when it came to the harsh necessities of prairie life. The Berrybender mess on the steamer was so prodigious as to destroy all sense of scarcity — Lord Berrybender had filled one whole keelboat with claret, as well as some champagne and port.

"What, travel without my claret? What a thought, sir!" Lord B. would have said, had anyone pointed out that the boat might have been filled with more humble necessities — potatoes, for example, or oranges, the lack of which was already causing grumbling from Bobbety and Buffum.

These culinary broodings, prompted by the shocking threat to her dog, could not long distract Tasmin from the prospect that must be faced. Either she had to persuade her prairie protector to take her to Santa Fe with him or she had to say good-bye to him and resign herself to the tedium of the boat.

"Mr. Snow, I quite regret that I've had so little

64

opportunity to hear you preach the Word," Tasmin said carefully. "I'm sure a sermon or two would improve my character immensely — besides, I have two sisters who entirely lack religious instruction. You could have a splendid parish if you would ever consent to be our chaplain."

In fact she could not imagine him putting up with the raucous Berrybenders for ten minutes; she was rattling on merely to stall his departure, which she knew might come at any moment; and once those great gray prairies swallowed him up, she would be unlikely ever to see the Raven Brave again, a thought that made her unaccountably low — she who could casually dismiss in an instant most men of her acquaintance.

"I'm a bad hand in a crowd — I get riled too easy," he said, glancing for a moment at the steamboat.

"But you said that you sometimes guided parties of traders — could we English really be so much worse?" Tasmin asked. Some devil in her insisted that she keep pressing the man, although there was no logic to it.

Though Jim Snow didn't answer, Tasmin thought he was beginning to feel, a little, the difficulty of the moment. Perhaps despite himself he had begun to like her at least a bit — he looked to the southwest, as if weighing in his mind's eye the difficulty of attempting to convey such a troublesome baggage as herself across those barren miles.

"It's too early to head to Santa Fe," he repeated. "If we was to leave now our animals would most likely starve, and we would too."

Though it was clear that Jim Snow could not be immediately persuaded to take her with him, Tasmin nonetheless felt a little encouraged by his patience in explaining to her the folly of what she contemplated — she felt she might even be growing on him a little.

"I'll put it to you plainly, Mr. Snow," she said. "I can't tolerate that boat. I didn't come all this way to the New World to listen to my family pursue their usual quarrels. If you won't take me to Santa Fe, then I'll hire Monsieur Charbonneau to guide me — he's quite experienced, I believe."

"Sharbo, that old fool! Why, it would be the end of you in a week!" Jim Snow said, his voice registering a high degree of indignation, though, fortunately, not religious indignation this time.

"But he traveled with Lewis and Clark," Tasmin pointed out. "I suppose he must know these prairies rather well."

"No!" Jim Snow said. "It was the captains that kept Sharbo alive! He can speak Mandan and Ree and a few words of Sioux, but if you took him ten miles off the river and spun him around a few times, I doubt he could even find his way to Saint Louis without starving."

"Then it's an impasse," Tasmin said, amused to have pushed the Raven Brave to such uncharacteristic volubility. "If I must go and you refuse to take me, then I fear I have no choice but to make do with inferior help."

Jim Snow, it was clear, was not much accustomed to lengthy conversations with women. Tasmin's careless refusal to abandon what to his eyes were almost suicidal plans was beginning to exasperate him. His jaw was clenched — he looked around the broad prairies as if about to flee.

"I guess I could send you Pomp, if I could find him," Jim Snow said. "Pomp's reliable — he might get you there."

"Pomp? Pomp who?" Tasmin asked, startled that he would wiggle out of her net by offering another guide.

"Pomp Charbonneau — he ain't a bit like his old fool of a father," Jim said. "Pomp was raised up over in the old country and knows a passel of languages, but he trapped with me on the Green River and lived to tell about it, which not many can claim."

"I'm sure young Mr. Charbonneau is all you say, but I'd still rather have you," Tasmin said, with a bold look — why not cast the fat directly into the fire?

For a moment Jim Snow looked entirely exhausted — probably until that moment his life had been entirely free of the kind of demands spoilt young females make. In no time, it seemed to Tasmin, she had worn the young man down — before he could recover, or reach a decision, a screaming was heard from the direction of the boat: here, to Tasmin's intense irritation, came Bobbety, Buffum, and Mary, the first two yelling at the unexpected good fortune of her rescue.

"Oh, damn them, the bloody little fools!" Tasmin said, unable to conceal her intense dismay.

In an instant she was being shaken like a rag by the Sin Killer.

"You're hell-bound for sure if you cuss like that!" he said. "I won't have no sinful speech!"

"It just slipped out, sir, I swear it," Tasmin said, timorously — her brains rattled like peas from the violence of his shaking, and her teeth cracked against one another.

"I'll do better — I promise no curse will escape my lips," she said, desperate to undo the damage her careless outburst had caused. But it was too late. Those flinty eyes looked into hers for a moment, and then the Sin Killer turned and left. Before her incompetent brother could properly beach the pirogue, the gray plains had swallowed him up.

"I say, who was that gentleman you were wrestling with, Tassie, in the year of our Lord 1832?" Bess asked, in her most grating tone. Tasmin at once slapped her sharply — she had quickly acquired the American habit of addressing all problems as violently as possible.

"When I require a calendar I can quite well acquire one from the stationer's, Bess," she informed her stunned sister.

"But Tasmin . . . ," Bobbety began; he

stopped at once when Tasmin doubled up her fist and shook it at him.

The wicked Mary smiled.

Tasmin raced as quickly as she could out onto the prairie. Mr. Snow had been gone but a minute, it seemed — perhaps she could catch him yet. Perhaps the temper aroused by her careless words would have cooled — if she could just find him, there might yet be hope.

Gone he was, though — as far as she could see there was nothing but the sighing grass. Tasmin could scarcely believe it — where had he gone? All around her was featureless plain and empty sky. So confused was Tasmin by this emptiness that, once she gave up and stopped, she would have been hard put even to find her way back to the river, had it not been for the loud braying of Tintamarre, who had found a muskrat hole and was attempting to bark its inhabitants to death.

"But who was it, Tassie . . . mayn't I even ask?" the tearful Buffum said, when Tasmin returned. Still in a dark temper, Tasmin did not reply.

"*I* know who it was — Sin Killer," the sinister Mary said.

Without another word being spoken, Tasmin rowed them back to the steamer *Rocky Mount* — all, that is, except Tintamarre, who was still barking into his muskrat hole.

8

In her red fury
Tasmin had forgotten . . .

Bobbety and Buffum Tasmin quite refused to forgive — in her view it was entirely their fault that
the Raven Brave had got away, leaving her to examine her own surprisingly turbulent feelings.
Could she be falling in love with this scarcely ar-
ticulate young American? Since she reached the
age of twelve, men Tasmin had no interest in had
been falling in love with *her* — could it be that
matters were now reversed? Had she been making
a fool of herself over a man who didn't want her?

Or *did* he want her? A day or two more and she
might have had him, she told herself. Three days
more and he would have been happy to take her
to Santa Fe, or Samarkand, for that matter.

Yet now the Raven Brave was gone, tramping
alone somewhere on the great pallid prairies.

Tasmin had yanked little Mary up by her
scruff and flung her into the pirogue, curious as
to how this malignant sprite could have known
that the man who was shaking her was called the
Sin Killer.

"Big White talks of him," Mary said. "All the
Indians do."

In her red fury Tasmin had forgotten that they

70

had three wild chiefs on board — all three had been to Washington to meet the president, and were being returned, under Monsieur Charbonneau's care, to their respective tribes. All three chiefs were old: they lounged around the lower deck all day, amid the greatest disorder, smoking long-stemmed pipes, spitting, snoring, painting themselves up most garishly, and occasionally rolling a kind of dice made from elk bones.

"And since when do you speak the languages of the Mandan, the Blackfoot, or the Sioux?" Tasmin asked. She knew that, in Master Jeremy Thaw's opinion, Mary was the family's best linguist, able to babble tiresomely in Greek, but Tasmin tended to disregard Master Thaw's opinion.

"Big White is teaching me Mandan, and the Hairy Horn helps me to comprehend the dialects of the Sioux," Mary said. "The only one who won't help me is Blue Thunder, who is a Blackfoot of the Piegan band."

"It is hardly ladylike to conspicuously display one's knowledge," Tasmin reminded her. "Do I flaunt my Portuguese?"

In fact she could scarcely utter a syllable in that peculiar tongue, though it was true that a skinny hidalgo, of a vaguely Iberian nature, had seen her once at a horse race and proposed marriage immediately.

"Are you going to fornicate with the Sin Killer?" Mary asked — she had ever been strikingly direct.

"Perhaps I shall — we'll see," Tasmin told her.

"If you plan to travel the prairies you had best take me," Mary said.

"You brash mite, why would I?" Tasmin asked.

"So you won't starve — I can sniff out tubers, tasty tubers," Mary said, as they pulled alongside the steamer *Rocky Mount*.

9

He lumbered away
like some small dirty bear . . .

Tasmin's first thought, once getting on board, was to rush down to the underdeck and question Monsieur Charbonneau closely about her new acquaintance, Mr. Snow — but of course she had scarcely stepped on deck when a garrulous regiment rushed at her, each member eager to relate to her various iniquities that had occurred in her absence.

"Why, Tasmin, you look wild as a deer," Lady Berrybender said — she was already walking unsteadily from the effects of her morning tipple.

"I was just picnicking, Mama . . . exploring the prairie glades a bit," Tasmin said — she had no intention of mentioning the Raven Brave to her mother, though she *did* gossip a little with Mademoiselle Pellenc, who drew her a bath and combed the many tangles out of her wild hair.

Mademoiselle Pellenc was the only female on board whose cynicism matched Tasmin's own. For all that, the violently hot-blooded Frenchwoman flew like a shuttlecock from Señor Yanez to Signor Claricia and back again; the latter was rather too garlicky, the former a good deal too quick, but Mademoiselle was not slow to inform

Tasmin that she had just acquired a fresh prospect.

Tasmin supposed for a moment that she might mean Lord B. himself, supposedly still fully occupied with the languid cellist, Venetia Kennet.

"*Non, non,* Herr Sten!" Mademoiselle said. "He presented himself to me in the laundry — he is a fellow of modest dimensions, I am afraid."

"I wouldn't expect too much in the way of passion from a Dane," Tasmin said. "What else is new that I should know?"

"The German slut, she gives herself to the big American — Big Charlie," Mademoiselle said.

Tasmin found herself completely unmoved by this news, or by various other tidbits of gossip that Mademoiselle offered. She no longer much cared what this rabble of displaced Europeans did with themselves. As soon as she was dressed in a clean shift she hurried down to the underdeck to locate Monsieur Charbonneau, the man who knew Jim Snow.

Toussaint Charbonneau was a tall, graying man of a decidedly shambling nature, kindly, but never really clean or wholly sober. His buckskin shirt was invariably stained, his leggings often torn. On this occasion Tasmin found him soon enough, sitting at a filthy table with his plump young Hidatsa wife, Coal. Old Gorska, equally untidy, had been sitting with them but he hastily moved away when Tasmin appeared; she had more than once given him notice that she would tolerate none of his low Polish insolence. He lumbered away like some small dirty bear the moment she appeared.

Tasmin liked Coal, a girl round of form and merry of eye; she was perhaps fifteen, and greedy for trinkets, an appetite girls seemed to share. Tasmin had won her for life by presenting her with a tortoiseshell comb, which she wore to splendid effect in her shiny black hair. To Tasmin it seemed a pity that such a lively creature had been taken to wife by this pettish old fellow, Charbonneau, no prize that Tasmin could see.

"Bonjour, monsieur," Tasmin said at once to the old tippler. "Could you please tell me what you know about the Sin Killer?"

Tasmin had spoken politely; she was hardly prepared for the pandemonium her words produced among the chiefs. The old Hairy Horn jumped up as if pricked, brandishing a gleaming hatchet. Big White rose too and took up his great war club, referred to as the "skull smasher" by Monsieur Charbonneau. The Piegan Blue Thunder looked wary — even a few of the *engagés* drew their knives, as if expecting immediate assault.

Old Charbonneau, the man to whom Tasmin had put her question, seemed, for the moment, quite paralyzed — the pinch of snuff he had been in the process of carrying to his nose rained like powder on his untidy tunic.

"Why, miss," he said, in astonished tones, "how would you be knowing Jimmy Snow?"

75

"I went rather adrift in my pirogue," Tasmin explained. "Mr. Snow found me and brought me back — if he hadn't come along I expect I'd still be adrift."

At that point Charbonneau, the Hairy Horn, Big White, and several *engagés* all rushed to the rail — they all stood gazing at the somber but empty prairie.

"Which way did Jimmy go, miss?" Charbonneau asked.

"I am not a compass — I did not ascertain his direction," Tasmin said — she had thrown the red nations into turmoil without learning even one useful fact about the Raven Brave.

"Jimmy's sly — he might be lurking — that's what's upset the chiefs," Charbonneau stammered. "Jimmy can sneak up on a prairie chicken and catch it, which is a rare skill. It's best to be watchful with Jimmy around."

At that point they all heard a high whistling — a great flock of swans, hundreds and hundreds, were passing directly overhead, a fact which seemed to stimulate even sharper anxiety amid the chiefs and the *engagés*. They clearly did not like being beneath so many swans.

To Tasmin all this stir and hubbub was quite ridiculous. It was a fine day — the boat was moving steadily — what harm could come from a flock of birds? What astonished her was that her rescuer, Mr. Snow — who was only one man — inspired such fear that half the men on the boat felt they must rush to arms — yet still, she didn't know why.

It occurred to her then that there *was* one person who might be helpful, the cheerful and muscular Captain George Aitken, the master of the steamer *Rocky Mount*.

Less than a minute later, to George Aitken's mild surprise, Tasmin presented herself on the bridge.

10

"Our West is not much like your gentle England."

Mr. Catlin's easel and paints were set up on the bridge, but of that silly cackler there was no sign — Tasmin was alone with sturdy Captain Aitken, who was studying the river with a practiced eye.

"Oh, Mr. Catlin — no, miss," he said. "Mr. Catlin's gone ashore with your father on a hunt. I believe they are hoping to scare up a bear."

"How thrilling — we've so few in England now — just what the Gypsies have," Tasmin said. "May I ask if you're acquainted with Mr. Jim Snow? I mentioned him to Monsieur Charbonneau and I'm afraid caused quite a stir."

"Jimmy, why yes, I know him pretty well," Captain Aitken said. "I thought that was Jim you set ashore this morning — bit of a tussle you were having, it seemed."

Tasmin blushed — she had not supposed this honest captain had seen her violent shaking. Of course he had a spyglass — no doubt an indispensable tool on such a river.

And yet Captain Aitken quietly went on with his job. He did not appear to feel that a tussle on a riverbank between a lad and a lass was a thing much out of the ordinary.

"That was my fault — I fear I let slip a mild oath — it was more than Mr. Snow could tolerate," Tasmin admitted.

"That's Jimmy — he's preachy unless he's drunk," Captain Aitken said. "Best not to cuss in his company unless you have to, though he's a rip-roaring cusser himself when his blood is up. Smacked you on the cheek, I see — didn't he, miss?"

Tasmin did have a bit of a bruise on one cheek, though this bluff professional man had been the only one to mention it. Her mother might well have mistaken it for dirt, but Mademoiselle Pellenc, no stranger to slappings, must surely have seen it for what it was.

Tasmin found that she liked Captain Aitken the better for his candor — she gave him a smile and he returned it.

"When I mentioned Mr. Snow's name belowdecks it stirred up quite a fuss," she said. "Can you tell me why?"

"Jimmy's an Indian fighter," Captain Aitken said, speaking as casually as if he had just informed her that Mr. Snow was a butcher, a baker, or a candlestick maker. "Oh, Jim can trap and he can hunt as well — he and Pomp Charbonneau have trapped all the way up on the Green River, and not many can say that."

"I have heard of young Monsieur Charbonneau," Tasmin said. "Is he an Indian fighter too?"

Captain Aitken looked at her for rather a long while — something of the weariness that had been in Jim Snow's face when she challenged him to take her with him could be seen in Captain Aitken's face as well, though the captain's gaze held no trace of unfriendliness. He just looked tired — nothing seemed to tire men so quickly as even a few minutes' questioning by a persistent woman.

"You're new to our country, Miss Berrybender," Captain Aitken said. "Our West is not much like your gentle England. If a man's got killing in him, the West will draw it out."

"And is Monsieur Pomp Charbonneau an Indian fighter too?" Tasmin repeated.

"Oh, Pomp will kill in battle, if he has to," the captain said. "So will I — and I have. But most sensible men will walk around an Indian fight, if they can. I will, and Pomp will too."

"But not Mr. Snow, I take it," Tasmin said.

"No, not Jimmy," the captain said. "It's the Indians who will walk around Jimmy, if he'll allow it."

"What happens when he won't allow it?" Tasmin asked.

The poor man heaved a sigh.

"When he won't, then there's likely to be hell to pay," Captain Aitken said.

11

. . . Cook brought up a squab
and a squash . . .

That Indians feared Jim Snow, the Sin Killer, did
not surprise Tasmin — she had seen the cold fury
in his eyes when he turned to face the four painted
warriors by the hill of devils. She very much
doubted that there were devils about that rocky
bluff that could have bested the Sin Killer when it
came to dealing out carnage. Perhaps he had only
held back that day because he didn't want her to
see him at his killing.

Once she left the bridge Tasmin spent the
morning sitting under a little awning outside her
bedroom, a victim of very uneven moods. She
looked far out onto the plains to the west, the
plains that she had trod but for a day. At lunch
Cook brought up a squab and a squash, the
latter article having been obtained from some
mild river Indians a few days earlier. Tasmin ate
only a bite or two. The appetite that had led her
to rip at a deer's liver with her teeth had now
quite deserted her. In a room nearby Buffum
and Bobbety were attempting their Latin, under
the droning instruction of Master Jeremy Thaw
— she could just make out rhythms that seemed
to suggest Horace. From time to time the boat

would have to back off a riffle, or else the *engagés* might need to saw off a snag. Fraulein Pfretzskaner and Master Thaw had their customary spat — the Fraulein wanted him to finish up with Latin so she could begin with their mathematics. At the end of the spat Fraulein burst into tears; salty floods drenched her great bosom, an interruption which gave Buffum and Bobbety time to attempt to make peace with their sister.

"We are so sorry, Tassie, that we interrupted you with your gentleman," Buffum said. "We will never be so brash again."

"What will *that* matter — as you can see, my gentleman is gone," Tasmin said, in her iciest tones.

"I suppose he meant to carry you away to Samarkand," Bobbety said, in his most grating voice.

"Samarkand is in Persia, you ignorant nit," Tasmin told her brother. "The city west of here where I had hoped to be taken is Santa Fe — but now you two have ruined everything."

"Perhaps Papa would hire you a guide," Buffum said. "It is said that Monsieur Charbonneau's son is a fine guide. He was brought up in Germany by a prince, I believe."

"Yes, the brilliant Pomp," Tasmin said. How a son of Charbonneau's had got to Germany was rather intriguing but it did nothing to mollify her for the loss of Jim Snow. Though her siblings were virtually prostrate with guilt, Tasmin did not immediately unbend — such pious virtues as forgiveness did not appeal to her. Besides, there was the distinct possibility that the Raven Brave was gone for good, driven off by her cursing. He may have felt that such a hell-bound woman deserved no guide.

These unhappy thoughts produced in Tasmin an almost unendurable restlessness. It was a sultry day — after a time she napped, slipping into an impatient, swollen dream. She seemed to hear great wings beating, and then a hand was on her, near the dark entry. She waited, but just then the steamer bumped hard against a riffle and Tasmin woke. Her sister Mary sat by the rail, licking clean the last greasy bones of Tasmin's squab.

"Who offered you my bird, you greedy wretch?" Tasmin inquired.

"The Hairy Horn says that we shall see a million pigeons this afternoon," Mary replied — of all the family she took the least notice of Tasmin's moods. "Old Gorska can easily shoot you some."

Tasmin, hungry again, made no answer.

"I expect you'll soon be leaving this old boat, won't you, Tassie?" Mary asked. She was but a little thing, yet she made up in ferocity what she lacked in size. Bobbety was of the opinion that she might be rabid — but of course, Bobbety's opinions were rarely accurate.

In this case, Mary was right. Tasmin did mean to leave the boat, which was just a floating

Europe. Even the smelly *engagés* were merely Frenchmen at one remove.

"The chiefs are hoping you will lure the Sin Killer on board," Mary said. "They hope to fall on him and kill him."

"Oh tush," Tasmin said. "The chiefs are old men. I doubt they would be a match for my Raven Brave."

"It is only the Indians to the north who call him the Raven Brave — Mr. Catlin told me that," Mary said. "And he told me why."

"Well, if Mr. Catlin said it, then it must be knowledge beyond challenge," Tasmin replied. "His learning is quite encyclopedic, in his own view at least."

"I like Mr. Catlin," Mary said. "Once we locate some buffalo he means to make me his assistant. We'll tramp off into the prairie and I'll carry his paints."

"If you're going to wake me up, stick to the point," Tasmin said. "Why do the Indians of the north call my friend Mr. Snow the Raven Brave?"

"Because there are no vultures in the north," Mary said, giving the bones of the pigeon one last lick. "In the north the raven is the bird of death."

"You needn't sound so melodramatic about it, Mary," Tasmin said. "Even in England crows are carrion birds. Nor is it a bad thing that Indians fear my friend. I myself would be a captive of the noisy Osage now, had Mr. Snow not saved me."

"Mr. Catlin says Papa is not to shoot the great swans," Mary said. "He says the Indians believe that swans are the carriers of souls."

"Tut, they only want to sell the feathers," Tasmin said. "Your new friend Mr. Catlin is a fine exaggerator. Take that plate to Cook and ask her to fix me a chop — a large chop."

"Cook was just thrashing Eliza," Mary informed her. "Eliza broke two plates this morning. If she is allowed to go on in this way we will soon be without a plate to our name."

"Trot along and do as you're told," Tasmin said, and then at once retracted her command, having just remembered something.

"Mr. Snow claims he saw you talking to a serpent," she said. "Is that true? Can you communicate with serpents?"

"It was merely a moccasin — I told it to go bite Bobbety, since he assaulted me with a frog," Mary said. "But the moccasin did nothing to Bobbety, otherwise he'd be dead."

"Mary, you are a violent brat," Tasmin said.

12

. . . far to the west, on a low hill, three antelope stood.

Long before the pigeons came, every member of the hunting party was in a crashing bad temper, none more so than Lord Berrybender, who was not accustomed to tramping around for hours without once firing his gun. He did not, at least, have to *carry* his gun — Gorska Minor shouldered the two fowling pieces, while Gladwyn took the rifles. Old Gorska had his own weapon, Belgian-made and of the finest workmanship; Mr. Catlin, who merely carried an ordinary musket, had several times complimented Gorska on his excellent Belgian gun. These compliments did not entirely please Lord Berrybender, who did not see why the help should have better equipment than his own, although it was true that the company would soon be dependent on the Polish hunter for meat, and possibly even for defense. Had he been allowed to blast away continually at buffalo and bear, or even antelope and elk, Lord Berrybender might have been less envious of Gorska's Belgian gun; but such, emphatically, had not been the case. The prairie grass that from a distance looked so silken was more nearly like a carpet of needles, and nothing appeared to be abroad to be stuck by the needles but themselves.

"I say, Gorska, can't you send that boy off to beat the bushes and scare up a stag or two?" Lord B. inquired impatiently.

"What bushes? No bushes," Gorska said. He had honed his hunting skills in the employ of a petty prince, ruler of a pocket duchy in the foothills of the Carpathians, in whose heavily forested glades it was easy to surprise the local game: boar, stag, even bear. But how was anyone to surprise game on this treeless prairie, where the wind was always blowing, for hunting purposes, from the wrong direction and where the animals — who, after all, were not blind — could see the hunters coming when they were still far out of range of even the best Belgian rifle?

"Well, if there are no bushes, then it's somebody's fault," Lord B. complained. "Poor planning, I say. Somebody should have come out here and planted a few bushes."

George Catlin, though he considered Lord Berrybender to be a rude, crusty old fussbudget, also knew that he was reputed to be one of the richest men in England; a hand-to-mouth painter such as himself, often dependent on extremely whimsical patronage, could not afford to be rude to the richest man in England, however great a fool he might be.

"Of course, of course — such an excess of visibility is a great inconvenience," he said. "It's a pity Mr. Jefferson was never in the West — I imagine he would have at once foreseen the necessity of bushes."

Just then Old Gorska held up a hand: far to the west, on a low hill, three antelope stood.

The efficient if moody Gladwyn, who was never more than a step behind Lord Berrybender, immediately held out a rifle.

"Antelope . . . about time they showed up," Lord Berrybender said.

"We're in luck, sir," George Catlin said. "Saddle of antelope is a most excellent American dish . . . first rate, excellent, tasty." When nervous, and he was usually nervous, George failed to see that his habit of using three words where one would have done was apt to irritate some people.

"They are a mile away," Old Gorska pointed out — he saw no hope of a successful approach to the jittery antelope.

"Quite inaccurate, they are but half a mile from us at most," Gladwyn said. He did not approve of the Pole.

"Mile," Gorska repeated, though he had no idea how far away the animals were.

The antelope appeared to be watching the English party — to George Catlin's eye they seemed poised for flight.

"My gun won't shoot a mile — or half a mile either," Lord Berrybender said. "The beasts must be brought closer."

"There's an old hunter's dodge that sometimes works with antelope," George said. "I believe the mountain men use it with frequent success . . . they're curious, you see, the prong-horns. I will advance a little way toward them and then stop and stand on my head. If I waggle my legs at them they may be disposed to come and investigate. Crouch down and have your guns ready while I make the attempt."

"All right," Lord Berrybender said. "Perhaps I'll just say a prayer or two, while I'm kneeling. I've been rather wicked with Venetia lately."

George Catlin advanced some fifty steps and then, laying aside his floppy hat, quickly stood on his head. The antelope had not moved. Carefully, he began to waggle his legs and was just getting the hang of it when the antelope, unattracted, turned and fled.

Sobered by the suspicion that he had not only lost three antelope but several fat commissions as well, George Catlin brushed the grass off his hat and rejoined the group.

"I fear they winded us," he said.

"Next time I'll bring my horse — at least I could chase the brutes," Lord Berrybender said.

Gorska Minor proceeded to kick up a badger, an aggressive creature who bared its teeth and snarled. While Gorska Minor poked at it with his ramrod the sky darkened; the sounds of millions of beating wings was heard. From the north the pigeons came, in a cloud that blocked the sun and cast a shadow far across the prairie. The hunting party stood and looked — some half an hour passed and still the cooing pigeons came.

"Where are they going, Catlin?" Lord B. inquired.

"Perhaps Indiana — someplace where there's grain," George said.

Lord Berrybender took his fowling piece and fired carelessly into the air: twenty-two pigeons rained down. Gorska Minor was forced to scamper, in his efforts to gather them up.

"It won't do, Gorska — I think I might have hoped for something better than squab," Lord Berrybender said, turning in disgust toward the river and the boat.

13

. . . news of the Sin Killer's approach had stirred them up.

The *engagés* were bitter because the English lord was so stingy with his grog — the splenetic Mery-Michaud, who had never been closer to France than the Hudson's Bay Company's trading post at Three Rivers, had heard of a big revolution and wanted to cut the old lord's head off. He came to Toussaint Charbonneau ranting about grog and beheadings; it was a message the tired interpreter received more and more wearily, every evening. The chiefs were in a disorderly mood too — news of the Sin Killer's approach had stirred them up.

It seemed to Charbonneau that he had spent far too much of his life listening to the endless complaints of *engagés* and Indian chiefs. If it wasn't grog they lacked, it was women, or money, or vittles.

"Shush that blab, Mery, unless you want a fine flogging," Charbonneau said. "I ain't the boss of His Lordship's liquor — there's a whole keelboat of it, alongside. Go steal some if you're that dry."

Big Charlie Hodges smiled at that suggestion — if Charbonneau had ever been fully sober himself he would have realized that the *engagés* had been going regularly over the side, to nip bottles of Lord Berrybender's claret from the keelboat. Charlie Hodges was the only American among the crew — George Aitken had hired him because he needed at least one boatman who spoke English, to give him precise information about the riffles and the snags.

Charlie didn't care much for the *engagés*, but he had a certain sympathy for Sharbo, an old, tired man, not unkindly, who had the hard job of managing the three surly chiefs and the English family too.

"That liquor boat is already sitting higher in the water — I'm surprised nobody's noticed," Charlie said.

Tim, the stable boy, who looked after Lord Berrybender's two thoroughbreds and his fine pair of carriage horses, knew that the rascally Frenchmen were stealing the old lord's liquor, but he hated the old man, who had often cuffed him rudely, and didn't care.

"How long before it's all gone, Charlie?" Tim asked.

"A month, maybe," Charlie said. "I expect most of the *engagés* will be long gone by then — they'll want to be trapping up the Red River of the North."

Though he didn't say it, Charlie Hodges meant to be long gone by that time too. Tim could stay in his stables and play the beast with two backs with Miss Elizabeth Berrybender all he pleased — Charlie had heard them huffing and grunting several times. Tim, for his part, had been equally discreet when he saw Fraulein Pfretzskaner slipping Charlie Hodges a big sausage or a leg of goose. It was clearly Charlie that the Fraulein favored — he was the only man on board built to her own ample dimensions; the day rarely passed but that she found a way to offer her Charlie some tidbit from His Lordship's table. Most nights they managed to enjoy at least some fleshly probings in a private corner off the pantry.

Charlie Hodges, though he closely concealed his intentions from everyone, did not intend to remain much longer with the steamer *Rocky Mount*. Charlie was no river man — he had headed west to farm, having heard that the Ioway soil was rich and fertile. The forests were said to be light, the Indians not too fierce. Though fond of Captain Aitken, Charlie did not feel he could allow such an opportunity to be missed. Somewhere above the mouth of the Platte, a stream they would very soon pass, he meant to leave the boat and tramp off to the east. His hope was to find land close to the Mississippi, which would make for ease of shipping, and as surely as he would need a plow, he would also need a wife — and he wanted no skinny slip of a girl, either. What he wanted was a fine sturdy woman of height and heft, someone who would bear him six to a dozen children to help him work the land. For such a task the big Fraulein seemed ideal; she hissed like a kettle whenever he touched her, steamed like a stove when they could enjoy a full embrace. For the Berrybenders, her employers, the Fraulein expressed only loathing. She would leave with her Charlie in an instant — if it should be that they must escape with only the clothes on their backs, then the Fraulein was ready. She could cook, she could sew, she could wield an axe; no more lessons with the stupid English children, no more quarrels with the skinny, stuck-up French whore. Charlie's secret was safe with her — it was her secret too.

Meanwhile Charbonneau, tired and tipsy, was trying to convince the Hairy Horn that the Sin Killer would not attack the boat.

"Jimmy's got no call to fight us," he said. "He just found that English girl and brought her back, that's all."

"A warrior who has eaten the lightning doesn't behave like other men," the Hairy Horn said. He himself had no fear of the Sin Killer. Such a warrior would gain nothing by killing an old man like himself. His interest was mainly in the lightning. Among his own people the belief was that a warrior who had eaten the lightning and survived was impervious to ordinary weapons. In the Hairy Horn's long lifetime he had known only one other man — a Sioux named Burnt Eagle — who had been struck by lightning and lived to fight again. Burnt Eagle had finally been killed by a white bear, but not before he had stolen many horses and counted plenty of coups.

"Only the white bears can kill a man who has eaten the lightning," the Hairy Horn remarked, before retiring to his blanket for the night. What he really wanted was for Sharbo to offer him his woman; such a fine plump girl would be good, but Sharbo, though he had lived long among the Mandans, was like other whites in that regard. He did not share his woman, which was a pity. A girl so young and bouncy would be a good thing, for an old man.

When the old chief left, Gorska walked over to Charbonneau.

"When the buffalo?" he asked, in his limited English.

"I can't say," Charbonneau admitted. "It's been a wet year — lots of the little water holes are full. The buffalo don't need to come to the river yet."

Gorska shuffled off, not satisfied. Every day Lord B. asked about the buffalo. He seemed to think it was Gorska's fault that there were none for him to shoot.

Charbonneau walked over and said a few words to Big White, repeating what he had told the Hairy Horn about Jim Snow. Big White hardly listened — he was a vain old fellow who still believed that the strength of his own arm was all the security he needed against an enemy. He had even put it out that he had single-handedly killed a white bear with his great club, a claim that made even his own young warriors snicker: they knew that the bear was barely

95

quarter grown, little more than a cub, and had been groggy from a winter's sleep when Big White clubbed it.

Charbonneau understood that Big White, the Mandan, was a braggart, and that the Hairy Horn was just a loquacious old man who babbled on to anyone who would listen to him. The only one of his native charges who worried him was the Piegan, Blue Thunder, a powerful man given to sudden, explosive rages. The first wisdom he had been offered about the tribes on the upper Missouri was that the Blackfeet were those who should be given the widest berth. Though there were many beaver in the streams west of the Yellowstone, few white men had harvested many and escaped with their own hair. Captain Clark had particularly warned the English lord about the Blackfeet, but who knew what an English lord would do?

The tall Piegan had passed through Washington in silence — the president's flattery had not impressed him, though he did consider the white man's axes very superior tools and had been quick to gather up a good supply.

Though Toussaint Charbonneau had been up and down the Missouri River more than twenty times he had never enjoyed the luxury of such a fine boat as the steamer *Rocky Mount*. He and Coal had a snug bunk under an overhang. Coal kept their baggage neat, busying herself to see that he was as comfortable as possible; though her efforts were appreciated they did not keep

Charbonneau from feeling old, tired, and over-burdened; he felt he might be making his last trip up the capricious river on whose banks he had spent much of his life. It seemed to him that there was a sadness about these long plains that seeped into men who traveled them too long. That sadness had seeped into him. Too much was expected of him — too much. In his memory Charbonneau had begun to loop back to the time when he and his Bird Woman, Sacagawea, whom Captain Clark called Janey, had made the great trek to the ocean, with their boy, Pomp, just a baby on Sacagawea's back. Of all the women he had known, his Bird had been the quickest of mind; even when she did not know the words that were being spoken she could figure out what was intended, what was at stake. None of his other women had had so lively a mind.

Coal knew that her husband was a man of many sorrows, sorrows too old for her to grasp. Her main hope was that she would soon be with child. She dreamed of a fat little boy — once her husband saw that he could still be a maker of sons some of his sorrow might go away. To insure that there would be a child, and a male child, Coal did everything the old women told her to do. She watched the moon, she took certain herbs. Sometimes when Sharbo was drinking with the boatmen Coal would try to entice him away before he became too tired. Sometimes when he came to their pallet ready to sink into sleep Coal would manage to arouse him just enough that he could be a man for a few moments, long enough to fill her with his seed.

Yet Coal sometimes felt that her husband's sadness must have come into her, along with his seed. She was by nature a cheerful girl, and yet, sometimes, lying by Sharbo and listening to him snore, she could not keep sadness away — could not choke back her tears. Her husband was old, he might get drunk and fall overboard; someone might kill him; he might simply die, as old men did. Then, whether she liked it or not, she might have to become the wife of some cruel warrior, like Blue Thunder. Every night Coal listened carefully to the call of the night birds; she was listening, particularly, for the trumpeting of the great tundra swans, birds that came every year to the Swamp of the Swans. The old women told her that if, mating, she heard the call of the tundra swans, it would be the best of omens. Then she would soon deliver a fat little boy; then maybe her husband would cheer up.

14

. . . George Catlin, his death at hand, took the only course open to him . . .

George Catlin felt bold enough one morning to ask Lady Tasmin at breakfast if she would care to sit for her portrait — he was at once rebuffed so rudely that he promptly went below and cajoled — with an offer of a new musket and some blue beads — the Piegan Blue Thunder to sit in her stead. After all, it was Indians, not English ladies, that he had come west to paint. Mr. Gainsborough had painted plenty of the latter.

Tasmin knew that the cranky painter was becoming rather too fond of her — even sharp rudeness didn't really discourage him. A week had passed since Jim Snow returned her to the boat — a week during which she had remained so snappish and surly that both family and servants did their best to stay out of her way.

"Blue Thunder will be my first attempt at a portrait of a Western Indian," George said — he did not allow himself to be discouraged by Tasmin's rudeness and had gone back upstairs to finish his coffee. "You can come and watch me work, should you care to, Lady Tasmin."

"Why would I want to watch George Catlin paint a picture of an Indian when I can see the

Indian for myself?" Tasmin asked Mary, when George had gone off to assemble his equipment.

Nevertheless, since there was little to do on board except stare at the muddy water of the featureless prairies, Tasmin and Mary drifted down to the lower deck. The Piegan was painting his face in vivid reds and yellows, in preparation for the sitting. Big White and the Hairy Horn ignored these preparations — both were sulking because the painter had not chosen them instead of Blue Thunder.

"I think you and I should gather up our kit and immediately leave this boat, taking only Tintamarre as our protector," Mary said.

Tasmin ignored the comment. For a week she had thought of nothing but escape, and yet she had had just enough experience of prairie life to convince herself that escape, at the very least, might prove impractical.

"Eliza has now broken three more plates," Mary continued. "Mama and Papa will soon be eating off the bare boards — and besides, if we don't hurry, we'll never catch your Mr. Snow."

"In a logical universe I would not be pursuing Mr. Snow, Mr. Snow would be pursuing me," Tasmin observed, noting that the painted Piegan was a strikingly handsome man.

"Perhaps he's following us, even now," Mary said. "Perhaps he means to kidnap you and ravish you."

Tasmin could not suppress a laugh at the wildness of the little creature's imagination.

"You've been spending too much time with Vicky Kennet," Tasmin said. "It is she who secretly dreams of wild ravishments — I believe she is growing rather tired of our old papa."

On the lower deck, near the rail, Mr. George Catlin was waiting with clear impatience for Blue Thunder to finish adorning himself. The Piegan wore a beaded war shirt and had draped himself with a great necklace of bear claws.

"I do believe it will take him longer to paint himself than it will take me to paint *him*," George said.

"I wouldn't mind sitting, I suppose, should you tire of painting these aboriginals," Venetia Kennet, a new arrival, declared. She had unloosed her auburn hair, which fell well below her waist. Both Señor Yanez and Signor Claricia had offered to slave untiringly for her throughout their lives, and yet neither had yet been admitted to the sanctum of her boudoir.

"I'm surprised you aren't at your scales, Vicky," Tasmin said. "Such a demanding discipline, the cello."

Venetia Kennet ignored that thrust. The humid air induced in her a heavy languor. For Tasmin Berrybender she felt the blackest hatred, of the sort one beauty is likely to harbor for another. Vicky's principal hope was that Lord B. would soon get off on a hunt, sparing her, for a day, his heavy but inattentive embraces.

Just then Mademoiselle Pellenc came down from Lady Berrybender's cabin carrying Prince

Talleyrand, the ill-tempered old parrot, to allow him his daily airing. Mademoiselle detested the flea-bitten old bird, but Lady B. insisted that Mademoiselle be the one to air him — after all, they both had French names.

No sooner had Prince Talleyrand been released from his cage than he hopped up on the rail near where George Catlin was rapidly sketching in Blue Thunder's wildly tinted profile. The parrot seemed to take more interest in the likeness than any of the other spectators — the scraggly old bird tipped his head curiously, from side to side.

"Good morning, Prince Talleyrand," George said, hoping that a great eagle might sweep down and relieve them all of the filthy bird. It was hard to get a profile right while enduring the scrutiny of a querulous old parrot.

"*Schweig, du blöder Trottel!*" Prince Talleyrand said, raspily but distinctly — even Mary Berrybender gaped with astonishment, while Fraulein Pfretzskaner, who sometimes amused herself by teaching the bird random insults, blushed a very bright red.

"What did he say?" George asked, in shock at having been rudely addressed by a parrot.

Holger Sten, the Danish painter, let out a roar of laughter — to his mind the parrot's remark was quite appropriate.

" 'Shut up, you silly fool,' that's what he said," Holger informed them.

"It's just a country phrase — customary,"

Fraulein Pfretzskaner mumbled, departing at once to seek her Charlie.

George Catlin, always a quick worker, thought he had Blue Thunder's profile just about right — it only needed a little lengthening of the chin. He was well aware of native impatience; for the moment speed was more important to him than finesse — he could always touch up the likenesses once he got back to Philadelphia. He meant to call his portfolio *Vanishing Races*, and he knew the native races *would* vanish — the very fact that he was traveling up the Missouri in a steamboat meant that, for these wild, warring peoples, the end was not far off.

Lord Berrybender, trailed by his man Gladwyn, came slowly downstairs, feeling rather heavy in his bowels, just as George Catlin finished his adjustment of Blue Thunder's chin. Lord B. tramped over to the easel and took a look.

"Why, hark the heralds, you've got the brute to a T," His Lordship remarked.

Pleased by this unexpected compliment, George Catlin picked up his little canvas and handed it to his sitter, Blue Thunder, hoping the Piegan would like it too. In this he was to be disappointed: instantly the Piegan's passive manner turned to one of horror and rage. He slapped at his painted cheeks, as if to assure himself that they were still part of his face; then he grabbed a hatchet and advanced on the horrified painter, uttering a high, chilling shriek —

103

George Catlin, his death at hand, took the only course open to him, which was to vault over the rail into the river.

Lady Berrybender had been following her husband down to the lower deck, a glass of gin in one hand. Blue Thunder's wild shriek startled her so that she missed her step and plunged straight downstairs, knocking Mademoiselle Pellenc into Señor Yanez, who in turn fell against Gorska Minor, who had been cleaning a gun. People toppled like dominoes; Big White and the Hairy Horn dashed to Blue Thunder's side, and the three of them began to gobble like angry turkeys — at least that was how it sounded to Tasmin's ear. Blue Thunder seemed disposed to leap into the water and finish off the sputtering painter, and he might have, had not Monsieur Charbonneau rushed up and restrained him.

"I say, what a racket — what's upset them, Charbonneau?" His Lordship asked.

"Why, it's just that in the picture Blue Thunder only has half his face — that's the cause of the racket," Charbonneau explained. "Blue Thunder thinks Mr. Catlin has stolen the other half of him — once he *feels* himself good and knows that he's all there, I believe he'll quiet down."

Holger Sten turned to wink at Piet Van Wely, who shared his dislike of the cranky Catlin — but Piet Van Wely was staring hard at the fallen Lady Berrybender, whose eyes were open, whose mouth gaped, and whose neck was bent at a most startling angle.

"Oh, Constance is always fainting; eats too much," Lord Berrybender said, hardly glancing at his wife. "Gluttons frequently faint.

"Do get up, Constance," he insisted. "I'm about to leave for my hunt — mademoiselle, perhaps you might better fetch the smelling salts."

But Mademoiselle Pellenc, Señor Yanez, Signor Claricia, Gorska Minor, Tasmin, Mary, and even Bobbety and Buffum, alarmed by the Piegan's shrieks, all knew what Lord Berrybender had not yet realized, which was that his wife, Lady Constance Berrybender, a heavy eater, would never need smelling salts again. She lay on the lower deck of the steamer *Rocky Mount*, stone dead of a broken neck.

15

. . . Mademoiselle Pellenc, whose duty it had been to tend the bird . . .

It was hours later — after the dripping George Catlin had come back on board, after peace had been restored with the chieftains, after Lady Berrybender had received one last kiss from each of her children, after her hair had been combed one last time by Mademoiselle Pellenc, after her shroud had been sewn tightly shut by the skilled seamstress Fraulein Pfretzskaner — that someone happened to remember Prince Talleyrand, Lady Berrybender's parrot. A search was made, but to no avail. Prince Talleyrand had evidently flown away.

"It seems you were right to begin with, George," Tasmin said to the painter, so stunned by what had happened that he had not even bothered to change out of his wet clothes.

"It *is* the river Styx we're traveling on," Tasmin continued. "Not only has it taken poor Mama in the general direction of Hades, but we've lost her parrot too."

George Catlin was silent, for once. His comment about the river Sticks had been only a rather poor jest.

"As for Prince Talleyrand, good riddance, I

say," Bess piped. "Smelly old bird."

But Mademoiselle Pellenc, whose duty it had been to tend the bird, could not accept the loss of her once-despised feathery charge.

"Now I am the only French," she cried.

"Well, no, there are the *engagés*," Tasmin reminded her, but she gave the poor half-crazed woman a comforting hug anyway.

16

Now, in the bright morning,
a grave was being dug . . .

Jim Snow watched the burial party from a sizable thicket of plum bushes. For a moment he feared the big red dog might catch his scent, but the dog merely looked his way for a moment before trotting off behind a large procession of children and servants, their goal a low bluff where several *engagés* were laboring to dig a grave.

The old parrot had alighted at Jim's campfire the night before. Now that the family whose pet the old bird had been were trooping up a hill, in plain sight, Jim rather expected the bird to rejoin them, but the parrot showed no interest in the grieving group. Instead it happily plucked the ripe, tart plums.

Though Jim Snow had walked briskly south most of a day he had been unable to get the bold, barefoot English girl in the muddy dress off his mind. In truth, his conscience was bothering him somewhat, where Tasmin was concerned. When she cursed he had shaken her so hard he feared she might have cracked a tooth; and yet he doubted that his shaking, or anything else, would long prevent her from leaving the boat and striking out for Santa Fe. Clearly she was a young woman of uncommon determination. Jim could not imagine why such a girl, or such a family, would be traveling up the Missouri River with winter coming on. There was nothing to be expected in the high Missouri country except wild tribes and bitter cold. Santa Fe, with its bustling trade, made a far likelier destination, and yet the big steamboat had already passed the usual embarkation points for Santa Fe. What the passengers meant to do in such wild country was a puzzle to Jim. Of course, the men could hunt, but it was hardly necessary to travel two thousand miles upriver to find good prairie hunting — the Osage were even then killing buffalo in abundance not a day from where the boat floated.

After a night of brooding — a night spent so close to the Swamp of the Swans that he didn't dare make a fire — Jim had retraced his steps to the Missouri. He caught up with the steamer on the afternoon of the fifth day, watching the prairies carefully for any sign that a party had headed west. Since then he had quietly followed the steamer, expecting, any day, to see Tasmin and some of the company disembark and strike out. When the old bearded hunter, the great lord, and the others had tramped ashore to hunt, Jim hung well back, watching. It was obvious that none of the party had the slightest notion of how to conduct a prairie hunt. The old lord tramped around smoking a long pipe, whose smoke any animal and many men could smell from a great distance; besides that, the group had made no effort to keep quiet. The most they could have expected from such a noisy approach was to surprise a greedy black bear in a plum thicket. Bears were sometimes inattentive, but deer and antelope, hearing such loud voices, would be unlikely to linger until the hunters came in range.

Jim had hidden himself in an overgrown buffalo wallow while the hunting party passed — the old lord was upbraiding his servants at every step. They passed within forty yards of him, quite unaware that they were being watched; for Indians bent on war they would have been easy prey. A little later, while the party was returning to the boat, Jim killed a young antelope with an arrow. He considered taking a haunch out to the boat, but decided against it, and dried the meat. If he went to the boat it would only stir up the three chiefs, whom he could see plainly enough, standing in their blankets and paint. He felt it would not be long before the adventurous girl came ashore — maybe, despite the risks, he could devise a plan for taking her to Santa Fe. He was wading across a little creek when he heard, just faintly, the Piegan's high war cry and saw a man jump off the boat into the river. The Piegan was enraged, that was clear, but Jim could not make out what had stirred him up. From the boat there came a babble of voices but there were no more war cries; the hubbub soon died down. The steamer made no progress for the rest of that day. At dusk Jim waded into the river and gigged a fine catfish, using a gig made from a two-pronged willow branch. He was eating the catfish when the old parrot sailed in and made himself at home.

Now, in the bright morning, a grave was being dug and a line of mourners was filing up to it, led by the old lord, who was still smoking his long pipe. Someone was dead, but Jim could not determine who it might be. Tasmin strolled behind her father, followed by her brothers and sisters, several servants, Charbonneau, the chieftains, and George Aitken, the captain of the boat. Behind them came a tall girl carrying what appeared to be a giant fiddle.

Jim kept low — he knew that if one of the Indians saw him there would be a great uproar. He worried that the parrot, who fluttered boldly about the plum bushes, would give him away, but none of the mourners noticed. Soon there was hymn singing — then low, sad-sounding notes from the big fiddle. The burying didn't take long. The mourners, in scattered groups, were soon filing down the long slope to the boat. Charbonneau had been entrusted with the big fiddle. The young woman who played it was strolling arm in arm with the old lord.

"You best go back — they'll be leaving you," Jim said, giving the parrot a nudge.

"*Schweig, du blöder Trottel!*" Prince Talleyrand replied.

17

"Merely fornication
— wouldn't interest you, Bob."

"Let us declare war immediately, savage war!" Tasmin said, addressing herself to Bobbety, Buffum, and Mary. George Catlin came around the corner just at that moment and heard the shocking comment.

"War?" he asked. "War with whom?"

George had a jumpy look — having a war hatchet raised over his head had been an irregularity from which his nerves had not recovered.

"That comment was not meant for your ears, George," Tasmin said. "Do go along."

"Why must he twitter so?" Bess asked, when the painter had taken himself away.

"Oh, the artistic temperament, I suppose," Tasmin said. "Artists ain't rough, like us aristocrats."

She had summoned her closest siblings for a council of war. Lady Berrybender had been in her grave less than half a day, and yet Venetia Kennet had already moved herself and her cello into Lord B.'s stateroom, with the plain intent of becoming the next Lady Berrybender. Lord Berrybender, their father, was, as they all knew, no sentimentalist. His true feeling for his deceased wife, whose loins had yielded him four-teen children, had been summed up at breakfast, which Lord B. had tucked into with his usual appetite just before the funeral.

"Constance, your dear mother, had no head for cards," Lord B. remarked, as Cook served him his kidney. "An even weaker head if she happened to be drunk, which was often the case. I could always beat her at whist — don't recall dropping a single hand these past twenty years. Very comforting to have a wife one can invariably beat at whist — so relaxing."

Tasmin doubted that the import of that remark was lost on Venetia Kennet, who possessed an excellent head for cards.

"The point of this savage war is to prevent Vicky from marrying Papa," Tasmin told them. "Should that dreadful event come to pass I fear we should all be put to work in the scullery — Vicky has many insults to avenge."

"*Your* insults, Tasmin," Buffum said. "I am always most polite to Vicky myself."

"Oh, slap her, Bobbety," Tasmin said, and Bobbety *did* slap her, though not hard.

"Why can't we just kill her?" he said. "Any of the *engagés* would be glad to do it."

"No, let's sell her into slavery, perhaps to the violent Comanches," Mary suggested. "She would be sure to suffer gross indignities — ravishment among them."

"Do shut up about ravishment, you don't even know what it means," Tasmin said.

"I do — it's what Buffum suffers at the hands of Tim, down in the horse stalls," Mary said. "It makes her whimper and squeal."

"What *is* she talking about?" Bobbety asked. He spent his days cataloguing his growing collection of snails and spiders, a pursuit that left him little time for shipboard intrigue.

"Merely fornication — wouldn't interest you, Bob," Tasmin said. She was beginning to regret having called the council. Help from her siblings was apt to be sporadic at best. If they meant to compromise Venetia Kennet it would be best to do it soon, before the conniving cellist managed to get with child. And Mademoiselle Pellenc had assured her that the statuesque Vicky was quite expert at the seductive arts.

"I wish Mr. Snow would come and take me off this dull boat," Tasmin said. "The parched prairies would make a nice change."

"They ain't parched, it just rained yesterday," Buffum reported. "You are so bossy, Tasmin, and that's the very reason men don't like you."

"The fact that I don't fornicate with stable boys doesn't mean that men don't like me," Tasmin replied cooly.

Just then George Catlin came round the corner again, looking distressed.

"There's been rather an uproar," he said. "Mademoiselle flew at Fraulein and scratched her cheeks quite badly — then Fraulein snatched up a club belonging to one of the chieftains and smashed Master Thaw with it. Master Thaw lies unconscious, bleeding from both ears. Fraulein vows to leave the boat at once, and Mademoiselle declares that she will not travel another mile until Prince Talleyrand is found."

"If Master Thaw is injured, that means no progress with Horace," Bobbety said.

"I've a fine suggestion," Tasmin said. "The Missouri River has two banks — deposit Mademoiselle on one and Fraulein on the other. Then we'll never have to listen to their wild harpings again."

George Catlin gave a start. A tall man had appeared on the western bank. He thought it might be the frontiersman who had brought Tasmin back, but before he could comment the steamer struck a sandbar so violently that they were all thrown off balance. When George recovered his footing and looked at the western shore again, the tall man was no longer visible.

"I say, Tasmin, I thought I saw that fellow who brought you back," George said.

"What? Where?" Tasmin said, rushing to the rail.

"I saw him just as we hit the riffle," George said. "Can't seem to spot him now. He can't have gotten far."

Tasmin wasted no words and no time. In a flash she was in her stateroom, rummaging up a kit. She grabbed a laundry sack and stuffed a few articles of clothing in it. If she could just get ashore quickly, perhaps she could catch Jim Snow.

She went racing down to the boat's ladder, trailed closely by Mary and Tintamarre, only to discover to her vast irritation that two *engagés* had taken the pirogue some distance off, in order to probe the sandbar with long poles.

"Bring back my boat this minute!" Tasmin shouted, with such outrage in her voice that the *engagés* immediately obeyed. One man was so abashed that he jumped out of the boat and was soon mired in mud up to his thighs.

"I'm going along, you'll need me to find the tubers," Mary said. The second *engagé* was about to relinquish the pirogue when Captain Aitken, looking rather at his wit's end, came rushing down to stop them.

"You mustn't go now, miss — there's weather coming," the captain said.

"Look, Tassie — what a violent cloud," Mary said.

Tasmin saw that a great black cloud, with lightning dancing in it, and thunder rumbling, had stretched itself across the whole of the northern horizon. The sight vexed her extremely — why *would* such a storm come just when she had a chance to rejoin the Raven Brave?

For a moment she was of half a mind to go anyway — what could a storm do but get her wet? It was true that the wind, merely a breeze with the breath of summer yet in it, had increased in force and become as chill as November, but what was a bit of a blow compared to the loss of this miraculous opportunity?

Sensing the drift of her thoughts, Captain Aitken went so far as to grasp her arm.

"You mustn't try it, miss — there's apt to be terrible hail!" he said. "We've all got to batten down and stay inside."

Just then there was a thunderclap so loud it seemed it might split the earth. The rain was advancing rapidly across the river, a wall of gray water hiding the brown Missouri. The *engagé* who had foolishly jumped out of the boat was struggling desperately to get aboard. Captain Aitken rushed over and threw him a rope, shouting for the other men to pull. Even Old Gorska took a hand — the poor muddy fellow was reeled in just before the torrent struck. Tasmin, though bitter, realized she had to give way. She and Mary and the dog raced for the cover of the lower deck. After a brief violent deluge the wall of water passed them — tiny hailstones the size of peas began to pepper the steamer, striking the water like a million pebbles. Mademoiselle Pellenc was wild with fright, the Hairy Horn hid under the stairway, the *engagés* cried out to their God for mercy, and the size of the hailstones increased, first to the size of pigeons' eggs, then to the size of ducks' eggs; at the climax of the storm the hail was as large as turkey eggs.

"We shall be battered to bits! We have come to the end of days!" Mary whispered in mad glee — there was a light in her eyes that Tasmin couldn't regard as entirely sane.

The roar of the hail became so great that no speech would carry. Big White and the Piegan drew their blankets over their heads, and Charlie Hodges, snug under the stairs with the Hairy Horn, was heartily glad he had resisted the Fraulein's demand that they leave the boat summarily. On the open prairie, hail was what all animals feared — even elk and buffalo fled such storms.

Then the hail slowed, became intermittent: soon the hailstones were merely peas again, and the cloud, still black, now darkened the plain south of them — the plains were as white as if there had been a snowfall. On the lower deck some of the *engagés* crunched the smaller hailstones when they walked.

So intense had been the storm that when it passed no one moved at once. They sat as though numbed, at first scarcely able to credit that they were still alive and the boat not smashed. Tasmin, who had resolved to put out for shore the moment the storm passed, found that she had lost some of her resolve. The impulse that seized her so strongly had diminished as the storm battered its way past them. Her hastily assembled kit sat at her feet, but she made no move to rush to the pirogue.

"Ain't we going, Tasmin?" Mary asked.

"In a bit, perhaps," Tasmin said, feeling decidedly glum. Where would Jim Snow have got to, in such a storm? Were there not other men on the Western plains besides her Raven Brave?

118

Trappers were always passing them, headed downriver with peltries piled high in their small boats. Probably it hadn't even been Mr. Snow that George Catlin saw. The thought, logical and sensible as it was, made Tasmin want to cry.

"I wonder what Papa is doing," Bobbety said, wandering up. "Do you suppose he misses the mater?"

18

Another half minute and the thing would have been achieved . . .

Lord Berrybender, in fact, had been indulging in a leisurely act of fornication with Venetia Kennet when the violent clatter of the storm struck their roof. In Lord Berrybender's case it was a particularly ill-timed clatter — surrounded by such a roar, he lost his stroke; the fires so regularly induced by Venetia's white languor were damped by the pounding of hail just at the moment when Lord B. himself should have been pounding.

Another half minute and the thing would have been achieved; and yet, though Vicky Kennet turned quite rosy, the thing had *not* been achieved; her sly attempt to lock him in with her legs did not deceive Lord Berrybender, an amorite of vast experience. Noise of such a level was, at such a moment, unwelcome. He seemed to recall that a cannonade — where had it been? Egypt, perhaps, or was it the Peninsula? — had once had the same effect. In that case there had been no remedy, Lady Berrybender, with the help of her laudanum, having dropped into a deep unconsciousness, leaving Lord B. alone with his disappointment.

In the present instance, though, there was still

hope. His ingenious Vicky had invented a little variation which sometimes stimulated His Lordship to second or even third efforts.

"Venetia, that damn storm undid me," Lord Berrybender said. "Do be a good thing and get your bow. I believe success is still within my grasp if you'll just help us a bit with those ticklish horsehairs."

Oh rot! Venetia thought but she obediently slipped from the bed. Tired as she was of the old fool's sluggish embraces, she had no intention — with Lady Berrybender miraculously removed from her path — of allowing the richest man in England to escape her. She took up her cellist's bow and returned to the bed.

"Mustn't get it sticky now, Your Lordship," she said. "I fear my Haydn would suffer."

She drew the bow just lightly a few times across Lord Berrybender's floppy member. Reaction was not immediate, but Venetia — employing just the lightest of touches — persisted. Though other methods of resuscitation were available, she put her trust in her bow, deftly devoting a stroke or two to His Lordship's hairy balls.

"That's it, that's a good girl," Lord Berrybender said. "I believe I feel life returning."

"Now just lie still, this is merely the overture," Venetia said. "Soon we'll get along to the first movement."

"First movement be damned, we had *that*

before the thunder," Lord B. said. "It's the crescendo or whatever you call it that's wanted now."

A few more strokes and the laggardly organ gained at least a rather knobby strength; when Venetia Kennet judged that it was as high as it was likely to rise she carefully put down her bow — *not*, of course, the bow she actually played Haydn with — and flung herself astride His Lordship before he could go floppy again. If there was seed in the old brute she meant to have it; and very soon, the thing was, after all, achieved.

"Damn useful that you're a fiddler, Vicky," His Lordship said, before dropping off to sleep.

19

She would not trade her Pope . . .
her Akenside or Shenstone . . .

Mademoiselle Pellenc could not be calmed. Buffum, who could usually mollify the high-strung *femme de chambre,* was helpless before her abject despair. The loss of Lady Berrybender, coupled with the departure of Prince Talleyrand, had quite undone the poor woman — the violent hailstorm seemed to have been the last straw. She raced around the boat in hysterics, scaring the *engagés* and demanding to be put ashore to search for the lost bird. Big White wanted to strike the noisy woman with his big club, the very club that, in the hands of Fraulein, had deprived Master Jeremy Thaw of his powers of speech. Charbonneau pleaded with the irritated Mandan, a warrior not easily restrained.

"She'll run down soon, I expect," Charbonneau said. "Women do, you know . . . like clocks. They run down."

"She grieves for our dear mama," Bess said. "Such anguish is most affecting. Since we're stuck on a sandbar anyway, couldn't we mount at least a small expedition and go in search of Prince Talleyrand?"

Tasmin found, to her considerable vexation,

that she herself could think of little besides the Raven Brave. Never before in her life had a man occupied her thoughts for any length of time. Master Stiles, at best, seldom lasted half an hour. Various balladeers, poetasters, Portuguese, Frenchmen, or the male nobility of England could rarely tempt her from her studies for more than an hour. She would not trade her Pope, her Erasmus Darwin, her Akenside or Shenstone, her Scott or her Byron for all such male attentions. Yet now, in America, through the caprice of travel, she had stumbled onto a man she could not get off her mind.

But where was he? The American plain was vast, her own experience slight. The terrible hailstorm had reminded her of how vulnerable one was on the naked American plain.

"I suppose I could just ask Captain Aitken how long he thinks we might be stuck," she said. "If it will make Mademoiselle feel any better I suppose we could go tramp around a bit."

She found Captain Aitken sitting on the bridge, smoking a pipe so short it almost seemed an extension of his chin. The poor man looked exhausted, and no wonder, with such a bunch to supervise. Below them, in water as brown as burlap, a number of *engagés* were pulling with great ropes and pushing with long poles — but to no avail. The steamer *Rocky Mount* was firmly stuck.

Tasmin could not but like Captain Aitken. By dissuading her from her impulsive dash he had probably saved her life — but that was not why she liked him. What she liked was his evenhandedness, a rare quality in men of her acquaintance. He neither ranted nor fawned; the excitable, even hysterical behavior of the Europeans neither impressed him nor offended him, as far as Tasmin could tell.

George Catlin had set up his easel some ways down the deck — he wanted to capture the summer plains covered with white hailstones. Piet Van Wely stood behind him — he liked to study the painter's effects as he worked. If George Catlin minded the plum botanist's scrutiny, he didn't show it.

"I have to thank you, Captain — what a fearsome pounding we had," Tasmin said. "If I had pulled for shore I fear the consequences would have been dire."

Captain Aitken tipped his hat.

"You've no experience here, miss," he said. "Probably the weather's not so fickle, in England."

"It's certainly not so violent," Tasmin replied. "A storm such as that one would have broken half the windowpanes in London."

"Yes, and it damaged two of our paddles, as well," the captain said.

"Mr. Catlin spoke of seeing a man on shore just before we struck the sandbar," Tasmin said. "Did you perhaps see him too?"

"I saw him — that was old Dan Drew," the captain said. "He's a hunter — supplies passing boats with game when the season's fair. Dan will soon be round, I expect, once he sees we're stuck. Perhaps he'll bring us an antelope."

Tasmin's glumness returned. It had not been the Raven Brave after all, just some ancient hunter. Her wild impulse had only been folly, after all.

"Since we're stuck we were thinking of going ashore for a bit, to look for Mama's old parrot," Tasmin said. "Perhaps we'll meet this Mr. Drew."

"If you do he'll talk your ear off," the captain said. "Dan gets lonesome, walking the river. I wouldn't mind a word with him myself — he keeps up with the moods of the tribes . . . knows who's at war and who ain't. It's useful information."

"I wonder if he knows Mr. Snow?" Tasmin asked.

Captain Aitken gave her a thoughtful look. Tasmin felt awkward — perhaps too much eagerness had showed in her face or her voice.

"Dan buried Jim Snow's parents — they were massacred by the Kickapoo," Captain said. "Jimmy was just a babe. They hid him in a cactus patch — was Dan found him and took him to the Osage, who adopted him. He was pretty full of stickers before he got out of that cactus, Dan said."

"My goodness . . . what horror," Tasmin said. She waited, but Captain Aitken volunteered no more information, so she went down to call for the pirogue.

Gorska Minor, who was occasionally disposed to be helpful, brought the pirogue round and helped Tasmin store her kit, which she decided to bring along just in case. Gorska Minor had a tendency to leer at the girls — he often stationed himself just below stairs, the better to peer up petticoats; it was he who spread the rumor that the massive Fraulein Pfretzskaner had quite dispensed with undergarments.

Tasmin, Bobbety, Buffum, Mary, Piet, and the hound all came trooping down to the pirogue, but there was no sign of the hysterical French maid.

"Where *is* she, drat her?" Tasmin asked.

"Locked in her room — I suspect she is taking poison," Mary said.

"Quite likely it's merely constipation," Bobbety declared. "I suffer from it myself."

"It's this American diet," Piet suggested. "What we all need is some good cabbage soup."

"I am hardly in the mood to delay this trip just to hear you two speculate about Mademoiselle's bowels," Tasmin said, as she took up the paddle and commenced to row toward the distant shore. "If Mademoiselle wants to join us in the search she'll have to swim."

Almost at once there was a loud splash from behind them.

"She's swimming," Mary said.

20

Jim Snow had known
the storm was coming . . .

"Ever been in a cloud, Jimmy?" Dan Drew asked. The two of them sat out the big hailstorm in his dugout, cozily enough; but the hail had receded and it was possible to converse again. Dan Drew was not one to waste an opportunity, conversation being one of his favorite pursuits.

"I can't fly, Dan — how would I get in a cloud?" Jim asked. The dugout, which Dan Drew claimed had once been a snake den, was hidden beneath a low shelf of rocks on a little ridge. Quite a few hailstones had bounced into the dugout. Now and then Dan picked up one of the smaller hailstones and crunched it between his teeth.

"Well, the way to get in a cloud is to climb up one of the Rocky Mountains," Dan went on. "I've been in several clouds in my day — I've even been above them. I was right on top of a storm like this trying to get up one of them high peaks near the South Platte. I was up there looking for eagle eggs."

Jim Snow had known the storm was coming when he crossed a prairie dog town without seeing a single prairie dog. When the burrowing

128

creatures went to ground it was time to seek shelter. Dan Drew's dugout was not far away, so Jim ran to it, accompanied by the old parrot, who resisted all efforts to make him return to the boat. With the storm no longer a danger Jim was impatient to be off, but no one escaped Dan Drew without hearing seven or eight of his stories — most of them stories Jim didn't believe.

"Why would you want eagle eggs?" he asked.

"Oh, they weren't for me, they were for the professor," Dan said. "Tom Say his name was — he was traveling with Major Long, collecting birds' eggs and such."

"Why take birds' eggs, with a hunter like you to kill game?" Jim inquired, to be polite.

"They didn't gather them to eat, they gathered them to study," Dan informed him. "The professor particularly wanted eagle eggs, but the best I could do was an eaglet. It worked out well enough, though — Major Long tamed the eaglet. The major would stick bacon in his hatband and that eaglet would fly around his head and even land on his shoulder, trying to get the bacon — it made a big impression on the Indians. None of them had a tame eaglet."

Jim was ready to crawl out of the dark little room — it was lit by a single candle, floating in a cup of tallow.

"That professor even collected bugs and mites," Dan said. "He caught a louse and put it under a microscope — he let me look but it was a thing I didn't like to see. Bad enough to have to live with lice — why study them?"

"The storm's over, Dan — I'm off," Jim said. "Will you be visiting that steamer anytime soon?"

"I might, if I can knock down a deer to sell them," Dan said. "There's a passel of grandees on that boat. I expect George Aitken has his hands full with 'em."

"This old bird belongs on the boat," Jim said. "I'd be obliged if you'd return it for me — I suspect it's somebody's pet."

The parrot pecked at some of the smaller hailstones, crunching them much as Dan did.

Dan Drew reached over to get the bird, but the parrot waddled out of reach.

"I don't know, Jimmy — I think that old rascal has adopted you," Dan said.

"Well, I can't be bothered to keep up with somebody's parrot," Jim said, irritated that the bird would behave so queerly.

"Old critters have minds of their own," Dan said. "I expect this one's going to go where he wants to go."

No sooner had the two of them crawled out of the dugout than Prince Talleyrand took wing, flew high, and was soon out of sight.

21

A bloody death fit for an opera
seemed the only way to proceed.

Mademoiselle Pellenc locked herself in her room, meaning to cut her throat in privacy. Feeling that Lady Berrybender's death had deprived her of any reason to live, she meant to finish herself with some darning scissors. As Lady Berrybender's *femme de chambre* she had naturally stood first among the servants; but with her mistress gone the skinny young Frenchwoman knew that she could only expect the worst. Cook, who hated her for her finical demands, would give her only gristle and gruel. Señor Yanez and Signor Claricia had already grown bolder in their advances. Lord Berrybender, who had once dallied with her familiarly, was now besotted with the tall, untalented cellist, a woman who seemed quite unfamiliar with any music except Haydn's. And now the German slut had smashed the head of Master Thaw, the one nice man among the Europeans. Master Thaw had often paid Mademoiselle fine, elaborate compliments, but now, thanks to Fraulein, he had lost all power of speech.

A bloody death fit for an opera seemed the only way to proceed.

The darning scissors, however, quickly proved

inadequate to the task Mademoiselle set them. They were quite dull; they wouldn't cut. Instead of a great operatic gush of blood, the scissors merely pinched, raising an ugly bruise, which she was forced to slap over with powder before rushing out to join the boating party, her suicide postponed.

Mademoiselle was no sooner out the door than she saw that the pirogue had departed without her, an injustice that quite wrung her heart. It was her compatriot, Prince Talleyrand, that they were searching for. Mademoiselle had often fed the old bird hazelnuts — she felt quite sure he would come to her call. But there the boat went. Lady Tasmin hadn't waited — Lady Tasmin never waited! Without a moment's hesitation Mademoiselle jumped over the rail, realizing only at the last second that she might have been wiser to descend to the lower deck before jumping. But the die was cast. She jumped, she was falling!

Toussaint Charbonneau, Old Gorska, and the diminutive Italian, Signor Claricia, were all standing at the rail smoking when the skinny Frenchwoman came falling and fluttering right past them, to strike the sandy water with a resounding splash. They were all astonished — none of them had ever seen a *femme de chambre* fall out of the sky before.

"Now *that* was a splash, Gorska," Charbonneau said. "I was near to getting water in my eye."

Mademoiselle was not hurt by her wild leap, but neither was she pleased to find herself the cynosure of so many masculine eyes. Big White, the Hairy Horn, and even Charlie Hodges rushed to witness this curious spectacle. Mademoiselle had jumped into no more than three feet of water; the channel was not deep enough for easy swimming. The laughter and ribald comments of the *engagés* she ignored, but just as she struggled into deeper water, something brushed her leg; with her wet hair in her eyes Mademoiselle could just distinguish three ominous gray shapes. Convinced that they were crocodiles, she emitted a wild shriek and began to swim toward the pirogue as fast as she could, while behind her, the three gray logs floated silently on.

22

Hearing the wild shrieks . . .

Hearing the wild shrieks, Tasmin stopped the pirogue until the crazed Mademoiselle Pellenc swam, waded, and floundered her way to them. Getting her on board was not easy — as she crawled in, Tintamarre leapt out, amid a general splashing that left no one entirely dry.

Though the smaller hailstones had by this time melted, some of the larger ones remained. Soon, once the bank was reached, Bobbety and Buffum amused themselves by throwing hailstones at each other.

"What sport, we can pretend they're snowballs," Bobbety said, only seconds before Buffum hit him smack in the forehead with a well-directed hailstone the size of a goose egg.

"You're a regular David without the slingshot, Bess," Tasmin said. "Goliath now lies vanquished."

"Come along, Piet, it is time we sought the delicious Jerusalem artichokes," Mary commanded. "Come along — we'll dig together."

"Is she not uncanny, the little one?" Piet said, before stumbling away.

"It is not every day that I have hailstones to fling," Bess said, looking down at the unconscious Bobbety. It was her habit never to admit wrongdoing directly.

"The crocodiles wanted to eat my legs off," Mademoiselle Pellenc insisted, as she got undressed. Wet clothes were intolerable to her, far more so than immodesty. The sun was now bright. She soon had her dress spread on the grass to dry and surveyed the empty skies clad only in her chemise, hoping to see a flash of green.

Tasmin fervently hoped that Jim Snow was not witnessing such dubious proceedings. They had been ashore no more than five minutes and yet, already, her brother was unconscious, a lump almost as big as the hailstone rising on his forehead. Mary and the botanist had disappeared, Tintamarre had managed to get a thorn in his foot, and the *femme de chambre* was almost naked.

"Mademoiselle, why is it that you have hardly any bosom?" Buffum asked.

"It is because I am so intelligent," Mademoiselle responded, icily. "The brain gains, the bosom loses."

Tasmin, occupied for the moment with her whimpering hound, did her best to ignore both women. In fact she had already decided to take the pirogue and leave them. Other boats could be sent ashore to pick them up when evening came. The balm of summer was still on the prairies. Tasmin had stuck some biscuits in her kit bag; she had in mind to sleep in the pirogue again. Perhaps the miracle would repeat itself;

perhaps the Raven Brave would appear again in the splendor of the dawn. Other, less happy possibilities — bears, Indians, floods, snakes, chiggers — she refused to allow her mind to dwell on. The prairie at least offered the hope of surprise, pleasant or unpleasant, ecstatic or fatal, while their little floating Europe offered only sameness: quarrels, sulks, spite. In the freshness of the West old ways could be peeled off as easily as Mademoiselle had peeled off her wet dress.

"Voilà! Voilà! L'oiseau!" Mademoiselle Pellenc exclaimed, pointing to the far, far distance.

Tasmin looked: the bird in question was so far away as to be no more than a black speck in the sky.

Bess had meanwhile been making a mud poultice for Bobbety's great lump. Though the trip ashore had been her idea, finding Prince Talleyrand had not been her main motive. She had come ashore in hopes of locating a shaggy frontiersman who would shake her and slap her as Tasmin had been shaken. Hearing of Tasmin's shaking, all the women aboard the boat had become deeply envious; they all hoped to get ashore and find men who would shake them thus dramatically. Buffum was particularly anxious to find such a shaggy swain; Tim the stable boy's rough embraces had become rather too mechanical; a good shaking by a passionate frontiersman might yield tremors far more interesting than anything Tim could induce.

Clad only in her chemise and her shoes, Mademoiselle Pellenc had begun to hurry across the prairie, on toward the distant speck, crying, *"L'oiseau! Voilà!"* as she ran.

"It's a *oiseau* all right, but I doubt it's Mama's parrot," Tasmin said. "More likely just a crow. Go get her, Buffum — if we're not careful she'll get lost. These plains are quite featureless, I assure you."

"But our dear brother is stricken — what if his brains ooze out?" Bess complained.

"Oh, stop dithering, he's merely got a little bump on his forehead, and you put it there," Tasmin said. "Go after Mademoiselle and don't lose sight of her — we're in danger of becoming dispersed."

"Pythagoras," Bobbety muttered. He often spoke in his sleep, intoning the names of the great.

Bess left reluctantly. She didn't trust Tasmin, who would no doubt desert them and take off in search of her young man; but in fact Mademoiselle was racing on across the prairie and could not be callously neglected. The need to recapture the old bird lent strength to Mademoiselle's skinny legs. Bess began to run too — if the indispensable *femme de chambre* should be lost, who would comb their hair in the morning, or before balls?

The prairie, which had looked so level, wasn't, and the grass, which, to the eye, seemed so silky, was full of unexpected brambles which scratched her calves as she ran. In what seemed like seconds Bess began to feel that she was being swallowed up by the Western distance, as Jonah had been swallowed by the whale — though being inside a whale might be cozy, whereas being on the great prairie alone was *not* cozy. The sky above her seemed larger than England itself. She seemed to have suddenly been sucked into a great emptiness as by a gust of wind — and what would the outcome be? When she began to run she had looked back often to the river, but now she feared to look back. What if she only saw the same distance, the same grass?

The only element of hope was Mademoiselle Pellenc, who showed signs of having run herself out. Now she was merely trotting. Soon she stopped altogether. Bess saw, as she approached, that the same brambles that had scratched her calves had torn the poor Frenchwoman's chemise away. Her skinny legs were naked, her small bosom heaved, and her wet hair was much in need of a combing.

Bess had every intention of delivering a stinging reprimand, informing Mademoiselle in no uncertain terms that her mad pursuit of Prince Talleyrand was a capricious act for which serious amends must be made. Bess considered herself a polished deliverer of reprimands. Among the servants only Cook — who possessed powerful powers of retaliation — was spared. But on this occasion, alone with the sweaty

Frenchwoman on the vast prairie, Bess realized that she lacked the breath required for a proper reprimand. Though sentences of censure formed distinctly in her mind, she could not get them past her lips. She was out of breath.

Mademoiselle, who had been more or less stumbling along, suddenly stopped stock-still.

"I think we should go back now, *oui?*" Mademoiselle said, in a small, subdued voice. "Yes, at once, let us return to *le bateau.* It is almost time for tea."

"Yes, let's return — it was foolish of you to venture so far," Bess said, and stopped. Running, she had seen nothing on the prairie; stopped, she suddenly saw the men, risen as if from the earth. There were six of them, small and dark — their scrawny horses grazed nearby. A great shaggy carcass lay on the prairie; the dark men had been cutting it up, their arms bloody from the task. All had stopped their work, dripping knives in hand. They looked at the two stunned white women silently.

"Yes, mademoiselle, let's excuse ourselves to these gentlemen," Bess said, taking Mademoiselle's arm. But when they turned to leave, the prairie was empty. There was no sign of the Missouri River, of the steamer *Rocky Mount,* of Tasmin, Tintamarre, Bobbety. There was no sign of anything.

The six dark men watched.

"Mademoiselle, we must run for our lives," Bess said.

Mademoiselle Pellenc, French and fatalistic, shook her head.

"I am runs out," she said. "I have no more runs."

Bess had no runs herself, but it didn't matter. The two of them were in the belly of the prairie — before they could stumble ten steps, in a rush the dark men came.

23

Scamper off?

Scamper off where?

The sight of the dead, butchered buffalo enraged Lord Berrybender so terribly that he threatened to thrash Old Gorska with his stick — and perhaps thrash Gorska Minor too. Informed by Captain Aitken that repairs must be made before the steamer could proceed, Lord Berrybender had at once insisted on setting out on a hunt; he even insisted that Monsieur Charbonneau, the expert plainsman, accompany the hunting party.

"You ain't from Poland, you'll find me buffalo, won't you, Sharbo?" His Lordship said.

Somewhat to his own surprise, Toussaint Charbonneau did just that, and almost immediately, too. The only trouble was that the buffalo, a nice young cow, was not only dead but thoroughly and competently butchered, too. Tongue, liver, sweetbreads, haunches, and saddle had been neatly removed by people who knew their job.

"They left the guts, that's unusual," Charbonneau observed.

"Why, I don't see that it's odd," Lord B. said. "I always leave the guts myself, when I kill a stag. Rather foul on the whole. Not much Cook could

141

do with a great pile of guts."

"Indian children slice them in sections and eat them quick as candy," Charbonneau told him. "My boy, Pomp, was always mighty fond of gut. Captain Clark always saved a good section of gut, when he killed something, just for Pomp."

"What do you say to this, Gorska?" Lord B. said, pointing at the carcass. "I've been telling you all along there were buffalo here, and this proves it — only this one's already dead. I'd like you to scamper off now and find me a live one to shoot."

Old Gorska looked around at the prairies, endless and empty, and felt his heart sink. Scamper off? Scamper off where? No buffalo were in sight. Nonetheless, there was little he could do but obey. He shouldered his fine Belgian gun and was about to tramp away when Charbonneau stopped him.

"Might be best to wait, Your Lordship," Charbonneau said.

"Wait? I'll be damned if I'll wait!" Lord Berrybender said. "I've traveled from England to kill buffalo and by God I want to kill some. Finding them's Gorska's job — why shouldn't he do it?"

Charbonneau had never ranked himself high as a tracker, but with the prairies muddy from the recent rain, it would have taken a blind man to miss the horse tracks around the carcass. Several Indians had run the cow down and killed her, leaving only the guts. They might have run the cow several miles before making the kill. Undoubtedly the hunters had a camp — it might be a mile distant, or it might be forty. No doubt the hunters were aware of the steamer, which had been belching black smoke all afternoon. Once the boat left, the Indians might come back for the tasty innards, not to mention the useful sinews and such. What was left of the buffalo cow might not interest a white man, but that didn't mean it wouldn't interest an Indian.

"From the look of the tracks six or seven hunters made this kill," Charbonneau said. "They haven't been gone long. If Gorska was to go rattling off now he might be in for a scrap."

"What of it? The man has a weapon!" Lord Berrybender said, his fury rising. "I suppose my expensive hunter's capable of beating off a few savages — if not, then I've wasted money bringing him all the way from Poland."

"I will go!" Gorska said, fed up with the insolent old brute.

"It is my fate," he added somberly, once again shouldering his gun.

Once Gorska left it occurred to Lord Berrybender that Charbonneau might be right — it would be a nuisance to lose his hunter to some wandering band of savages.

"Gorska Minor, step lively . . . go with your father," he said. "Gladwyn, give the boy a fowling piece — I'm in no mood to shoot birds."

Gladwyn at once handed the shotgun to Gorska Minor, who looked surprised.

"Go, boy . . . find me some buffalo and do try to guide them back this way," Lord Berrybender said. "I won't be satisfied until I've brought one of the shaggy brutes down."

Gorska Minor was startled by his new assignment. Every few days he was required to clean all His Lordship's weapons, but he had never even been allowed to fire a pistol. The sight of the great dead beast with a huge pile of guts beside it had very nearly undone him. The thought that it was now his duty to tramp across the empty prairies, locate such a beast, and somehow urge it back within range of Lord Berrybender's gun was terrifying — but his father was moving at a steady pace across the grasslands and he had no choice but to follow.

The Poles had scarcely left when Charbonneau's eye fell on a piece of white cloth, stuck on a bramble not far from where the buffalo lay. It was only a scrap, but it reminded Charbonneau that Lady Tasmin and her party were somewhere onshore. The possibility of kidnap did not at first occur to him — plenty of Indians had cloth of one kind or another, from the traders, and in any case, it seemed unlikely that the girls from the boat would have advanced that far into the prairies. The scrap of cloth was no more than a reminder that the young ladies had to be safely rounded up when the hunt was over.

"I believe Lady Tasmin and some of her sisters and that jumpy Frenchwoman are around here somewhere," he remarked.

"Looking for that damn parrot, I suppose," Lord B. said, gesturing for Gladwyn to set up his hunting seat, a small leather folding seat with a sharp point that could be thrust into the ground; the nobility customarily used such seats at horse races but Lord B. found them perfectly suited to hunting, as well. When Gladwyn had the seat ready, Lord B. was more than glad to sit down — there had been that trouble with the fornication, requiring rather prolonged exertion. Having his nice sturdy seat was a handy thing. He felt, all in all, rather tired — from now on, with the hunting prospects improving, he meant to hunt first and fornicate later. A solid hunting seat, when a man was tired, was a mighty welcome thing. Lord B. sank onto his gratefully; a bit of rest wouldn't hurt.

"Gun, Gladwyn . . . gun!" he said. "I want to be ready if a great shaggy herd comes loping by." Gladwyn provided a gun; Lord B. yawned and took it. Even keeping his eyes open was proving rather difficult.

Charbonneau took his knife and went over to the buffalo and cut off a few sections of gut. As a part-time cook for the famous Lewis and Clark expedition he had once been rather famous for his *boudin blanc,* which needed fresh buffalo gut to be done properly.

While he was slicing, Charbonneau heard an unusual sound — a snore. Lord Berrybender, his head tilted back, his mouth wide open, was fast asleep and snoring loudly.

"I guess a nap won't hurt him," Charbonneau remarked.

"Possibly not, sir," Gladwyn said, in a chilly tone. As His Lordship's man he felt it best to stand aloof from the help — particularly the American help.

"A nap never hurt anyone," Charbonneau said, turning his attention to the gut pile.

A moment later he was proven wrong. Lord Berrybender, dreaming of buffalo, allowed his rifle to droop. While he dreamed, a horsefly settled on his hand. Lord Berrybender twitched, the fly rose, Lord B. twitched again, and the gun discharged. Lord B. fell off his seat and writhed on the ground — he had discharged the heavy ball directly into his right foot.

"I guess naps ain't as safe as all that," Charbonneau amended.

"Clearly not," Gladwyn said.

Charbonneau had scarcely had time to run to His Lordship and assess the damage — three toes, at least, seemed to be missing — when they heard the sound of running feet.

"It's Gorska, he's carrying something," Gladwyn said, in a weak voice. The sight of His Lordship's noble blood — at the moment gushing out of the wounded foot — caused him to feel rather faint.

"Must have kilt an antelope, or maybe a doe," Charbonneau said. He was in the process of making a tourniquet, using his own belt.

"Or even a buffalo calf," he added — Gorska had something across his shoulders, but Charbonneau, busy with his tourniquet, could not tell what.

A moment later Gladwyn fainted dead away.

Old Gorska, drenched with sweat, very red in the face, stumbled through the high grass and dropped his burden, which proved to be his son, Gorska Minor, a short, bloody arrow through his throat. Charbonneau saw at once that the boy was dead.

"Well, now that's a great pity, Gorska," he said, carefully twisting the tourniquet. Lord Berrybender had lost most of a foot — it wouldn't do to misapply the tourniquet and have him lose a leg. Charbonneau considered himself a fair doctor, having been trained by the great Captain Lewis himself.

"And now His Lordship's shot off his foot, too," Charbonneau said. "I guess we're having us a day."

24

Tintamarre barked from a distance; Bobbety occasionally uttered a Greek name.

Tasmin's escape succeeded, with only the mildest effort. Buffum and Mademoiselle were gone in one direction, Mary and Piet in another. Tintamarre barked from a distance; Bobbety occasionally uttered a Greek name. The lump on his forehead was of a size to be of interest to science, Tasmin felt sure, but no scientist was there to appreciate it. She waded out to the pirogue, shoved it into the stream, and was soon drifting pleasantly away, a circumstance which brought her deep relief. Above her, swans were calling, and geese as well. A great yellow fish, of ugly demeanor, surfaced briefly beside her boat — a harmless big fish with whiskers. With the sky bright above her and the air balmy, Tasmin felt that few things could be better than floating in a boat. The beauty of the day was extraordinary. She wondered how far New Orleans was — there were said to be some very distinguished Creoles in New Orleans.

It was a little gusty. The pirogue rocked this way and that; occasionally a small wave splashed her, but Tasmin didn't care. She thought of taking a swim, but felt too lazy. Being away from her family, with their interminable screechings and whinings, was rather sedative. The warmth of the sun and the gentle rocking of the pirogue lulled her into what seemed the briefest of naps. For a few moments at most she closed her eyes, and when she opened them, the miracle she had dreamt of happened. Jim Snow, in water to his waist, had hold of her boat and was pulling it to shore.

"Why, hello!" Tasmin said. "My chevalier has come to save me, just as I had hoped."

Jim Snow was not amused. His look was iron. Tasmin was at once reminded that he was not an easy man.

"You need to stop this wandering off, you little fool!" he said.

The cutting way he said it caused Tasmin's temper to flare.

"Don't speak to me that way, Mr. Snow," she said. "I'm a free woman and I'll go where I please. Why *are* you taking me ashore — I *was* ashore."

Jim Snow flashed her a look, but was too intent on the business at hand to respond.

"Get out of the boat and don't be talking," he whispered. "You've got one of them carrying voices."

Tasmin, still rather miffed, grudgingly stepped out of the pirogue. To her astonishment Jim Snow at once hacked a sizable hole in it and sent it spinning back out into the current, where it slowly sank.

She was about to protest this ruthless scuttling of her vessel, but for once held her tongue. Jim Snow seemed to know exactly what he was doing, and he was in a hurry to do it too. The decisiveness of his actions convinced her it was no time to bicker. Instead of pulling her ashore he hurried her, still in the shallows, upriver for a hundred yards or more, where the bleached trunk of a tree was lodged against a muddy point. His rifle, pouch, and bow and arrows were there, nicely concealed. He listened for a moment, put his finger to his lips, and then, bending low, led Tasmin across the prairie, pausing when a clump of weeds offered a little cover, to listen and look.

From upriver Tasmin noted some stir about the steamboat, which was still stuck. Various canoes, keelboats, pirogues clustered around the main vessel, but Tasmin could gain no conception of what was wrong. Though the country still seemed empty and peaceful, both the Raven Brave and the people on the boat seemed to be acting in response to unseen threats.

Their silent but purposeful travel continued for another half hour. Though somewhat exasperated, Tasmin kept quiet. They had drawn almost level with the steamboat when Tasmin saw an unexpected flash of green amid the gray prairies — it was Prince Talleyrand, sitting on a rock. The old bird seemed to be waiting for them. Before Tasmin could comment Jim Snow pushed her into a kind of hole, under the little ridge of rock where the parrot sat.

"But I don't want to go into a hole," Tasmin protested. "I've always been singularly afraid of holes."

"It's all right, Tassie . . . it's quite roomy once you've squeezed in," said her sister Mary, from somewhere in the bowels of the earth.

"Get in — they're close now," Jim whispered.

"Well, I do hate holes," Tasmin repeated, wondering who it could be that Jim referred to. The Raven Brave observed no niceties. Once Tasmin dropped to her knees he put his hands on her rump and shoved her into a dimly lit chamber, he himself crowding close behind — Prince Talleyrand soon waddled in too, avoiding Mary, who sat with a number of smelly wild onions in her lap.

"Where's Dan?" Jim Snow asked Mary. "And where's the little fat man?"

"Mr. Drew was of the opinion that he ought to have a look around," Mary said. "Piet suffers violently from claustrophobia, so he went too, though I don't think Mr. Drew much wanted him."

"All this I find quite puzzling," Tasmin said. "I was enjoying a peaceful boat ride and now I'm in a hole in the ground with my wicked sister. What's it all about?"

"You are *so* impatient, Tassie," Mary said. "It's the reason you are rarely well informed.

Buffum and Mademoiselle have been kidnapped by the red savages, Gorska Minor has been killed quite dead, and Papa has shot most of his right foot off — all this while you were boating."

Tasmin's inclination was to disbelieve every word the little wretch said — Mary had long been noted for the extravagance of her reports. But then there was Jim Snow, who offered no contradiction, and who *had* exercised unusual caution in pulling her off the river and rushing her into this hole.

"The Pawnees and the Osage are at war," Jim said quietly, as if discussing a change in the weather. "Them and some Kickapoos. The Bad Eye has stirred them up."

"Who is the Bad Eye, may I ask?"

"An old prophet — he's made a war prophecy," Jim said.

Tasmin felt that somehow events which belonged only in the fantastical fictions of Mr. Cooper or Mr. Irving had somehow surged into her well-ordered English life. Instead of rejecting suitors in Berkeley Square or Northamptonshire, she sat in a hole in the dirt, somewhere in America, being asked to believe things which hardly seemed credible. Her sister and the *femme de chambre*, last seen chasing a bird, had somehow been kidnapped? A harmless Polish boy killed? Her own father abruptly and inexplicably minus a foot? And all this had happened in the brief, happy hour she had spent drifting in her boat on the brown muddy river?

"May I remind you that this is the child you claim talks to serpents," she said to Jim Snow. "I wouldn't believe a word she says."

"Oh hush, Tassie — I scarcely said two words to that snake," Mary protested.

Jim Snow's thoughts, as usual, were severely practical.

"That fat fellow should have stayed here," he said. "There are Indians on the prowl all along the river — that's why I sank your boat. If they'd seen it they'd be trying to hunt you down."

"If they find me I'd rather like to run," Tasmin said. "I can't run far in this hole."

"No, Tassie . . . we are in sanctuary," Mary said. "Mr. Drew says no savages will bother us here."

"Be that as it may, I still don't like holes," Tasmin repeated.

All the same, she was pleased that the Raven Brave had taken it on himself to rescue her. She had convinced herself that he was hundreds of miles away and indifferent to her fate — but it wasn't so. She felt a sudden urge to comb his long, tangled hair, though she knew that it was a license unlikely to be permitted.

Prince Talleyrand suddenly fluttered out of the cave.

"Be quiet," Jim Snow whispered. He was listening hard, a wariness in his look. Tasmin found him intensely appealing.

"Jimmy, you there?" a voice asked.

"We're here — is it safe to come out?"

"It's safe, the Pawnees have gone north," Dan Drew said. "We best be getting these young ladies back to their boat."

The prairie sun, once Tasmin squeezed out, was so intense after the dimness that for a few moments she had to shield her eyes with her hand. Only slowly did her focus accept the strong light. Jim Snow seemed to have forgotten her. He stood some distance away, talking to a tall, kindly-looking old man with gray hair down to his nape, whose buckskins were very well kept, in contrast to Jim's.

"That is Mr. Drew," Mary said. "He is extremely knowledgeable — he has already taught me how to whistle prairie dogs out of their holes."

"Very useful, I'm sure," Tasmin said. "I hope he won't mind escorting you back to the boat so that you will be out of harm's way."

"Where will you be, Tassie?" Mary asked.

"Oh, hereabouts, I suppose . . . I do hope for a moment or two with Mr. Snow," Tasmin said. "We have our trip to Santa Fe to plan, you know?"

"He seems a rather stern gentleman," Mary said. "Probably he'll get round to giving you another good shaking, very soon."

"Get back on that boat, you impertinent brat," Tasmin said.

"You don't seem very concerned about Buffum and Mademoiselle," Mary said. "Very likely they are enduring cruel ravishments, even now."

"It's only your opinion that they were taken, and your opinions are rarely reliable," Tasmin said. "If they *are* taken I will immediately ask Mr. Snow or Mr. Drew to arrange their release."

"I must get Piet — he was intending to hide in a plum thicket," Mary said. "It would be most vexing to lose our botanist at this early stage of the trip."

The old hunter, Dan Drew, in conversation with Jim, stopped and made Tasmin a very decent bow when she approached. For a man who lived in dangerous country, he seemed mild — lazy, even.

"How do, miss?" he said. "The little one and I will just go locate that Dutchman and then I'll get them back on board — I guess Jimmy will look after you, in the meantime."

"I hope he won't mind," Tasmin said. "I know that I'm rather a lot of trouble."

Jim Snow ignored her remark. He seemed rather embarrassed about something — Tasmin couldn't guess what, though in fact she felt rather embarrassed herself, a condition she rarely experienced. Usually she preferred to brazen her way through dubious situations, and yet now she felt constrained and rather uncertain. What would happen? It had been an afternoon of kidnap, injury, and violent death. All logic suggested that she ought to hurry back to the safety of the steamer *Rocky Mount* as rapidly as possible; and yet, if there was one thing she *did* know, it was that she didn't want to hurry back to the boat just yet. Though hardly tranquil in spirit, she felt she was exactly where she wanted to be: on a small ridge above the Missouri River, in a country filled with warring savages, and in the company of her unusual gentleman, Mr. Jim Snow.

25

. . . and here was
this talky girl again.

When it came to Indians, Jim Snow trusted old Dan Drew's judgment — if he said they were safe for a time, then they were — but the mere fact of safety did little to relieve the turmoil in his spirit. What *was* he doing, standing there with this English girl, a troublesome sort he had supposed himself well rid of ten days earlier? Why *wasn't* he rid of her, when it was clear that the safest place for her was on the boat? The Osages, Kickapoos, and Pawnees were at war, with the Omahas and Otos likely to be drawn into the conflict. Even the river wasn't safe, but it was far safer than the prairies. Two women had been taken already — at least that was Charbonneau's opinion, and Dan Drew's as well. A boy had been killed, by which tribe no one knew.

Jim had known nothing of these tribal warrings until he had happened to spot a dozen Osage warriors, moving north and painted for battle. He hid, and once the war party passed, sought out Dan Drew, who knew the various Indian bands well; he often brought meat to them in times of famine. Because of his great generosity Dan Drew was safe, where other whites would soon have come under attack.

Now the immediate danger had passed, but not without cost to the English, who had casually drifted ashore right into the thick of things; and here was this talky girl again. Though Jim Snow liked Pomp Charbonneau and Kit Carson and some of the other trappers, and could even tolerate talkative old Dan Drew, the fact was he usually liked to keep some distance between himself and his fellows; and yet that rule did not apply to the English girl, who had somehow taken over his attention in a way no one else ever had. There she stood, meek — for the moment — as a doe, having contrived to show up alone in her boat again just at the most dangerous moment possible. He *should* send her back to the steamer, and yet he didn't want to. There was something about her he liked — why else had he come back for her?

Tasmin, who had been censured countless times for her impatience, now waited patiently for Mr. Snow to decide their fate. Defiant when he awakened her in the boat, she now felt calmly passive. Whatever course of action they were to pursue was for Jim to suggest.

"You still ain't got no kit, but at least you've got shoes, this time," he said, with an effort.

"I *had* kit — you sank it when you sank my pirogue," Tasmin said pertly. "It's probably rather soggy now but if we could find the boat we'd find my kit."

"I'll get it tonight," Jim said.

Without another word he turned and started walking away from the river. Tasmin felt confused — was she to be abandoned again? Had he rescued her only to leave? Disappointment was so sharp that tears started in her eyes, but then Jim Snow stopped.

"Ain't you coming?" he asked.

Tasmin came — so little was her Raven Brave a man of words that he had not thought to ask her — and yet he must have followed the boat for days, waiting for an opportunity to see her, a realization she found deeply satisfying.

When she caught up, Jim set a steady clip straight out into the prairie. Though she wore shoes this time, Tasmin still found it a rather scratchy experience.

"Are you taking me to Santa Fe after all, Mr. Snow?" she asked.

"Nope — just want a look at that dead buffalo," he said.

"Oh, did Papa at least kill one — he's been so keen to," she said; and then she saw the butchered beast itself, stiff in death, dried blood everywhere, and a vast cloud of black and green flies buzzing over the carcass.

"He didn't kill this one," Jim said, lifting a snatch of white cloth off a weed. He had handed it to Tasmin.

"This might be from Mademoiselle's chemise," Tasmin said. "She was in a rather immodest state, I'm afraid. I sent my sister Bess to make sure she didn't get lost."

Then, to her surprise, Tasmin saw her father's fine leather hunting seat, poked into the ground some little distance away. The sight startled her far more than the little scrap of chemise, for if there was one thing her father was particular about it was his sporting equipment. A catastrophe so great as to cause him to forget his hunting seat must have been a very considerable catastrophe indeed.

"Why, they left Papa's seat, careless fools," she said. "We had better return it, when we go back, else someone will probably be flogged."

But *were* they going back? she immediately wondered. She could not in the least predict what Jim Snow's intentions might be. The discovery of the scrap of chemise and the hunting seat was enough to convince Tasmin that something pretty drastic had occurred on the prairies. Jim Snow had walked off to the north, scanning the terrain. After a time he returned.

Feeling a little weary, Tasmin sat for a moment on her father's seat. The emptiness of the country seemed brutal — indeed, overwhelming. Tasmin, who had seldom been at the mercy of anything more powerful than her own moods and passions, felt suddenly at the mercy of those great prairies and the wild men who inhabited them. The plains had power of a different order than any landscape she knew; they made her feel melancholy and small. Without warning, her spirits slid. Had she been alone she might have cried, in puzzlement and misery —

but she wasn't alone. Jim Snow was nearby, looking rather carefully over the ground. He stooped and picked up a piece of black ribbon, which Tasmin at once recognized. Buffum had worn it as a choker, when in dramatic moods.

"That's my sister's ribbon — she's excessively fond of black," Tasmin said.

"Whoever took 'em went north," Jim said. "Probably those scoundrelly Kickapoos."

On the steamer *Rocky Mount* all the talk of kidnap by wild savages had served mainly as a source of stimulation — idle blather from the women of the group. Tasmin had given the matter no real credence. Of course, they were forging into a stark frontier, where such things as abductions by savages were bound to happen now and then; but gleeful talk of ravishment and speculation about native proclivities and equipment had only been a mildly titillating part of shipboard life. Even now, holding what was plainly her sister's ribbon, Tasmin could not quite accept the fact of kidnap. Bess might merely have dropped it — perhaps she and Mademoiselle had just taken fright and scampered back to the boat.

"But it's only Monsieur Charbonneau's *opinion* that they were taken," Tasmin said. "They might be on the boat — someone ought to look, at least, before leaping to dire conclusions."

In fact she didn't want her tiresome sister or the frantic maid to have been kidnapped — it might produce a disappointing interruption of her time with the Raven Brave.

"Nope, they're gone," Jim said. "Charbonneau was right."

"But how do you know — you said yourself that he was a fool," Tasmin argued.

"He *is* a fool, but not that big a fool," Jim said, surprised yet again by Tasmin's determination to argue every arguable point. Neither of his own wives, Sun Girl and Little Onion, both Utes, had exhibited anything like such a level of temperament. But then, the two Utes had been trained to obedience, whereas this good-looking English girl had evidently been encouraged to dispute even the most obvious facts.

"Look at the tracks, miss," he said. "There were six Indians here, with horses — they ran down the two women and they took them."

"You need to get better sense," he added mildly, a comment that stung Tasmin to sudden fury. She jumped up, yanked her father's hunting seat out of the ground, and faced her rescuer.

"Do please stop accusing me of lack of sense!" Tasmin raged. "I won't hear it! If there is one point generally agreed on in our family it is that I am the one with sense.

"It's not that *I* lack sense, it's that this dreadful place lacks *everything!*" Tasmin continued, fiercely, bosom heaving. "There's not even a magistrate to summon, which is the usual procedure in instances of kidnap. If my sister's gone, then there's nothing at all to be done about it, that I can see."

Still in a high fury, she flung the leather seat as far as she could throw it.

"I came ashore hoping that I might find you and that we might have a nice time together," Tasmin said. "I assume you must want something of the sort, since you troubled to follow our boat. *Don't* you want a nice time with me, Mr. Snow? I want our nice time very much, and I'm disgusted with my blinking sister for getting abducted and spoiling everything."

Tasmin felt the anger drain out of her — dejection immediately took its place. She it was who had insisted on her own good sense, and yet what sense did it make to have so strongly declared herself to a man she scarcely knew? A man, moreover, who had no fondness even for conversation and who seemed to possess nothing except a rifle and a bow — not much to put against the Berrybenders' vast estates.

Jim Snow flushed — it was such a long speech to sort out — and yet he was not one to deny joy when he felt it; and he *did* feel it.

"If you mean you want to marry up, I'll do it — sure!" he said. "I thought you might want to marry up with me — that's why I followed the boat. But right now we need to go — this is warring time. More Indians could show up, and catch us like they caught your sister."

Tasmin was stunned. Did she, as he put it, want to marry up? Whatever could it be like, to marry, in such an absence of all context, this appealing but perplexing young man, when what she mainly wanted was to trim his hair and beard? Though the impulses that brought her such an unexpected proposal seemed wildly fanciful, Tasmin was pleased — deeply pleased — by Jim Snow's frank statement. Dejection and rage turned to joy — though joy not unmixed with confusion. Her Raven Brave *did* want to have a nice time with her — it was the most honest acceptance Tasmin had ever received, a big improvement over the sort of fopperies that had come her way in England.

But before the nice time could happen, the warring time had to be surmounted. She no longer felt the need to dispute it. It was time to trust the Raven Brave.

Jim picked up the hunting seat, took Tasmin by the hand, and led her quickly back toward the river, stooping low and stopping whenever there was a bit of cover, to scan the prairies around them for whatever enemies might be.

26

Alarums of the most violent kind were heard from the near shore . . .

Captain George Aitken, with the patient exercise of care and skill, had at last managed to ease the steamer *Rocky Mount* off the clinging sandbar when, it seemed, pandemonium suddenly rained upon him. Alarums of the most violent kind were heard from the near shore, shortly after which a canoe arrived, aslosh in bloody froth from Lord Berrybender's foot, which seemed half shot away. Charbonneau was doing his best to manage a tourniquet, but the old lord's outraged thrashings made it difficult. Venetia Kennet, leaning far over the rail to catch a glimpse of the nobleman she intended to marry, saw the bloody froth and the mangled foot and fainted dead away, toppling over the rail just beside the boat. It took three *engagés* to retrieve the heavy but momentarily lifeless cellist.

Hearing the hubbub and sensing that something was terribly wrong, Fraulein Pfretzskaner began to blubber, upsetting Cook, who seized her heaviest ladle and rushed out on deck, prepared to defend her honor and perhaps even her life. Cries and lamentations soon reached the ear of George Catlin, who was on the upper deck —

165

he was near to finishing the landscape he had labored on since the hailstorm passed; rattled by the intolerable noise, he ripped the canvas up and flung the pieces overboard. The pieces drifted down toward a pirogue that seemed to be filled with blood, from which several *engagés* were attempting to lift the body of Gorska Minor; the boy, an arrow through his throat, was evidently quite dead. George regretted the hasty destruction of his landscape — it had not been *that* far off — but how could a painter be expected to make delicate adjustments amid such a racket?

Just then Captain Aitken came off the bridge, surveying the chaos below with his usual calm.

"I believe there's been an attack, Captain," Catlin said.

Captain Aitken continued his calm inspection.

"Well, the West ain't Baltimore, Mr. Catlin," he said. "These English *will* go ashore."

He went down to the lower deck and administered the violently annoyed lord a dose of laudanum sufficient to put an elephant to sleep; then he attempted to comfort Gorska, who was crying out to his God and weeping bitterly over the loss of his son.

"Who was it killed the lad?" the captain asked, once they had carried the old lord up to his stateroom, where he sprawled, mouth agape, across his bed in dope-induced sleep.

Toussaint Charbonneau had no sufficient answer.

"Gorska never saw an Indian — just looked around and saw the boy gasping for breath — that arrow cut his windpipe," he said. He had been attempting to instruct Gladwyn on the correct use of the tourniquet, but Gladwyn was so worn out from having to help carry his master over more than a mile of prairie that he was in no state to comprehend a lecture on medical technique.

"A Polish hunter wouldn't know one Indian from another anyway," Captain Aitken said. "Is someone bringing the young ladies, or are they dead too?"

"Well, Lady Tasmin and little Mary are fine — Jim Snow and Dan Drew have them," Charbonneau said. "I don't know about the other two — most likely they were taken."

"Taken?" George Catlin said. "Taken?" Suddenly the stories of kidnap took on a different weight.

Before Charbonneau could say more, Venetia Kennet, her clothes soaking, her long hair a wild wet tangle, stumbled into the stateroom, eyes wide with shock. Lord Berrybender's right foot, or what was left of it, was extended off the bed, dripping into a bucket — the sight filled her with sudden horror. Her husband-to-be, once the handsomest nobleman in England, was now a deformed old man.

"It's only toes, mainly," Captin Aitken said. "Many a man has lost a few toes, Miss Kennet. In a month His Lordship will be as good as new."

167

Black bile rose in Vicky's throat and she stumbled away.

"He's not bleeding much now — ease off the tourniquet," Captain Aitken said. "You best go talk to the chiefs, Charbonneau. I imagine they want calming."

"Yes, and so do the tribes," Charbonneau said. "Dan Drew thinks it's a general war — Osage, Pawnees, all the fine tribes."

When Charbonneau got downstairs he found every man on the lower deck armed to the teeth, which rather vexed him. Señor Yanez, evidently convinced that attack was imminent, had distributed muskets freely to the *engagés*, many of whom had only a rough idea of how to use them. The lower deck bristled with muskets and knives, a grave danger to the English party but hardly a threat to the Indians, who, in any case, were not in evidence.

Worse yet, in the confusion, they had lost a chief: Big White. Either from impatience with being stuck on so many sandbars, or from disgust with the noisy company, he had taken his great war club and gone. Neither the Piegan nor the Hairy Horn expressed the slightest interest in Big White's whereabouts or intentions. And yet Big White was the chieftain Captain Clark had strongly urged Charbonneau to protect. Charbonneau, calm in the face of the old lord's injury, the young ladies' kidnapping, and the young Pole's death, was rattled considerably by the disappearance of his famous charge.

"I was told not to lose him and now I've lost him," Charbonneau said. "If he gets kilt there'll be hell to pay with the Mandans. I better go locate him, if I can."

At this Captain Aitken balked.

"Sharbo, I can't spare you," he said. "I've got to have somebody handy who can parley with the red men, if they come. Big White's an able man — I expect he can look out for himself."

"Damnation, I had meant to have him sit," George Catlin said. "Full face, of course — no more profiles. I've learned my lesson."

In fact George was talking mainly to distract himself from a painful attack of nerves. Lady Tasmin had not reappeared, nor the brash little Mary, and as for Bess Berrybender and Mademoiselle Pellenc, the general view was that they were quite gone — "taken," in the stark expression of the frontier.

Toussaint Charbonneau and Captain George Aitken, each with his own worries, ignored the talkative painter — in Charbonneau's view the man was lucky to be alive anyway, considering the rash liberties he had taken when he attempted to paint the volatile Piegan.

Just then a second pirogue came slowly back from shore, this one carrying old Dan Drew, Mary Berrybender, a dazed, semiconscious Bobbety, and a rather scratched-up Piet Van Wely, his face much marked from the thorny thicket in which he had hidden during the time of anxiety, while the Indians were milling about.

"Oh good, there's Dan . . . just when we need him," Charbonneau said. "Dan knows the country as well as any Indian — perhaps he'll hunt Big White for me."

"If it comes to a choice, I rather hope he'll help us to get the young ladies back," Captain Aitken said. "Wouldn't want them to be ill-used, any more than we can help."

"Drat Big White anyway," Charbonneau said.

27

He thought he might just have a nip of grog — maybe two . . .

Bobbety Berrybender claimed that the blow from the hailstone had left him afflicted with triple vision.

"Trios, trios, I only see trios," he insisted. News that neither Tasmin nor Mademoiselle Pellenc were there to make him poultices alarmed him so much that Captain Aitken gave him a dose of laudanum not much weaker than that he had given the old lord himself, after which Bobbety was deposited on the upper deck with Master Jeremy Thaw, whose power of speech had still not returned. Piet Van Wely, iodine on his scratches, joined them, the little group being viewed with stern contempt by the unmarked and fully operative Holger Sten.

Charbonneau disarmed as many of the *engagés* as possible. Señor Yanez and Signor Claricia, both very drunk, inquired about the fate of the missing women; both still had passionate designs on Mademoiselle.

"But what of Lady Tasmin?" George Catlin inquired.

"Oh, I wouldn't worry about that pretty lass," Dan Drew said. "I expect she and Jimmy

171

Snow are just courting."

"Courting? Surely not!" George said, much disturbed by the suggestion. Bold as Lady Tasmin might appear, it was scarcely credible that she would have started a romance with some raw product of the Western frontier.

"It's the other two that worry me," Captain Aitken admitted. "I suppose there's no hope of bargaining for their return?"

"Plenty of hope, if we can find 'em," Dan said. "I imagine they've taken them to the Bad Eye — he's the main trader in women in these parts. I expect when you get upriver you can strike a bargain — if that's where they are."

"We'll be three weeks to a month getting to the Bad Eye," Captain Aitken said. "And that's if we're lucky with the currents. Rather a long time for two tender ones to suffer."

Dan Drew didn't answer — a month's captivity was not long, as captivities went. It was white women who had been held a year or two that there was scarcely any good reason to bring back. They were usually broken by then, not equal to the scorn of their luckier sisters, once they were returned.

"The Sin Killer might get them back," Charbonneau said. "Jim throws a powerful fear into some of the tribes."

At this Mary Berrybender broke into her strange, high laugh.

"But the Sin Killer is Tasmin's new gentleman," she said. "She is unlikely to allow him time off just to rescue her sister — though I suppose Mademoiselle is another matter."

"Why'd that be, little miss?" Dan asked.

"Why, because Mademoiselle is so good with Tasmin's hair," Mary replied.

She then raced upstairs to have a look at Bobbety's lump.

"Who makes a warmer friend, an English girl or a fish?" Captain Aitken asked, once the strange child was gone.

Charbonneau didn't answer. The day's disturbances had left him weary. He thought he might just have a nip of grog — maybe two nips — and then retire to his cozy pallet. Perhaps Coal, his bright-eyed wife, would bring him his pipe and some vittles — she might even rub his aching feet.

28

For a moment she had hoped there might be a kiss . . .

When she saw that they were making for the river, Tasmin became fearful that Jim Snow — in the interest of her safety — might mean to return her to the boat after all. She didn't want to go back to the boat, and was much relieved when he merely hid her in Mr. Drew's cave while he went downriver and retrieved her sopping kit.

Tasmin spent the little wait feeling rather blank — she had often been accused of dissecting her suitors rather as if they were frogs. But now something momentous had happened — a man of whom she knew almost nothing had offered to marry her, a thing so surprising that all capacity for analysis seemed to have left her. She merely waited. In Jim Snow's presence past and future got squeezed out. The present — intense, exciting, huge — took all her attention.

"Come out," he called, when he returned. "You'll want to spread these clothes to dry."

Tasmin at once squeezed out of the cave. The sun was just setting — afterglow was golden in the Western sky. Over the river a bright moon had risen. Jim quietly helped her spread her wet clothes on the grass to dry. His wariness had left him; he seemed to feel confident that the warring tribes would not disturb them.

"We've got no vittles tonight," he said. "I might try to gig a fish."

"There's something else I'd like you to try," Tasmin said mildly.

Jim looked up, curious but not hostile.

"I'd like you to call me by my name, Tasmin — you've never said it," she told him. "It would please me if you would just say my name."

"Tasmin, okay — I'm Jim," he said. "Pleased to meet you."

To Tasmin's astonishment he took her hand, shook it firmly, and returned to his task of spreading out wet clothes — she had packed only the roughest and simplest. For a moment she had hoped there might be a kiss — but for that, it seemed, she would have to wait. She hardly knew what frontier custom allowed to the betrothed; perhaps she could not immediately expect any kissing. She found herself assailed by powerful doubts. Perhaps his offer to marry up with her had been only a momentary inclination on his part — perhaps he had only said it to calm her fury. It had *felt*, at the time, like a true offer, but was it? Did he still want to?

"Look here, Jim — did you mean it when you said you'd like to marry up with me?" Tasmin asked, feeling that she might burst into tears if the matter were not immediately confirmed.

"I meant it — I sure did," Jim said, as if surprised that there could be the slightest doubt about the matter.

"So we're truly to be married? I need to know it!" Tasmin said. Some jelly of doubt would not quite leave her; she wanted to be fully convinced that Jim Snow intended to make her his wife.

"That's right — we'll get hitched," Jim said, smiling at her for the first time — a shy, becoming smile.

"The only reason I followed that boat was you," he admitted. "I've a notion you'll make a fine wife."

"Well, I do hope so," Tasmin said. "As your fiancée, then, might I just ask one favor? Might I just trim your beard a little, so as to see your face better? I have some scissors with me — I'm just in a fever to do it."

Jim was a little startled by Tasmin's request. He had never given a thought to his beard — it was just there, like the hair on his head. So far it had required no attention; neither of his Indian wives had even mentioned it, and yet Tasmin, his new bride-to-be, was waiting expectantly. She would surely think it rude if he said no — perhaps, independent as she was, she would even refuse to be his.

"I guess you can cut it, if you want . . . if it will please you," he said.

"Oh, it will please me exceedingly," Tasmin said, immediately getting out her scissors, at the sight of which Jim Snow looked startled.

"You mean cut it now?" he asked.

"Why yes, at once — just sit on one of those rocks," Tasmin said. "I shan't take long."

"But it's nearly dark," he said. "Wouldn't the barbering go better in the morning?"

"Sorry, can't wait," Tasmin said. "There's plenty of light, really."

Jim obediently sat on one of the rocks near the entrance to Mr. Drew's cave and Tasmin was at last allowed to do what she had been longing to do since the day they met; she got her fingers in Jim Snow's tangled beard and began to comb it straight.

"Don't take too much off, now," he said, very surprised to find himself the object of such attentions.

"Hush now . . . how can I trim a beard with you chattering?" Tasmin said.

Jim made no further protests. Tasmin stood so close to him that he could smell her; she had a light fragrance, probably from the use of some fine soap. She wasn't greased like his other wives. She was quick with the scissors too — masses of his beard seemed to be falling away. It seemed to him that she hardly meant to leave him a beard at all.

"There . . . I'm rather content with the beard," Tasmin said. "You are so handsome, Jim, only one could scarcely see it for the tangles. Now you could pass for a prince in any court in Europe."

The compliment embarrassed Jim deeply — he doubted that anyone would ever mistake him for a prince. But he liked it when Tasmin stood so close.

"Now that the beard's right it's obvious that you have rather an excess of hair," she said. "Do be sweet and oblige me for just another minute — I mean to give your hair just the lightest trim."

Jim didn't protest. He had given himself over to a new power — a good-smelling power, Tasmin, his wife-to-be. Soon again the scissors snicked and his hair, like his beard, seemed to fall in masses. Tasmin snipped, she didn't speak. She had rarely felt happier than at that moment, while at the simple task of barbering the young man who was to be her mate.

"There, you're sheared, Jim," she said.

Her eyes seemed to have widened, as she stood close. To Jim they seemed as large as the moon.

"I just must kiss you — I must," she said, and she did kiss him, his fresh-cut locks tickling her cheeks.

"I should have brushed you off, you've hair everywhere," she said, lifting her face from his. But then, hair or no hair, she kissed him again.

"Jim, when can we marry?" she asked, her voice rather husky. "I fear I'm cruelly impatient. I don't want to wait too long to be made a wife."

"Old Dan can marry us, when he comes back," Jim said. "He was a justice of the peace, back in Missouri — he's married up two or three of the boys."

"I hope he hurries back, then — I am so impatient," Tasmin said.

29

. . . soft echoes of pleasure
that left her rather dreamy . . .

Dan Drew married them just as darkness fell, using Jim's little Bible. Then he lent them his cave for their nuptial night, and appeared again shortly after dawn, with three rabbits and two fat grouse as wedding presents.

"Well, you're hitched now — first couple I've married in five years," Dan observed, once he had a rabbit and a grouse cooking on a spit of wood.

"I guess that means the country will soon be settled up," he added, with a smile.

Tasmin could still feel the effects of the hitching in her body, soft echoes of pleasure that left her rather dreamy but also keenly hungry. She could hardly keep from grabbing the grouse. Jim Snow was washing himself in the river. He claimed that most of his hair had gone down his shirt and was itching him ferociously. Tasmin watched him bathe with a proprietary eye. By the time he came back, his newly cut hair shining with droplets of water, Tasmin was already ripping into the first of the grouse. Though grateful, of course, to the tall frontiersman for marrying them and then supplying their wedding breakfast, Tasmin was rather hoping that the old fellow would soon run along. She wanted to be alone with her husband, to kiss him and kiss him, and more.

Of the steamer *Rocky Mount* there was no sign — it had disappeared into the early morning mists — the day promised to be cooler; the breeze held a hint of autumn.

"They'll pass the Platte today, if they don't stick," Dan said. "Big White's loose somewhere — jumped ship during the commotion. Charbonneau's mighty upset about it."

"That boat's stuck most of the time," Jim said. "Big White probably thinks he can make better time afoot."

Like Tasmin, Jim was hoping Dan Drew would soon go on about his business. Decisions would soon have to be made, but for the moment he felt too lazy to think about them. It would be nice just to sit with his wife for a while, watching the river flow. Eventually he and Tasmin would decide which way to go: back to Council Grove, across to Santa Fe, or upriver to the Mandan villages, where Tasmin's sister and the Frenchwoman were most likely being taken.

Tasmin was impatient with any mention of the steamboat, or her family, or Monsieur Charbonneau and his problems. She had escaped that world, that tiresome fuss; now that she had secured her prize, a fine young husband, she meant to glut herself with him. The Berrybenders, with their endless complaints, were fetters that she had at last shaken off.

"George Aitken's exercised about the two women — I told him I'd help try to get 'em back," Dan said. "The old lord's roaring about lost dowries and such."

Tasmin, sucking the greasy bones of the fat grouse, could not but be amused at this report. It was not hard to imagine how loudly her papa would roar if he knew that she herself, who would surely have commanded one of the most lavish dowries in Europe — from a Bourbon or a Borghese, a Hohenzollern, a Romanov, from any number of Hapsburgs — had married, willingly and boldly, a penniless American, who probably didn't even know what a dowry was. The virtue that might have brought the highest price in Europe had been given away for love. There was much that she meant to teach her young husband, and much that he must teach her about prairie ways — but the base, at least, was solid; the sweet ache in her body told her that.

Dan Drew knew that the young couple wished him gone. Oh, they liked the breakfast he had brought them, but they wished him gone. They had just discovered each other — they wanted no one else. It was only the way of the world. The young lady was too absorbed in the love that was just beginning to really grasp her sister's peril, or that of the Frenchwoman.

With a smile, Dan stood up and turned to go.

"Where will you be heading, Dan?" Jim asked.

181

"I may go parley with the Bad Eye — buy those girls back, if that's where they are," Dan said.

"I may have to go kill that old liar, someday — he's bad about spreading false prophecies," Jim Snow said casually, as he took the rabbit off the spit.

Such talk made Tasmin uneasy — she wished Mr. Drew would just go. She liked her mild Jim best; surely their raptures would soon gentle the Sin Killer. She didn't want her husband to be seized by violent passions. She wanted to tame him with passions of another kind. Wrapped in her young arms, flushed by her quick kisses, rocked in her eager loins, he might soon lose his dangerous impulses.

Dan Drew gave them a nod and turned to leave.

"Good-bye to you, young folks," he said.

"Thanks for hitching us, Dan," Jim said, as the old plainsman turned and walked swiftly away.

Tasmin at once laid her cheek against her husband's soft wet beard.

"You smell so sweet when you're clean, Jimmy," she said.

Just then the old green parrot flew down and settled on the rock by Dan Drew's cave.

"Go away, filthy bird!" Tasmin demanded, but the parrot took no heed.

30

The stars above were secure in

their courses . . .

At night, with the steamer *Rocky Mount* safely moored, George Aitken liked to sit on deck and study the stars. With his erratic crew he could do little; with his even more erratic passengers he could do nothing. His relaxation came at night, when he could get out his little book of tables and constellations and contemplate the heavens. As they moved north of the Platte the North Star, his favorite star, seemed to increase in brilliance nightly. Captain Aitken respected the river, but he loved the stars. As summer passed into autumn the nights grew chill, but Captain Aitken had a great thick coat; he wrapped himself up in it warmly, filled his short pipe, and let starlight be his balm.

No one else on the boat, it seemed, was susceptible to being soothed by the heavens. Since the capture of the two young ladies and the departure of Lady Tasmin, the painter George Catlin had become increasingly frantic. He often interrupted the captain's restful stargazing with futile pleas involving Lady Tasmin — he wanted a search mounted, an effort Captain Aitken knew to be quite futile. Lady Tasmin had left of her own accord — if she ever reappeared it would also be of her own accord.

"The ice, Mr. Catlin — the ice," Captain Aitken repeated. "We mustn't let the ice catch us. We must get to the Yellowstone, where there's a fort. If the ice catches us with no fort to winter in, the Indians will pick us like berries. They'll not only take the rest of the women, they'll take the guns and all the provisions. We'll be eating shoe leather, if we ain't lucky."

George Catlin scarcely listened. The loss of Bess Berrybender and Mademoiselle Pellenc was bad enough, but Tasmin's apparently willing departure shook him so badly that he considered going ashore himself to mount a search; he was only dissuaded by Toussaint Charbonneau, whose own efforts to locate the missing Big White had convinced him that the shores were too dangerous to risk. Charbonneau said the prairies were cut by many horse tracks, signifying warring bands, who would not be likely to deal gently with a white man so green as to suppose a huntsman could attract antelope by wiggling his legs.

"Best to stay aboard, Mr. Catlin," Charbonneau advised. "Probably we'll find the young ladies when we get to the Mandan villages — there's a pretty brisk trade in captives goes on there."

Old Gorska, since the death of his son, had given himself up to drink and weeping, weeping and drink. Over and over again he repeated to anyone who would listen that he had never seen an Indian — he had merely looked around and discovered that his son was dead.

Mary Berrybender was devoting a great deal of time to the Hairy Horn, receiving instruction in the Sioux language. With Lady Berrybender dead and Lord B. just able to hobble about with the aid of a crutch fashioned by the skillful Signor Claricia, chaos had descended on the English company. The boy Seven, he of the cleft palate, could not be located — one theory was that he had been playing near the great paddle wheel and had been swept over and drowned. Others thought that the Piegan, who disliked the boy, had quietly dispatched him and dropped him overboard. The loss — if it was a loss; Seven had always been adept at hiding — weighed on Captain Aitken particularly. His employers in Pittsburgh were not paying him to lose noble English passengers — this George Aitken well knew. They were not much past the Ioway bluffs and several were already dead, missing, or damaged — Master Thaw still showed no signs of recovering his power of speech.

And now Dan Drew, who showed up occasionally to sell them meat, insisted that Lady Tasmin and Jim Snow were married — Dan himself claimed to have officiated. If true, this represented a calamity for Lord Berrybender's dynastic hopes — so great a calamity that no one had yet worked up to telling the old lord, the brunt of whose towering ill temper, since his accident, had been borne by the increasingly haggard cellist, Venetia Kennet, now constantly subject to the old nobleman's many whims, some of them decidedly gross in nature. Lord Berrybender could scarcely walk, which meant that he couldn't hunt, which left the two of them nothing to do all day except to play whist and copulate. Though perfectly willing to lose at cards, as Lady Berrybender had obligingly done for years, Vicky Kennet found to her horror that, despite herself, she sometimes won, Lord Berrybender's attention sometimes wavering just as he had to play the critical card.

"What . . . you treacherous wench, I'm sure you cheated!" Lord B. would yell, when he noticed to his distress that Venetia had actually won a hand, after which he was apt to pinch her cruelly the next time he had her alone — and he always had her alone. Venetia, so recently determined to marry Lord B. at all cost, had come to doubt that even the vast acres, the carriages, the castles could really be worth such constant stains to her dignity.

It was just after a rather onerous afternoon of fornication that Venetia happened to hear the *engagés* shouting about something. Looking out the stateroom window, she saw a buffalo standing in the water not fifty yards away. At once she yelled for a gun — Gladwyn, hurrying in with a rifle, was rewarded with a glimpse of her white bosom before she could cover herself. Lord B., naked except for the bandage on his foot, took the gun, opened the window, and shot the buffalo, a bit of marksmanship that improved his mood immensely.

"By gad, that's the answer!" he said. That evening claret flowed — the next morning Lord Berrybender settled himself in a chair on the lower deck. In the course of the day he shot two elk and a beaver — Cook was rather put out at being asked to cook the beaver tail; Charbonneau, who had cooked many, was finally allowed to assist. Lord Berrybender even offered a slice to Old Gorska, in an effort to cheer the old hunter up.

"Now, Gorska, that boy of yours is gone," he said. "My Constance is gone, my Bess is gone, the Frenchwoman is gone, and it appears that even my son Seven may be gone. We all must live with our losses, we all have crosses to bear. I myself have to put up with a damnable woman who cheats at cards — you must buck up, man, the hunting's just starting."

Gorska declined the beaver tail — he had no intention of bucking up.

"But what of Lady Tasmin?" George Catlin put in. "Lady Tasmin is not presently among us, as I'm sure Your Lordship has noticed."

Lord B. gave an airy wave.

"Oh, Tasmin's just picnicking," he said. "No worries on that score. I'd like to see the savage who could handle Tasmin — there's no one in England who can handle her, else I'd have collected a fine dowry by now. She's a peach,

Tasmin is, matrimonially speaking, and I'm not one to sit by and allow matrimonial fruit to grow overripe. Pluck it, I said, just as I plucked Lady Constance. I liked that fine bosom of hers."

That night Captain Aitken sat long on deck — the North Star and its millions of pale companions cast a fine light over the swelling prairies. He and his party would be among the river Indians soon — the Arikaras, then the Mandans, plus whatever tribes might have come to the river to trade — the Teton Sioux perhaps. Though the river Indians had long been accustomed to trading with the whites, the possibility of some sudden conflict was always there. Some of the young warriors, hot to prove themselves, were likely to be indifferent to trade; they might prefer to take scalps. Or one chief might seek to gain position over another by demonstrating his boldness with the whites. Indeed, the very size of their party might be taken as a threat. The Hudson's Bay Company wisely sent their traders south in twos and threes. Greedy for goods, the tribes saw no reason to fear two or three Frenchmen; but a whole boatful of Europeans might be seen as a threat, as it had been ten years earlier, when the Arikaras had soundly defeated General Ashley and his company of mountain men.

Fortunately the English lord, on Captain Clark's advice, had laid in an expensive stock of presents and trade goods — perhaps lavish bribery would work, as it had before.

Despite the solace of the stars, Captain Aitken

found himself assailed by doubts. The stars above were secure in their courses, whereas, on the Missouri River, nothing was secure. Lord Berrybender had not yet grasped that he had come to a place where English rules did not apply. The rules of the wilderness were less forgiving than those of any Parliament or Congress. It might be that, of them all, Lady Tasmin was best off — no one was abler on the prairies than her chosen companion, Jim Snow.

The fading moon was just being reddened by the rising sun when Captain Aitken rose from his chair and went back to the bridge to refill his pipe. He was just tamping in a shag of tobacco when a shot rang out from the lower deck — Lord Berrybender, up early, had evidently found something to shoot at.

Charbonneau, hearing the same shot and fearing trouble, jumped up at once; but it was only the old lord, his hair wild, in a bed suit of red flannel, brandishing his rifle. On the bank lay a dead wolf.

"Got him! Would you just be a good fellow and go fetch him, Sharbo?" Lord Berrybender asked.

"If your cook won't broil a fine beaver tail I doubt she'll appreciate a wolf," Charbonneau said, a little puzzled by the request.

"Oh, I don't want to cook him, man — I mean to stuff him!" Lord Berrybender said. "My first wolf — gets the blood up, you know. I believe I'll go wake up my cheating Vicky and show her a thing or two."

31

The plains were covered with the great brown beasts . . .

Bess steeled herself — the fat, friendly puppy was licking Mademoiselle Pellenc's face. Mademoiselle could not seem to move; she let the puppy lick her.

"Mademoiselle, we *must*," Bess said, well aware that the half-breed woman, Draga, was watching them impatiently. Any delay and Draga would seize a stick from the fire and beat them with it — beat them with the smoldering stick until she could no longer lift her arm. Then Draga might direct one of her daughters to seize other sticks and continue the beating until Bess and Mademoiselle were scorched, scarred, and almost insensible.

"*Mademoiselle, s'il vous plaît!* Draga is watching," Bess insisted. Finally Mademoiselle seized the puppy and held it firmly. Bess at once hit it sharply in the forehead with the blunt end of the hatchet. The puppy barely squealed. Mademoiselle flinched, but at once took up the skinning knife and began to skin the warm, limp carcass of the little dog.

Draga stood by the campfire, watching. Bess glanced at her fearfully — Draga was just waiting for some sign of sloth, waiting for any excuse to beat them — even without an excuse she would beat them, sooner or later. Bess had become inured to the blows themselves, but not to the hot sticks, which left blisters all over her back.

"Maybe they will let us have a little of the *petit chien*," Mademoiselle said. In three weeks she had gone from being a woman of such refined appetite that she had thought nothing of returning a loin of pork to Cook if she thought it a moment overdone to a woman so racked with hunger that she would eat anything — bones, guts, any cast-off morsel. Always skinny, Mademoiselle had grown so thin that the warriors scarcely bothered to amuse themselves with her anymore — the chubbier Bess drew more of their attention now. Terrible at first, these assaults had come to seem minor when compared to the threat of Draga, who had left no doubt in either of their minds that she would beat them to death, stab them, or even burn them alive if they faltered and were slow to do their chores.

"Hurry, Mademoiselle — she's watching," Bess said.

Mademoiselle hurried — in her country childhood she had often watched peasant women cutting up hares or lambs; she soon disjointed the puppy and took the pieces to Draga, who dropped them one by one into the stew pot.

The weather had turned cold — there had even been sleet in the afternoon, which meant a hard night for Bess and Mademoiselle. They had

191

to huddle together in whatever little nest they could make in the long grass. They had no blanket but had managed to capture a deer hide that the dogs had been worrying. Mainly they used it to wrap their feet, which were bloody, scratched, and cold. They had to be up early, to scour the plains for firewood. Both of them knew they would die when the real cold came, unless they were rescued or managed to escape. In the night, whispering, they talked only of escape but had not been able to develop a plan that offered much hope of success. Mademoiselle wanted to try and steal a horse, but Bess could not convince herself that such a plan would work. Neither of them had any idea where to go if they did escape; and if they fled and were recaptured their punishment would undoubtedly be terrible, perhaps fatal. Even if they somehow reached the river they would have no way of knowing whether the steamer was upstream or downstream. Nor were their captors the only Indians in the area — twice other raiding parties had stopped at their camp. Bess and Mademoiselle had been made available to the visitors but the raiders had been hasty and skittish. They didn't linger.

Twice buffalo were killed. The plains were covered with the great brown beasts but the raiders who had taken them were not mainly on the prairies to hunt. They traveled hard and made only hasty camps.

Since escape seemed at least as perilous as

captivity the two women did not attempt it. They did whatever chores were set them, and endured the beatings and indignities as stoically as possible. Never friends, or even amiable when on the boat, adversity soon brought them close. They agreed that, had either of them been taken alone, they would have died, from hopelessness, filth, violation, hunger, chill, and Draga's implacable cruelty. Together, they had survived, and had forged an intense determination to keep surviving. Degraded they might be, but they were alive.

At night, huddled with their deerskin, they whispered and made various plans, most of which were abandoned in the morning. Their only real plan was to live, and if possible, to be revenged on Draga, the cruel old half-breed woman who blistered them with hot sticks and laughed with her two dusky daughters when one or another of the warriors took a lustful interest in them. Mademoiselle's tenacious haughtiness provoked Draga's most violent attacks.

"If only Tasmin would come with the Sin Killer," Bess said. "I'm sure he'd soon put these brutes to flight."

Mademoiselle didn't answer. She didn't think anyone would come — not until they reached the trading place, where she supposed they were being taken. Monsieur Charbonneau spoke of it often, the big trading place of the Mandans. He said Frenchmen often came there from the north, a fact which gave Mademoiselle hope.

How far away it was she didn't know, but she hoped it was not many more days. She feared the coming cold; every morning the frost on the grass seemed heavier. Soon a big snow might come. And how would they survive a big snow?

"I want to be warm again, Bessie," she said. "That's all. Just to be warm."

32

Near the Little Sioux,
not far ahead . . .

Dan Drew smelled smoke — not much smoke, but enough to alert the curiosity of a hunter with a sensitive nose. He was near the Little Sioux River — game had been scarce along the Missouri so he had moved farther out, away from the big river. So far he had encountered four raiding parties, none large, none threatening to him, and none with any white captives to trade.

Near the Little Sioux, not far ahead, was a fine grove of willows, which was where the smoke came from. Dan went tramping loudly toward the smoke. In his view it was better to announce oneself as noisily as possible when approaching a camp, even a very small camp. In warring times folks were apt to get jumpy.

He thought he might find some Omahas or Otos, smoking a deer or an antelope, but to his surprise, the solitary man by the campfire was Big White, Charbonneau's missing Mandan. Big White was cooking himself a fat duck for breakfast.

Dan reckoned he and Big White were about the same age; over the years they had encountered each other many times, usually in the

195

Mandan villages, where Big White had long been a prominent chief, much spoiled and flattered by the subtle French traders who had been slipping down from Canada along the Red River of the North.

"I'm surprised you ain't home by now," Dan said. "I heard you was lost."

Big White didn't answer. The notion that he might be lost in his own country was an absurdity. He was annoyed that the old hunter had stumbled on his camp. What was he doing on the Little Sioux anyway? Big White was on a serious vision quest; the last person he wanted to see was Dan Drew, a good hunter but a man who talked much and said nothing important. Among the tribes he was known as White Tongue, because of his loquacity. It was true that he was generous, often sharing his meat with the Mandans and other tribes. For that reason Big White didn't wish to be rude to him, although he was already impatient for the man to go.

"I am fasting," he said. "I don't know why I killed this duck. You are welcome to it if you are hungry."

"Let it cook awhile," Dan said. "Sharbo's looking for you — he's upset that you left the boat."

"If you see him tell him to leave me alone," Big White said. "I have to make a fast. I am not going home right now."

Then he turned the duck. Actually he was hungry — he didn't believe in fasts. But it would be worth a duck to get Dan Drew to leave.

"They've lost a passel of people off that boat," Dan said. "Two dead at least, maybe three. And two white women taken — they may be dead too."

"No, Draga has them — she is with some Gros Ventres," Big White said, annoyed that he would have to interrupt his meditations to explain even the simplest things to Dan Drew.

"Uh-oh, Draga," Dan said. "That vile old hussy needs killing."

Dan knew Big White wanted him gone, but the fat duck smelled better with each turn of the spit.

"Why ain't you going home?" he inquired.

"I waited too long to return — Captain Clark couldn't find me a boat," Big White said. "All the boatmen said the Sioux would come and kill them if they carried me. Even old Lisa said it — even old Lisa was afraid of the Sioux. This boat took me but now it is too late."

"Why, it ain't too late," Dan said. "You still got your hair, and you could still bash heads with your war club."

He saw the great war club, propped near a log nearby.

"I have been gone too long," Big White said. "Probably my old wives are dead. No one in the village will want to see me. They have a new headman. None of the young warriors will remember my deeds. The young women won't want me. I am old. Everything that I did has been forgotten."

He looked at the old hunter, who had pulled off a leg of the duck and was munching it. In fact, Dan Drew was one person who had known him long. Dan Drew would remember his great feats. He wondered if he ought to trust the hunter with a potent piece of information. He wanted to tell it to somebody.

"A bird spoke to me this morning — a meadowlark," he said. "He spoke to me in my own language."

Dan Drew had a cold feeling suddenly. He wished he had not found Big White. When Indians spoke of talking birds who could speak in Sioux or Mandan, the message was never likely to be good. Birds only talked to those who would soon be dead.

"What business has a meadowlark got, blabbing to people?" Dan asked. "Meadowlarks should mind their own business."

Big White could tell the old hunter didn't really want to hear the meadowlark's prophecy, which had been bad. No one wanted to hear bad prophecies.

"He said I would soon be killed by a man from the south," Big White said — he wanted to tell someone what the bird had said.

"Birds can be wrong," Dan said. "Anybody can be wrong."

Big White didn't answer.

Dan Drew found that he had lost his appetite for duck. To be polite, he smoked a pipe with Big White and then got up and left.

33

Tasmin awoke shivering,
covered with goose bumps . . .

Nemba, the Oto woman Jim had insisted on visiting, was noted among the river peoples for her skill at working hides; the doeskin shirt she made for Tasmin was indeed very soft and supple, but also baggy, much too loose at the waist in Tasmin's opinion.

"Does she expect me to get fat?" Tasmin asked, once she put on the shirt.

Nemba had no fear of the Sin Killer, though she did fear the ruthless Sioux. She told Jim quickly, in sign, why she had left the doeskin shirt so loose at the waist. There was no end to the ignorance of white women, in Nemba's view. This one the Sin Killer had taken to wife did not even seem to know that she was with child, though only that morning Nemba had seen her puking near the corn patch.

Jim Snow was startled by what Nemba told him. A child already! The moon was only in its second cycle since he and Tasmin had been behaving as man and wife. Because the tribes near the river were warring he had taken Tasmin far out into the prairies, where no one would threaten them, to spend the last weeks of warmth. There they had only the roaring of the buffalo bulls to disturb them — they could behave as man and wife as often as they wanted. But frost had soon begun to whiten the grass in the morning. Tasmin awoke shivering, covered with goose bumps, so they had come back to the Oto village, to arrange with Nemba for warm skin garments, kit to protect them in the deep cold.

Tasmin felt a flash of jealousy — she didn't like it that the Oto woman was talking to her husband in sign; indeed, she was rather vexed by the whole business of skin clothes. On the boat there were plenty of warm clothes: great capotes, oilskin jackets, waterproof boots, all acquired by Lord Berrybender and his agents in Saint Louis. All they needed was to go upriver until they caught up with the boat; Charbonneau or Gorska or Gladwyn or someone could have brought them plenty of winter clothes.

But Jim Snow had brushed aside the option of provisioning themselves from the steamer; he brushed aside so many of Tasmin's suggestions that she had begun to wonder why she even made them. She loved her sweet-breathed husband and responded to him deeply when they were joined in love — her one serious frustration was that he had no use for words. He ignored her opinions and only occasionally responded to her queries. Tasmin had not forgotten her mild inquiry about theology and the slap that greeted it, but she was rapidly reaching the point where she had rather be slapped than ignored. And it seemed to her her objection to the baggy shirt was being ignored. Nemba was comely, though short and rather heavy — Jim seemed on familiar terms with her, which Tasmin found disquieting.

"What were those obscure gestures supposed to mean?" she asked, anger in her voice. Jim heard the anger — it was always a shock, how quickly women angered.

"She left the shirt loose on account of the baby," he said.

"Baby?" Tasmin asked. She looked again at Nemba, wondering if it could be true — and if it *was* true, how had the Oto woman known? Was *that* the reason for her nausea in the mornings — a recent nausea but consistent?

"A baby?" Tasmin said again, convinced suddenly that it *was* true. "But what will we do? We have no domicile — not even a cabin."

"I guess we won't need one, for a while," Jim said. "You'll be droppin' it in the warm months, at least."

"Drop it? Is that what I'm expected to do?" Tasmin asked.

All around them, when they were far out on the prairies, the cow buffaloes had been dropping their calves. Was she herself now locked into this old, inexorable cycle, expected merely to squat at some point and squeeze a human infant out of her body? She remembered the wild screams that had accompanied her mother's regular lyings-in. Teams of nursemaids brought water, toweling, sheets, steaming basins, while the two placid, hammy midwives sat in low chairs at the foot of the bed. Tasmin doubted that she would be able to avail herself of any such help, if indeed Nemba was right and a baby was coming. Would Jim help her? Would anyone?

In her time on the prairies with Jim Snow she had made some progress toward wilderness skills. She could clean a fish, remove the liver from a buffalo, and the tongue as well. Jim had even made her a bow and fashioned her some arrows. In time she felt she might be a decent archer, though, so far, her only victim had been a skunk, which she shot at as a joke but pinned to the earth.

All that had been fun, but she doubted that she was yet equipped to be her own midwife. The very thought of such a crisis made Tasmin a bit wistful for the Berrybender resources — at the very least, before her time came, she meant to pluck a servant or two off that boat. Probably Cook, herself the mother of twelve, would be the most practical choice. Of course it would enrage her papa — no English gentleman could happily tolerate the loss of his cook.

That night they camped on the river, some distance above the village where Nemba lived. Gray chill squeezed out the sunset; Tasmin was glad of her warm new shirt, even if it was baggy. The weeks on the prairie had been a time of deep content, but now she felt restless, tight, unsettled. Other than to reveal it to her, Jim had said nothing about the baby. Did it please him that a small human, conceived in their passion, was even now forming itself inside her? He had made no response at all — he just went about, securing the night's firewood, which he did every night, whether she was pregnant or not. Memory of the quick way Nemba had talked to him with her hands still annoyed her — it had put her in the mood to quarrel. Better a quarrel than long hours sitting in silence by a little fire, waiting for the stars to shine in their brilliance. Tasmin had never long allowed herself to be squelched by any circumstances, and she didn't intend to allow such a thing, even if her husband *had* been quick to slap.

"Was Nemba your woman?" she asked, abruptly.

Jim thought he must have misheard. "My what?" he asked.

"Your woman — wife, even," Tasmin said, making a blind strike.

"I've heard that many frontiersmen take Indian wives," she went on. "It seems quite reasonable, since no other wives are likely to be available." She tried, with no great success, to keep heat out of her voice.

"Oh no, not Nemba — she's just good with skins," Jim said. "I've got two Ute wives, though, up near the Green River."

They sat close together by the campfire. One of Jim's hands rested lightly on Tasmin's knee.

Instantly the knee was jerked away. Her blind strike had worked so well that Tasmin was completely stunned. She had thought she might provoke Jim into admitting to a dalliance with Nemba — caught the Sin Killer sinning, as it were. But Nemba at once vanished from the equation, only to be replaced with two wives, and a third who was dead. Tasmin was so shocked that she could not at once find her tongue. The man beside her, a self-confessed polygamist, had married her too, and got her with child, a child she was expected to "drop" somewhere, when the time came.

"Could you repeat what you just said, Jim?" Tasmin asked, not hotly. She was still stunned — her tone was subdued.

"I married two Ute women when I was up on the Green River, trapping with Kit Carson and Pomp Charbonneau," Jim said, pleasantly. "The women kept the camp, while we trapped."

"And did Mr. Charbonneau have wives too — they seem to have been so useful," Tasmin said.

"Not Pomp," Jim said. "Plenty of the Ute girls wanted him but Pomp's finicky. He wouldn't have them."

"How fortunate that you aren't so finicky, Jim," Tasmin said.

"Such an accommodating man you are. I fear I must be rather a disappointment to you, Jim. I have so few skills, compared to your other wives."

"You're learnin' quick, though," Jim said with a smile, giving her a pat on the knee.

At that Tasmin stood up and walked blindly into the night.

34

With her feelings so roiled, the fact of darkness was a comfort.

Tasmin spent a cold night huddled in the Oto corn patch. Several dogs snarled at her, and a few barked, but then they quieted down. She heard Jim calling for her, but she didn't answer. Her feelings were in riot — one moment she was hot with anger, the next chilled by the thought of her own folly. In Northamptonshire, English custom had somewhat kept her native recklessness in check; but she was in America and there was *no* American custom. What system of manners could possibly prevail in a place where there were only savages and buffalo? That she had rushed to accept Jim Snow as a husband now seemed absurd; and yet, only weeks ago, accepting him had felt right and felt wonderful. And as she herself had said only moments before the fateful revelation, it was no blemish on Jim's character that he had taken native wives — on the frontier *that* was customary. How could he have known that he would someday meet Lady Tasmin Berrybender — or any English woman? He had not tried to hide the fact of his Indian wives, particularly — to him it was a matter of so little importance that he had not thought to mention it — until questioned.

And the wives — two surviving — lived far away, in a place unimaginable to Tasmin, where the Utes lived.

With her feelings so roiled, the fact of darkness was a comfort. Tasmin needed time to think, to recover, if possible, her famous command of logic; but it was not easy to think logically with her emotions running first hot and then cold. They were hardly the small, quiet feelings that might be expected from some country squire's daughter. One minute her blood — whether Berrybender or de Bury — was up and she wanted to fight the man she had just come to love. The next minute the very forbidding facts of the actual situation cooled her anger and left a dull listlessness in its place.

The insult that had driven her away from the campfire — Jim's casual assurance that her progress at practical tasks meant that she might someday hope to equal the performance of his two native wives — had of course not been intended as an insult at all; it had clearly been meant as a compliment, and yet it was a compliment that starkly revealed to Tasmin that the great plains of America, where she had enjoyed several very happy weeks, were no wider than the distance that lay between herself and the young man she had joined herself to. Could the frontiersman from the New World ever really know and appreciate a woman of the Old World? And the child, when it came — which world would it belong to?

That query and others just as painful and perplexing raced through Tasmin's mind all night. She did not sleep a wink. Finally the sun came, and nausea with it. When Jim found her she was bent over amid the cornstalks, throwing up.

35

Then, out of nowhere, the storm came . . .

"According to your friend Nemba the steamboat passed several days ago, which means that it's upriver," Tasmin said. "I am going to it — if you have other plans, please pursue them.

"I'm afraid you married a very obstinate woman," she added, a fact that Jim Snow, halting and confused, could hardly have been unaware of.

Jim was purely stumped. He supposed most women were changeable but none he had met so far were nearly as changeable as Tasmin. When she learned from Nemba that she was with child, she was naturally a little startled, but seemed content enough. Then, out of nowhere, the storm came, and was still storming. She had first wanted to be taken to Santa Fe, a possibility now that fall had come; only now she *didn't* want to go to Santa Fe with him, or anywhere else with him, it seemed.

"The boat will be nearly to the Mandans by now, I expect," he said, confused. Tasmin had stuffed her kit into the sack she had brought it in. She showed every indication of being about to leave.

Jim had killed a small deer the afternoon before. He had been about to smoke some of the meat when Tasmin declared that she was leaving.

"What about meat? I can smoke you some," he said, deeply puzzled.

"I don't care to wait, thank you very much," Tasmin said. "I have my bow and arrow — perhaps I'll manage to pierce something a little more edible than a skunk."

There was a crispness in her tone which startled Jim — he had never heard a woman speak with such crispness. Her words were like shards of ice. He didn't want Tasmin to go, but he could not think of anything he might say or do that would cause her to change her mind. A fit of some sort had come over her — he decided it was best just to let her go. Once the fit passed she would probably come back.

Tasmin drew some faint amusement from the fact that she had managed to quell the Sin Killer. The terror of the prairies just looked tired and confused, and all it had taken was a little English ice.

All Jim could think to offer was a little practical advice.

"Stay on this side of the river," he said. "If you do the Sioux might let you be."

"Now, now . . . no instructions," Tasmin said. Then she walked away. Only two days before she could hardly get enough of kissing him — but now there she went.

When Tasmin had proceeded along the river some fifty yards she turned and looked back, half expecting to see her husband following her. But he wasn't following her — he was methodically smoking the deer meat. Her intent had been to leave him so broken that he would be incapable of practical actions — but in that she had failed. He might be heartbroken, but it didn't keep him from curing his jerky. She had no interest in justice — she had meant to break him utterly; that he was capable of merely turning to some mundane task was itself an insult. For a moment she considered turning back, for the sole purpose of goading Jim some more; but she didn't turn back — her pride wouldn't allow it. If her husband repented, let him track her.

A brisk wind, carrying more than a mild suggestion of winter, was in her face. Tasmin, still angry, struck a brisk pace. Twice she passed small groups of Oto women, gathering nuts and acorns from beneath the scattered groves of trees. She thought she might gather a few nuts herself, once she got farther from Jim.

As she walked her anger subsided. For six weeks or more she had scarcely been out of Jim's presence for an hour. He had only left her when he hunted, and then not long. Slowly, an old happy lightness infused her spirit, a joy much like that she had felt when she awakened alone that first morning in the pirogue. She felt again the happiness of being solitary — dependent only on herself and answerable to no one. It seemed strange, at that moment, that she had forged a union so intense as to make her forget how much she liked solitude — cherished it, in fact.

In her haste to be off the steamer she had failed to grab a book — once out on the prairie with Jim it was that oversight that irked her most. The great spectacle of nature was all very well, and Jim Snow's embraces were also very well; but she missed her books, her Scott, her Byron, Mrs. Ferrier, Southey, even silly Marivaux, whom she picked up at the urging of Mademoiselle Pellenc. Any book would have provided some diversion during the sultry prairie afternoons. The first thing she meant to do, once she got back, was lock herself in her stateroom and glut herself with reading. Her body had been sated on the prairies, but her mind had been starved; now she was anxious to get upriver and feed it.

Just as Tasmin was ripping along, buoyed by the thought of what a fine thing it would be to have a good soak and then shut herself in for an orgy of reading, she saw, not far ahead, a small, black-clad figure sitting on a fallen tree. It was a man, though a small man. Tasmin took up her bow. In such a wilderness all men were to be approached with caution; and yet Tasmin considered that it would be rather too theatrical if she were to stride up like Diana and loose an arrow at him. When she drew nearer she saw that the man wore priest's robes, and was doing just what Tasmin had been anticipating. He was reading.

When he looked up from his book and saw Tasmin he was very startled indeed and immediately stood up to greet her.

"Queen and huntress, chaste and fair," the small priest said. He had a narrow face, and a carbuncle on his chin.

"*Bonjour, mademoiselle,*" he added, with a quick, frank smile.

"I hope we can speak English, Father, since you seem to know it so well," Tasmin said. "What is that book you're reading?"

"Oh this, my little duodecimo?" the priest said, with a self-deprecating look. "Why, it's only Marmontel, the *Contes Moraux* — it would be *Moral Tales* if one were to English it. I cannot seem to get enough of him, ma'am — no author is more acute when addressing the challenges we all face in our attempts to lead a moral life."

Tasmin smiled. "I like the way you put that, Father," she said. "Got any more books with you? I've been touring the prairies and I confess I'm rather book-starved."

"Only a tiny Testament and an even tinier catechism," he said. "I am Father Geoffrin and you, I assume, are one of the missing Berrybenders."

"Yes, I'm Tasmin — eldest of that nearly innumerable brood," she said.

"I saw your esteemed father only the day before yesterday," Father Geoffrin said. "The brood is not quite so innumerable as it was. Your papa, I fear, is rather vexed with you for being so long about your picnicking."

Father Geoffrin had the habit of squeezing his own fingers as he talked — his fingers were long and thin, and the nails well kept, a novelty on the frontier, in Tasmin's view.

"Oh well, Papa is more or less always vexed," Tasmin said. "Fourteen children and nineteen servants hardly make for a simple life — but what's the latest?"

"The Fraulein is the latest," Father Geoffrin said. "She disappeared on the morning of my visit — eloped with one of the boatmen. Monsieur Charbonneau considers it a very ill timed elopement, due to the violent state of the tribes."

"That means we've lost both tutors — unless Master Thaw has recovered," Tasmin said.

Father Geoffrin shook his head. "Master Thaw, I'm afraid, remains as silent as the grave, mademoiselle."

"I'm no longer mademoiselle — I'm madame now," Tasmin corrected. Even if she never saw Jim Snow again she meant to insist on her married status.

Father Geoffrin was plainly startled by this news. He looked Tasmin up and down frankly — more frankly than was to be expected of a man of the cloth.

"Madame?" he said, lifting his eyebrows.

"Madame," Tasmin said firmly. "Would you have any food?"

"Only a humble corn cake," the priest said. "I was yesterday among the Omahas, attempting to harvest souls, and they pressed it on me."

He extracted the corn cake from a small pouch and handed it to Tasmin — though it looked rather grubby in appearance, she munched it hungrily.

Father Geoffrin was still pondering the unexpected news that Tasmin was a married woman. He looked intensely thoughtful, as if he were working out an equation of the higher mathematics.

"Have you met my countryman Monsieur Simon Le Page?" he asked, wrinkling his narrow brow. "Of course, he isn't really *my* countryman — he's a Québecois."

"Never heard of the fellow — what does he do?" Tasmin asked, to be polite.

"He's a fur trader," Father Geoffrin said. "From time to time he manages to ransom white captives. He is said to be making some effort even now, in regard to your sister Elizabeth and Mademoiselle Pellenc."

"Look here, Father, I'm feeling rather anxious to get back," Tasmin said. "Won't you come with me? I would like to hear more about Fraulein's exciting elopement — and I'm sure there are other scandals as well."

"Oh yes, your brother Seven has disappeared," the priest said. "Dire forebodings there."

"Tell me . . . but let's walk while we talk," Tasmin said. "You don't seem to be very busy here, on the whole. After all, you were just sitting on a tree reading a book of tales, when I came along."

"Ah, but Lady Tasmin, they were *moral* tales . . . *moral*," Father Geoffrin insisted.

"There's nothing very moral about a tale, that I can see," Tasmin said. "Not if it's a good tale."

Father Geoffrin looked rather downcast. He slipped the little book into a pocket.

"A fine, subtle point, madame," he said. "I'm a Jesuit — we thrive on subtle points. I suppose that's why I hate the wilderness so. There's nothing subtle about a tomahawk."

"I'm going, Father, subtle or not," Tasmin said. "Are you coming?"

"Happy to stroll along with you, madame," Father Geoffrin said.

36

. . . a company of fiends sprang from the dense morning mist . . .

Fraulein Pfretzskaner awoke to horror — a company of fiends sprang from the dense morning mist and began to hack at her Charlie — she saw his blood on their hatchets as they struck again and again. The trek east had exhausted them both. All day they had pushed on through heavy grasses, weeds, briars, little swamps, mud; everything that grew clutched at them — even the grasses were waist high.

"Charlie, we will have to do much chopping before we can farm," Fraulein said, looking far to the east and seeing only the high waving grass.

"Then we'll chop, I guess," Charlie Hodges said. He himself was a little startled to find the prairies so resistant, the going so slow. By nightfall they had scarcely traveled ten miles toward the distant Mississippi. The hard going had made them both ravenous — in one meal they ate nearly all the cold pork and thick sausages Fraulein had smuggled off the boat. They camped near a little copse of trees — Charlie thought he heard wild turkeys gobbling, not far away.

"Might get us a gobbler, in the morning," Charlie said, before falling asleep with his head on Fraulein's ample shoulder. She herself was still munching corn bread and sausage; she always liked to eat a bit before falling asleep. Better dreams came to sleepers with full stomachs. She munched as their campfire dwindled, the coals glowing. Being off the boat, in this wilderness of grass and weeds, had not yet brought the quick happiness that Fraulein expected. Of course it was good to be free of the English — the English she was done with. But the sky seemed too wide. Munching corn bread helped put down the occasional pulse of apprehension that rose in her now and then, like nausea. Afoot, far from the boat, the wilderness she had been observing seemed more threatening — less easily turned into a prosperous farm. Still, they had traveled only one day. Happiness needed patience. Soon they would build a snug cabin, clear a neat field, produce some jolly, chubby *Kinder*, stout boys who would soon grow big enough to help Charlie in the rich fields they would plant. They would be so happy together, she and her Charlie, on their good American farm.

By the time Fraulein awoke and began to scream the hatchets had made an end to Charlie — he opened his eyes in surprise just as death came. Fraulein Pfretzskaner fought to reach him — she wanted at least to close his eyes, but the Indians were around her like a wolf pack.

Pit-ta-sa, their leader, was surprised at the size of the white woman — usually it was easy enough to capture a woman once her man had been killed, but this large woman was willing to fight. She smashed Blue Blanket's nose with a skillet and hit Neighing Horses such a blow with her fist that the wind left him; he had to sit down. Pit-ta-sa himself grabbed the dead man's rifle and hit the woman three times with the butt; but even that, though it staggered her, didn't make her fall.

Blue Blanket bled so freely from his nose that thick blood covered his chest and belly. After that day he would be called Bloody Belly. Pit-ta-sa hit the woman again with the gun butt — the blow would have killed a deer, perhaps even a horse, but the woman only sank to her knees. She still held the skillet.

"I don't want her, let's go now — she would eat too much," Neighing Horses said, when he had regained his power of speech. The woman lurched over, on her knees, and closed her dead husband's eyes — or one of them, anyway. The other eye had been knocked partway out by one of the hatchet blows.

Pit-ta-sa ignored Neighing Horses, who often got discouraged if a fight didn't immediately go his way. Pit-ta-sa thought the big woman was about through fighting; she had begun to realize that her man would never be alive again. Her time with him was over; her fury was already changing to sorrow.

"No, wait a minute," Pit-ta-sa said.

Neighing Horses hated having his opinions questioned, but Pit-ta-sa was always questioning them. He had never seen a woman as large as the one there on her knees, sobbing over her dead husband.

"Put her on your horse, if you want to keep her," Neighing Horses said. "She is too big for my horse. She might break his back."

"I don't need to put her on any horse," Pit-ta-sa reminded him. "It is not far to the Bad Eye's camp. We'll just tie her good and let her walk."

None of the young braves wanted to use the large woman — they all said they had had enough of women for a while. Pit-ta-sa found this amusing. What they didn't want was to have their noses broken by a skillet.

Then Fraulein sat down. Her Charlie was dead; all her dreams were broken for good. No amount of corn bread, or sausages, or anything else could hold back her hopelessness. Nothing was any longer any good. When the skinny Indian came toward her with leather thongs, Fraulein meekly held out her hands and let herself be tied.

37

Draga, a violent woman whose origins were obscure . . .

Monsieur Simon Le Page, though a young man of only twenty-four years, considered himself to be a master of trader's protocol; he believed himself to have the delicate sense of precedence necessary to deal successfully with native tribes. He would have appreciated the assistance of some intelligent man with whom he could discuss diplomatic niceties and analyze strategies, when tricky situations arose — in a large trading encampment such as the Mandans', with many chiefs vying for position, tricky situations were bound to arise.

Unfortunately Simon Le Page had no such bright assistant — he merely had the phlegmatic, incurious, pipe-smoking Malboeuf.

"Malboeuf, do you even know what protocol is?" Simon had asked, more than once.

"Monsieur, I just row the boat or skin the beavers," Malboeuf replied. "I don't care for fine words."

Young Monsieur Le Page had scarcely walked into the large encampment — followed by a horde of filthy children and packs of skinny, slavering dogs — when a delicate situation came to his attention.

Draga was beating two nearly naked white women with a hot stick just pulled from a campfire. The women, filthy and bruised, seemed too glazed to respond. They each gave a grunt when a blow fell, but only a grunt. To Simon's eye one looked English, one French. He considered himself a fair student of nationalities, as any trader must be if he were to succeed.

"Look at the old slut, we should shoot her, monsieur," Malboeuf said. "Beating those pretty girls."

Simon merely nodded to Draga, who paused in her chastisement for a moment to look at him hostilely.

"If I shot Draga the Bad Eye would have us torn apart sinew by sinew," Simon reminded him. "I'll see what can be done for the young ladies in good time. First we have seven chiefs to visit, presents to distribute, and furs to inspect.

"That's our reason for being here, Malboeuf," he repeated. "Furs. Charity will have to wait."

In fact it was the distribution of presents that worried Simon most. He would need to make a careful assessment of the ever-shifting orders of precedence among the chieftains. It would be no easy task.

More than sixty solidly built earth lodges were scattered along both banks of the Missouri River. This great village of the Mandans had been a busy trading center for many years; from it thousands of choice pelts had made their way north to the Hudson's Bay Company's great depot at Three Rivers, the place from which Le Page and Malboeuf had been dispatched.

Young Simon Le Page stood high in the estimation of his superiors at the Hudson's Bay Company — otherwise he would not have been entrusted with the Mandan territory, an area where there was sure to be competition from many experienced traders.

Though Simon's future looked bright — he hoped to someday direct all the company's trading operations in the West — he knew that everything depended on precise and careful judgment. The Indian leaders were all jealous men; if one thought another had received better presents, then resentment might smolder or violence flare. Any slip — a musket with a broken trigger, blue beads given to a chief who preferred red beads, an insufficient offering of tobacco — could mean that, instead of a bright future, Simon might have no future. The order of precedence had to be estimated correctly — failure in this task might get one hacked, shot, scalped, killed. Simon was not fearful, but neither was he reckless. One must be supremely alert, and not allow oneself to be swayed by momentary sentiment, as Malboeuf had been when he saw Draga beating the two women.

Draga, a violent woman whose origins were obscure, could do what she wanted with captives — whip them, torture them, even burn them alive — because of her impregnable position with the Bad Eye, the old, blind, murderous prophet who stood first among the leaders whom Simon had to woo. The Bad Eye was convinced that Draga could talk with the dead and hear what they were plotting — for the dead were always plotting, in the Bad Eye's opinion. A woman such as Draga, who could inform him of the plans of the dead, was a woman who must be protected, which is why Simon Le Page walked past the two white women, as they were being beaten, without giving them more than the briefest glance.

"I don't like this Bad Eye," Malboeuf said, as they approached the old man's lodge, the whole surface of which had been piled with buffalo skulls, long since bleached white by wind and sun. There were said to be more than a thousand skulls piled on the humped, earthen lodge. Whenever a chieftain or leader wanted a good prophecy he brought the Bad Eye a buffalo skull. The old man — gross, surly, indolent, suspicious — would feel the skull carefully and then deliver his prophecy. Draga claimed to know what the dead intended. The Bad Eye, for his part, was said to know what the buffalo thought. Together they were capable of producing powerful fears.

"Do you think they fornicate? Draga and the Bad Eye?" Malboeuf asked.

"What a thought, Malboeuf," Simon said.

Did the prophet copulate with the witch? It was a distracting thought — so distracting that Simon at once put it out of his mind. He had his tasks to think of. He intended, personally, to inspect every peltry before allowing it to be sent north. This was the kind of thoroughness his superiors expected of him. If the trading went well, if the Bad Eye liked his presents, then it might be possible to do something for the two bruised white women, who were even then grunting under Draga's blows.

38

. . . that same long mane
of shining auburn hair . . .

The steamer was almost in sight of the Mandan
encampments — another day would have put
them there — when the scuffle occurred with the
Teton Sioux, six of whom Captain Aitken had
taken aboard as a courtesy three days earlier. He
had done so on Charbonneau's advice — a very
large party of Sioux, some two hundred,
Charbonneau thought, were milling around on
the western bank, showing every sign of hostility.

"It's take the six or fight the two hundred, I
expect," he said.

"The filthy wretches, what right do they have
to interfere with us?" Lord Berrybender said,
much vexed because the marauding Sioux had
driven all the game off the river, where he had
become accustomed to taking his sport. Almost
every day, from his position on the lower deck,
he had managed to bag a buffalo, an elk, or a
deer. With Gorska now a drink-sodden wreck it
was mostly helpful to have the game within rifle
shot — and yet this admirable system had been
disrupted by these wild men of the prairies.

George Aitken had been dubious about the
wisdom of taking the six Tetons aboard — but

the Sioux had spotted the Piegan and the Hairy Horn, one of their own chiefs, and were jealous. When the six came aboard no one was less happy to see them than the Hairy Horn himself, who refused them even tobacco. He was almost as annoyed at their arrival as Berrybender himself. In his view one Sioux on board the steamer *Rocky Mount* was plenty — and the Sioux should be himself.

"Six Sioux can get into a lot of mischief, Charbonneau," Captain Aitken said. But he knew the interpreter was probably right — better six minor miscreants than two hundred warriors bent on war.

George Catlin was the only one thoroughly glad to have the new Indians on board, for the simple reason that he was running out of Indians to paint. He and Holger Sten had set up rival ateliers on the upper deck, vying with each other to sketch such trappers or vagrant watermen as came on board. George and Holger had become rather chummy of late; soon they were trading brushes, critiquing each other's efforts, comparing techniques. George Catlin still mainly stuck to portraits, while Holger Sten executed many rather pallid landscapes. In the absence of Tasmin — an absence that had begun to vex Lord Berrybender exceedingly — both painters had been slyly attempting to get Venetia Kennet to let them paint her with her glorious long hair down.

"Why she's a very Rapunzel," Catlin exclaimed one morning — the two of them had caught a tantalizing glimpse of Venetia shaking out her auburn mane.

It was that same long mane of shining auburn hair, stretching down to Venetia's derriere, that produced the brief but unfortunate scuffle with the visiting Sioux. Venetia, feeling rather languid thanks to Lord Berrybender's excessive attentions, was standing outside their stateroom, brushing out her hair — a process that took a good hour — when a Sioux named Half Man walked up, saw the astonishing mane, and casually began to inspect it with fingers greasy from a scrap of pork Cook had flung at him.

Venetia, who was hard put to keep her lustrous hair clean in the primitive circumstances that prevailed on the boat, was so outraged by this indignity that she smacked the man hard with her silver-backed hairbrush.

"Leave off, you filthy savage!" she yelled, with such force that Lord Berrybender at once rushed to her aid, grabbing Half Man by the arm. Half Man was called Half Man because one of his testicles remained hidden in his body; spells, herbs, and incantations had failed to coax it down. Fortunately the novelty of a man with only one testicle greatly appealed to the Sioux women — Half Man had four wives and had been seduced many times by curious girls. He thought his novelty might appeal to the tall white woman with the long hair — he had been about to show himself when she whacked him on the hand, an insult not to be tolerated. Half Man at once drew his knife — he meant to kill the woman, scalp her, jump overboard, and wade ashore with his great trophy scalp; but the old white man lurched out of the cabin and was so rude as to grab Half Man's arm. Half Man's knife was sharp — he whetted it carefully every night, since skinning buffalo or other game could easily dull a knife. Half Man shook free, but the old man lunged for him, intent on getting him in a stranglehold. Half Man whacked hard at the hand, and his stroke was good. Three of Lord Berrybender's fingers dropped to the deck, among them his trigger finger, a sight which caused Venetia Kennet to scream at the top of her lungs — and her lungs were very healthy. Piet Van Wely, just coming up the stairs, saw an Indian with a bloody knife — Piet at once reversed direction. The deafening screams unnerved Half Man — instead of scalping the tall woman he quickly followed the small fat man to the lower deck, where he sought out his fellow Sioux. The six tribesmen, knowing that the old lord was a powerful chief, decided it might be time to go ashore. Charbonneau, without knowing the extent of the disaster — Miss Kennet was still screaming — at once saw that a boat was provided.

"I didn't hurt that old man much," Half Man explained to Charbonneau. "It was only three fingers. That woman is too loud."

"Well, she's a musician," Charbonneau explained.

Half Man was not mollified. "Who wants racket like that?" he asked.

Venetia Kennet's screams continued for several minutes. Tim, the stable boy, was forced to stuff straw in his ears, as a means of shutting them out.

Captain Aitken, meanwhile, had once again assumed the duties of a medical officer; he bound up Lord Berrybender's hand, in this task assisted by Cook, who had carved a great many joints in her day and was quick with opinions on matters of a surgical nature.

Venetia Kennet screamed from shock — then, once she stopped screaming, sobbed for quite some time, not from shock but because she was faced with a deeply unappetizing situation. The loss of half a foot had greatly increased Lord Berrybender's impatience; what tolerance could she expect now that he had lost more than half the fingers on his right hand?

The old lord himself wandered distracted around the upper deck, wondering whether the stump of what remained of his finger would be long enough to reach a trigger.

"*Can* I shoot — that's the question, Captain — can I *shoot?*" Lord Berrybender said. He had already disturbed Captain Aitken's neat bandage by trying to wiggle his trigger finger — or the stump that remained of it.

"You must just be patient, sir," Captain Aitken said. "Must not get the bleeding started up again."

"Patience be damned!" Lord B. cried. "Patient is the one thing I'll *not* be! Had my way more or less instantly my whole life — don't intend to stop now! Vicky, stop that bawling and get me Señor Yanez. He is said to be a fine gunsmith — perhaps he can devise me a trigger that I can reach with my little stump."

Later, after an extended conversation with Señor Yanez about modifications for the triggers of Lord Berrybender's many guns, the small Spaniard hustled off and got busy. The old lord, having, by then, drunk a considerable quantity of brandy, sank into a lachrymose state. As he wept, little Mary Berrybender plunked a mandolin lent her by her friend Piet.

"It's Tasmin's fault, don't you agree, Mary?" Lord B. said. "Filthy girl, always selfish, picnicking and gamboling about while her own father goes to rack and ruin."

"I expect she's been marrying her gentleman, that's what I expect," Mary said — "so Tasmin shall have no title, no throne, but there's a great fat dowry you won't have to pay . . . I suppose our wild girl's flown away, just like old Prince Talleyrand."

Lord Berrybender belched and gave a start. No notion had been farther from his head than that a daughter of his would betray his noble interests in that way. There had once, he knew, been murmurings about Master Stiles, but that was, on the whole, given country tradition, rather the expected sort of thing.

But an American? It was not to be tolerated.

"Pretty Tasmin, such a desirable girl," Mary said. "I doubt a Bourbon or a Hapsburg would give much for her now."

"Egad, how sharper . . . ," Lord B. said, before drink overcame him and he slumped down, dead drunk.

Having stirred the hornets' nest, Mary slipped down to the lower deck and had a very satisfactory hour of instruction in the Sioux tongue from the old Hairy Horn, who had just decided that he wished to spend the rest of his life aboard the steamer *Rocky Mount*.

39

His skull lodge stood well above the river . . .

"Most boats are quiet — why is this new boat roaring like that?" the Bad Eye asked. He could hear the steamboat plainly, belching like a great beast. His skull lodge stood well above the river — and yet the boat sounded like it was just outside his lodge.

"It's a new kind of boat," Draga said. "New and big."

"It must be big or it couldn't roar like that," the Bad Eye said. His lodge had a long mud platform on it, covered with buffalo robes. The robes were old, filled with fleas and lice, but the Bad Eye was not bothered by such trifles. He had grown so fat that he no longer cared for walking; his legs would still carry his weight, but they wouldn't carry it far. Though Draga still brought him women, he now had little interest in copulation. The Bad Eye had known the great boat was on its way to the encampments — he had had many reports. But he had not expected to hear a boat roar like a beast.

"How many men does it take to row it?" he asked.

"No one rows it — it is a steamboat," Draga

233

said. "It eats wood. If there is no wood it eats coal."

The Bad Eye didn't like the sound of that at all. A boat that ate wood could not be a normal boat.

"It sounds like a god," he said.

Draga was contemptuous of the old fat fool, a man who had spent an idle life making up prophecies that his people were superstitious enough to believe. Blind from birth, he had never seen the world. He learned what he knew by feeling — how a puppy was shaped, or a fish, or a woman — or by listening. He took in food through his mouth and knowledge through his ears. His hearing was very acute, so acute that he could hear a mouse scratch in its burrow or identify a fly or wasp or bee by the sound of its buzzing. Because he had never heard the sound of a steamboat, he thought the boat might be a god, or else a great water beast of some kind.

Draga came from the West, her father a Russian trapper, her mother an Aleut. As a young woman, coming south with the Russian fur traders, she had seen great seagoing ships in San Francisco Bay. She had come to the Russian River in a skin boat with her parents and some other Aleuts — but a great swell capsized the boat and only Draga made it to shore. For a time an old Spaniard kept her, but he choked on a grape and died. Draga, thinking herself Russian, tried to reach the Russian fort, but she first fell in with some Modocs and then with some Nez

Perce and gradually drifted east. Two white trappers bargained for her and kept her for a year, until one of them was killed by the Blackfeet. The other trapper hid his furs and fled, taking Draga with him; in time she came to the Mandans and the skull lodge of the Bad Eye. An old crazy woman of the Modocs, who had convinced herself she could talk with the dead, had taught Draga a few spells and recipes. The old one knew of a cave where there were many bats; she taught Draga how to pick the hanging bats like fruit, kill them, dry them, mix them in potions. The old half-crazed Modoc woman thought that the bat cave was connected with the world of the dead. Draga was not convinced, but she had learned early that she could either surrender herself to the appetites of men or else become a sorceress; the choice was not hard. She had a few dried bats with her, which she used to good effect in the Mandan village. She saw that the Bad Eye was as crazy as the old Modoc woman had been — only the Bad Eye was cruel as well as crazy. She herself saw him strangle two men and a woman — it was the Bad Eye's way of dispatching those who disregarded his rambling prophecies. Draga soon gained more power over the fat prophet than anyone had ever had. From listening to his ramblings she learned the names of many Mandans who had fallen in battle; it didn't matter to Draga whether these dead men had been great warriors or merely fools and braggarts: she gathered names as the other women picked berries, and used them to convince the Bad Eye that she was in communication with the spirits of the departed. In time he came to trust no one but Draga — in fact the Bad Eye was more than a little afraid of the strange sorceress from the Western waters.

Draga knew that the steamboat was just a boat. It posed no threat to the Bad Eye; the Mandans would never have let anyone harm their prophet. But the unfamiliar sounds it produced upset the old man. Draga thought it might soothe him to hear a rare but not wholly unfamiliar sound: the screams of a burning captive.

"I want to burn one of the white women — we have three now," Draga said. "Pit-ta-sa brought in a new one last night, a big one. Why not let me burn one? The cold is coming. The people would enjoy a good burning, before it gets too cold."

The Bad Eye had no intention of going along with that suggestion. The custom was to trade for captives, and these women had all come off the great belching boat. No doubt the whites would give many blankets, many rifles, to get them back. It irked him that Draga would even mention burning one of the whites. Let her go catch an Omaha or an Oto if she wanted to burn somebody. White captives were too valuable to waste. Besides, he himself had never liked the smell produced by burning people. A burned human left a bad smell in the village for days — a thing he had never understood. A roasting goose or haunch of antelope smelled good when it was cooking, but a cooked human left a sickening, sweet odor that was not pleasant — once it got into his nostrils it lingered for days.

"No burning — the Frenchman will buy these captives," the Bad Eye said. "We can sell them for a good price."

Draga knew the old man would reject her suggestion. He was greedy now for the things the whites gave him — guns he couldn't see to shoot, axes he couldn't see to cut with, beads whose color he could not define. She had mentioned the burning merely to remind him that there was another way to deal with captives: the old way, the way of the torture stake. Warriors used it to build their power. The wild tribes — those who grew no corn but lived by the buffalo — still used it: Sioux, Cheyenne, Comanche. Despite the power she wielded, despite her hold over the Bad Eye, Draga thought she might leave these corn-growers, these bargainers, someday. What the whites brought didn't interest her. She thought she might go west again, to a place where she could do what she wanted with a white girl, if she caught one.

"No burning, did you hear me?" the Bad Eye repeated. "Beat the women if you want but don't ruin them. I don't want any trouble with the whites on that big boat."

The Bad Eye waited, but there was no answer from Draga. Draga's breathing was husky — he could hear her if she was still there — but now he heard nothing; the sorceress had left. The fact that she left so silently made him a little uneasy. A woman who moved that quietly was a woman to beware of, particularly if she spoke with the dead.

40

"All those tears

over a little tupping."

"Oh fiddle, a pox on Samuel Richardson," Tasmin said. "I confess I could not get through *Clarissa*. All those tears over a little tupping. A great bore, I say."

The first of the low, brown earth lodges of the Mandans were visible not far upriver, and a trace of smoke in the air indicated that the steamer *Rocky Mount* was just around the next bend. The two of them, Tasmin and Father Geoffrin, had taken only two days to catch up with the steamer — days during which they had talked incessantly about literature, only pausing now and then to consider a collateral issue — that is, morals.

"Lady Tasmin, it is not the tears or the tupping, it is the sensibility of Clarissa one admires," Father Geoffrin protested. "A young lady of fine intelligence torn apart by virtue."

"Would you say I have a fine intelligence, Father?" Tasmin asked, with a smile.

"Oh, indeed," Father Geoffrin said. "As fine as Pompadour — *tendre et sincère*, as Voltaire said."

"Oh now, hardly *that* fine — you mustn't flatter me," Tasmin said. Indeed, the little priest had been a very fountain of compliments, so far. All her accoutrements, mental and physical, he judged to be of the finest. Tasmin's modest denials grew more and more routine. If this diminutive Jesuit wanted to be in love with her, so be it — but she still had no intention of indulging his taste for Samuel Richardson.

"I suppose I'm rather too hardy for all that moping and scribbling," Tasmin said. "If the lustful Mr. Lovelace wanted *me* so badly I'd find a bed and have him. Nothing wrong with a bit of pleasure, that I can see."

In fact the absence of just that sort of pleasure was making her a bit fretful. Her brief weeks of marriage had accustomed her to regular and fervent attentions in the arms of Jim Snow. From time to time she turned and looked back downriver, half expecting to see her husband trailing after them. In the heat of her jealousy at hearing of Jim's native wives, she had lashed out too cruelly. Life among the fourteen young Berrybenders had not encouraged in her any disposition to share. She did not regret marching off — it had been necessary to make her point. Pleasant as it was to talk about books with the little priest, Tasmin found that her attention kept returning to her husband and his other wives. Jim Snow had made their home on the Green River seem quite remote. Perhaps these distant wives no longer really existed. Perhaps they had taken husbands. Perhaps they had run away, been drowned, been eaten by bears.

"I expect you know your geography, don't you, Geoff?" Tasmin asked — they had quickly agreed to proceed on a first-name basis.

"I fear in this case that I am very vague as to longitude and all that," Father Geoffrin said. "The Green River is very distant — that I can assure you."

"I am equally vague when it comes to the Jesuit doctrines," Tasmin said. "What do you Jesuits think about polygamy?"

"Our doctrines are very complex," Father Geoffrin admitted. "Hopelessly complex, I fear. I myself have not mastered even the hundredth part of them."

They had just come level with the first of the Mandan earth lodges. Several filthy children were staring at them. An old crone was hobbling about, attempting to kill a skinny dog. The sight of these ragged scraps of humanity seemed to overwhelm Father Geoffrin. To Tasmin's astonishment, he suddenly burst into tears. One of the small, filthy children immediately threw a stone at him.

"Go away, you little wretches!" Tasmin yelled.

The children stood their ground. The old crone, more nimble than she had at first appeared, succeeded in braining the skinny dog. Father Geoffrin's sobs slowly diminished. He wiped his eyes on a corner of his robe.

"A mistake . . . ridiculous . . . a mistake," he said to Tasmin. "Do I look like a priest to you?

Of course I don't. I'm a man of the boulevards and the coffeehouses. By inclination and habit I am very clean — but in the wilderness it is rarely possible to remain clean. Then there are my skepticisms. I harbor the gravest doubts about the Deity. I have studied the works of the greatest thinkers and philosophes and yet I doubt."

"Geoff, this is ridiculous," Tasmin told him. "I merely wanted to know about one river."

Father Geoffrin ignored her.

"And then there are these people, these savages," he went on. "A little boy just then threw a rock at me. Am I to attempt to save his soul? I, who have no notion of what a soul is, or whether these savages *have* souls? It's all very well for Father de Las Casas to argue that they do, but then he probably knew better Indians . . . Aztecs, you know."

"Shut up, Geoff . . . this babble is intolerable," Tasmin said. "If you don't wish to be a priest, then you must simply leave the order."

Much as she liked the little Frenchman, her immediate urge was to give him a good smack. The steamer *Rocky Mount* was in sight, not a mile away. She herself had an inclination to cleanliness. Rather than stand around watching a dog being butchered, she wanted a good bath. She did not care to indulge Father Geoffrin in an ill-timed crisis of conscience.

The little father, however, was not to be easily checked.

"When I agreed to come among the Mandans I thought I might just manage a glorious martyrdom, but that won't do either," he went on. "Even the mildest toothache causes me to reach for my laudanum — I have some here in my pouch. If I were to suffer martyrdom my behavior would be anything but glorious. I would rather renounce many gods than suffer a twinge of pain."

All around them, in the strung-out village, heads were turning. Many Indians, their mood difficult to judge, were staring at the white woman and the priest. More and more warriors emerged from the lodges, men of uncertain disposition. The boat, which had seemed so close, now seemed far. A gauntlet of a sort would have to be run — or walked, at least — and her companion was hardly in a state to put a crowd of savages to flight.

"Hello, miss — you're back," a familiar voice said, from just behind her. She turned and saw Monsieur Charbonneau. Though he was as greasy and unkempt as ever, Tasmin was very glad to see him. He said a few words to the old crone and led them safely through the crowd.

41

Draga, spitting out teeth . . .

"No, no, Fraulein . . . submit!" Bess cried, but too late. Draga, for once, had misjudged the demeanor of her victim. All night Bess and Mademoiselle had tried to soothe Fraulein for the loss of her Charlie, but they made little progress. The Fraulein's grief was bottomless. When Draga took a stick and began to beat the new captive, Fraulein's grief boiled into anger. Draga at once discovered that she was beating a woman with the strength of an ox. Fraulein Pfretzskaner, eyes blazing with hatred, yanked the stick away from Draga and smacked her with it — right in the mouth, dislodging two of Draga's none-too-numerous teeth. Through a gurgle of blood Draga managed a strangled yell and several warriors came running, hatchets drawn. Fraulein Pfretzskaner whirled on them like a very Boadicea, knocking two men senseless with her stick. Draga, spitting out teeth, yelled at the men to catch her — she wanted a long revenge — and the men tried but failed. The Fraulein's arms were slippery with blood; they couldn't hold her. Pit-ta-sa thought for a moment that the huge woman might defeat them all, but then, as she turned, he saw his chance and killed her with a hard hatchet blow to the back of her skull. The other warriors, their blood up, continued to hack and slash.

Buffum hid her eyes through it all, but Mademoiselle Pellenc stared.

"The end came — they chopped her dead," Mademoiselle said to Buffum, when the yelling stopped.

"It was only one beating," Buffum said, her eyes still hidden. "She should have waited. The steamer's almost here — she might have waited. Think of the beatings we've stood."

"She wanted to be with her Charlies," Mademoiselle said. "Now she is with her Charlies. It may be for the best."

That same day, as they were selecting a dog for the stew pot, the young trader Simon Le Page came and got them.

"Mademoiselles, your liberty has been secured," he said, with a smile. "If you'll allow me I'll escort you back to the boat."

Draga, her mouth swollen, her eyes terrible, did not dare to interfere.

42

Venetia cast a look of great helplessness . . .

The grand reunion — or what should have been a grand reunion — on the steamer *Rocky Mount* was turning sour. Never had the various temperaments of the Berrybender ménage more glaringly failed to mesh, and this despite the fact that Cook, overjoyed to have the missing women back — Tasmin particularly — had outdone herself, preparing a suckling pig and a great haunch of buffalo. There were quantities of fresh smelly bread, and even some mint jelly. But only Tasmin, Mary, and Simon Le Page addressed these edibles with respectable levels of appetite. Bess and Mademoiselle, who had seen nothing of such rich food during the weeks of their captivity, barely managed a nibble. Mademoiselle, though Simon Le Page was paying her sensitive attentions, could not forget the bloody hatchets as they descended on the expiring Fraulein; the smells of the rich food were so overpowering that Bess had to excuse herself several times in order to rush to the rail and be sick.

Bobbety and Father Geoffrin, discovering that they shared a passionate interest in the new science of geology, talked of nothing but sediments and fossils.

"You *would* bring this Papist back to us, Tasmin," Mary said — "I fear you were never solidly lodged in the Anglican faith."

"Shut up, Mary, you're a rude brat," Tasmin said, carving herself another hot slice of the piglet.

Simon Le Page was at once dazzled by Lady Tasmin, but knew, sadly, that such a noble beauty was far beyond the aspirations of a humble young trader. Mademoiselle Pellenc, despite her ordeal, struck him as very pretty — there, he thought, there might be hope for an ambitious Québecois.

George Catlin's heart had leapt up when he saw Lady Tasmin come aboard with no young frontiersman in tow; he had rushed down and gushed out effusive welcomes, only to be greeted so coolly that he had spent the afternoon in a sulk.

Venetia Kennet, who had hardly drawn a bow across the strings of her cello since Lord Berrybender shot his foot, had been required to dust off her Haydn and play a bit for the reunited company, which she did embarrassingly badly, with many a piercing shriek from the cello as she mangled her chords. Venetia had rather hoped that Tasmin would come back humbled — skinny, bruised, and starved, like Bess and Mademoiselle. But Tasmin wasn't humbled — and even more annoying, she looked to be in vibrant health.

"Father, do have Vicky leave off the Haydn just this once," Tasmin said. "She's all atremble with happiness at our safe return, I expect — she can hardly be expected to control her fingers at a time of such abounding joy."

"She's just lazy, Vicky . . . ought to practice more," Lord Berrybender replied.

Tasmin saw Venetia Kennet flush at that remark — everyone on board knew what Vicky Kennet was required to do.

"You should try a few weeks ashore, as I just have, Vicky," Tasmin said. "The cool prairie air is such a balm to one's complexion — brings the color right to one's cheeks."

"Oh well, Tasmin, I have not got the milkmaid spirit quite to the degree that you have," Vicky said. "I should need a very trustworthy escort — in fact I've already had a horror of stepping in a bog. One could be so quickly swallowed up."

Venetia cast a look of great helplessness at handsome young Monsieur Le Page when she said it — a rather daring look, considering that Lord B. was alert to the merest suggestion of a rival. Simon Le Page thought it best to ignore the look; he continued his attentions to Mademoiselle Pellenc.

Lord Berrybender considered Monsieur Le Page — rescuer of his daughter and his *femme de chambre* — as something of a popinjay — but then, all French had a measure of the popinjay in them. Lord Berrybender had been assured by a local antiquary that, at some distant genealogical point, the Berrybenders themselves had been French, a suggestion he didn't welcome.

"Don't care to look behind me — no interest in the Conqueror or any of that 1066 rot," he said; he did, however, take pride in the fact that Berrybender seed had flowed only into the most dynastically appropriate wombs — bastards, of course, did not count in that reckoning. And yet there sat his daughter Tasmin — if she *was* his daughter; he was, of course, aware of certain rumors concerning Lord de Bury — so willful as to dare breach this long trickle of noble seed to noble womb. Lord B. had a bad feeling about Tasmin, and had had it from the minute she stepped on board, as casual after an absence of several weeks as if she had merely strolled down to the village to buy a ribbon or a sweet.

Lord Berrybender rarely suppressed an inquiry for more than a few seconds — and damn the company! — and yet he found himself unaccustomedly cautious in the matter of Tasmin's prairie marriage, a great calamity if true. Still, what evidence for it was there? Only Mary's comments — and Mary was known to be inventive, with a sort of genius for planting seeds of disquiet. Such seeds were even then sprouting like spikes in Lord Berrybender's vitals — he felt he might even be getting indigestion, though he had eaten very little of Cook's great feast.

Now, restless, drunk, troubled by a growing distemper, Lord B. reminded himself that he, not Tasmin, was lord of the manor. He looked directly at his daughter, hoping to catch her out, to learn the truth — but Tasmin, to his annoyance, merely stared straight back at him, bold as brass, with even a touch of defiance in her light smile. Spears of disquiet stirred even more sharply in Lord Berrybender's bowels. In his annoyance he remembered how casual his late wife, Constance, had been when it came to discipline, never smacking Tasmin as she should have been smacked. And now Constance was dead, Tasmin was grown, the days grew short, the winds blew cold, it was too late. Tasmin was not some social-climbing wench like Vicky Kennet, who would allow him any number of liberties in hopes of marrying him. Tasmin had no need to climb; unless she married some prince, she could go no higher. But the horrid thought occurred to Lord B. that Tasmin, in her defiance, might have climbed in the wrong direction: down, into the embrace of some American.

"Were you wanting to ask me something, Papa?" Tasmin asked. "It's rare we see you so deep in thought when the table is spread with such an array of excellent vittles."

"Ah, Tasmin . . . ," Lord B. said, appalled to discover that he was rather quailing before his daughter — he who had fought seventeen duels without a tremor.

"I expect Papa is fretting because you have not chosen to bring your gentleman home for inspection," Mary said. "Of course, he *isn't* a gentleman in our good English sense, though perhaps presentable in his own way."

Tasmin gave her sister's ear a cruel pinch.

"I would like to take you to a high place and drop you headfirst on a rock," she said. "Perhaps the Rocky Mountains will provide an opportunity — we'll see."

"What's this, Tasmin? A fellow of some sort? Not a bounder, I hope — shouldn't want my fine girl compromised," Lord Berrybender managed to mumble, well aware that Tasmin sometimes flew into prodigious rages when her behavior was questioned.

"Oh, no . . . I'm not at all compromised, just rather blissfully married," Tasmin said. "My husband, Mr. Jim Snow, is occupied at the moment with his many duties but I expect him in a few days. I do hope you'll approve of him, Father."

Her comment silenced the table. George Catlin started as if pricked with a pin — he felt all hope slipping away.

"And if I don't approve?" Lord Berrybender growled — the audacity of the girl was not to be borne.

"But Papa, why shouldn't you approve?" Tasmin asked, not about to be cowed by a drunken parent. "You can't have been planning to sacrifice me to our enfeebled nobility, once we get home, I hope — you know I can't tolerate these pale, sickly English nobles."

Venetia Kennet's heart gave a leap. Tasmin had ruined herself; that was clear. Venetia felt suddenly filled with new resolve; she *would* triumph, become Lady Berrybender after all. Lord B. *would* marry her yet!

Lord Berrybender could not immediately decide what answer to make to the insolent girl across the table. Sometimes, when he carelessly mixed brandy with wine, the combination made his head rather whirl. At the moment, despite a strong inclination to thunder and rage at Tasmin, not only his head but the whole table seemed to whirl. He gripped his chair firmly, but the whirling continued.

"Tasmin has been very bad, hasn't she?" Mary said. "Do rise up, Papa! Do produce one of your purple rages. Smite her hip and thigh! Reduce her to silence and shame!"

Father Geoffrin could not suppress a giggle.

"The *petite mademoiselle* is very quick to turn a phrase — she would be much applauded in France," he said.

Mary received this compliment coldly — she had no intention of accepting any familiarities from the silly Jesuit that Tasmin had dragged home with her.

Lord Berrybender stood up — stood up only to sway. The table was whirling, more or less like a carousel. Yet he knew that he must say *something* chastening to his upstart daughter. Rarely in a long life had his authority been so directly challenged.

"Can't allow it — not acceptable," he managed to mumble. "Have to throw the bounder out."

"Your opinion is quite irrelevant," Tasmin informed him. "The thing is done. I'm married."

"Then I'll *unmarry* you, you insolent wench," Lord B. managed to thunder. "You can't just fob off the nobility of Europe like that. I'll seek an annulment — consider yourself confined to your room.

"Here's a priest . . . he must know how to arrange annulments," he added.

Father Geoffrin merely chuckled.

"Oh, not I, Your Lordship," he said. "I should think you'd have to apply to the Holy Father directly, in a matter of that significance.

"The Holy See is unfortunately rather distant from the Missouri River," he added, unnecessarily, Mary thought.

"Wouldn't work anyway — not only am I married, I'm with child," Tasmin said. "Pregnant, to put it bluntly."

"What? You harlot, I'm ruined!" said Lord Berrybender. "Where is the fellow? I'll kill him!"

"You're not ruined at all, you're just drunk," Tasmin informed him.

Seconds later Lord B. began to sway, then to sway more, and finally to heave. The remains of his modest dinner, and a great deal of wine besides, came up in Simon Le Page's lap, to the horror of Mademoiselle Pellenc, who at once took command of the young trader and led him away, meaning to clean him up.

Tasmin found that she missed the clean, cool air of the prairies: no centuries of Europe, no squalid family scenes, no yelling. She took herself out on deck, followed by Mary and the hound, Tintamarre. It was snowing lightly, the breeze quite chill.

"I wish you would let off goading Papa," Tasmin said. "He knows well enough he can't tell me who to marry."

"Are you missing your husband, Tassie? Tell me," Mary said. She had become the meek Mary again.

"Yes, quite sharply," Tasmin admitted. "He can be a silly boy at times. I left him in a moment of pique."

"No doubt you were jealous of his other wives," Mary commented. "Monsieur Charbonneau mentioned them to me."

"I was, but it's hard to remain properly jealous of two brown women who may be a thousand miles away," Tasmin said.

"They can't be as pretty as you, anyway," Mary said. "Rather squat girls, I imagine."

Tasmin looked into the darkness. Snow was melting on her flushed cheeks, on her hair, on Tintamarre's red coat.

"This snow will make Captain Aitken very anxious," Mary said. "He fears we will get stuck in the ice and be unable to make our fort, in which case many of us will perish."

"None of that's happened yet," Tasmin said.

If she were with Jim, she reflected, they would be sitting close together, listening to the way the campfire spat as the heavy snowflakes fell into it.

"I do hope my Jimmy is warm," she said. "If I were with him I might at least keep him warm."

Mary went belowdecks, to seek the Hairy Horn. She never tired of conversing with the sly old chieftain.

Tasmin, with Tintamarre beside her, stood by the rail a long time, watching the snowflakes disappear into the dark waters. In her breast was a sharp regret. How silly she had been to leave her Jim.

43

Captain Aitken had no patience . . .

The day Old Gorska killed himself — messily, by cutting his own throat with a razor in his filthy closet on the lower deck — was a day so rife with alarums and distempers that no one had time to mourn the drink-sodden old hunter except Cook, who had lost two sons herself and knew the grief it brought. The silent arrow that killed Gorska Minor fatally pierced his father too.

What drew the company's attention away from the suicide was the untimely discovery of the parlous state of the stores — a discovery made on the very morning of the day when the seven chiefs of the Mandans and a few from neighboring tribes would be lining up to receive what they were sure would be splendid presents from the rich whites on the Thunder Boat, the name given the steamer by the Bad Eye, who was still much distracted by the belchings of the boilers. The great bulk of trade goods they had laid in in Saint Louis had not been examined since the voyage began. Toussaint Charbonneau was horrified when he saw the state of the goods. Rats had been into the blankets — half of them were riddled with holes. An undetected leak had left the crates of muskets covered with water, leaving the great majority of the guns too rusty to use. There were plenty of beads, of course, but the native women had been receiving regular deposits of beads from many sources — unless the beads were spectacular, the natives were apt to yawn and carp — and the Berrybender beads were the cheapest variety, thanks to Lord Albany's fine sense of economy; in his view a bead was a bead and a savage a savage. Instead of buying better beads he had bought himself a fine new rifle, made by a Pennsylvania gunsmith — even Gorska had conceded that it was a fine gun, though not, of course, as good as his own Belgian gun.

The Belgian gun was the first thing Lord Berrybender mentioned, when informed of Gorska's suicide.

"Bad news, of course, alas and alack — set in his ways, Gorska was," he said. "Preferred the Carpathian bear to the American bison — odd fellow. Doesn't do to be set in one's ways — life doesn't always go smooth . . . adjustments frequently necessary . . . I lost my Constance, after all, and the boy Seven too. Meanwhile, since Gorska will no longer need it, I'll just have that fine Belgian gun. Of course, it's selfish of me to mention it immediately . . . but then, why wait? Besides, I *am* selfish . . . ask Vicky."

Venetia Kennet set her teeth — she was not going to be tempted into a rash remark. She had already put up with much and was prepared to put up with more: she meant in time to be Lady Berrybender, and that was that.

Captain Aitken had no patience, either with the old lord or his aloof consort; but he held his temper. The company faced a serious threat — he determined to keep a cool head.

"Sir, there's trouble besides Gorska," the captain said. "The stores are mainly ruined and today is present day. The chiefs are expecting rather a lot — and we haven't got a lot."

"Why haven't we? I laid out quite a sum for presents, I recall," Lord B. said.

"Rats and leaks," Charbonneau said. "The blankets are chewed and the muskets rusted up. The chiefs are likely to be riled. All we've got that they like are axes and hatchets."

"What about grog — I suppose I could spare a few bottles of claret," Lord B. offered.

"No sir . . . if we give them grog they'll use the axes and hatchets on us," Charbonneau said. He was so appalled at the situation they were in that he had considered taking his two charges, the Hairy Horn and the Piegan, and leaving the boat. The Mandans knew him — they didn't expect *him* to provide presents. It was known that he was a poor man who worked for Captain Clark. Leaving might be the safest thing. Nothing enraged powerful chiefs as quickly as inferior presents.

"This is somebody's fault, I'm sure," Lord Berrybender said. "Gladwyn, what about it?"

"Why, sir, Señor Yanez is the gunsmith — the muskets were his responsibility," Gladwyn said, smiling a thin smile. "But I fear Señor Yanez rather scorns the muskets — he says they aren't really guns, just clubs that shoot."

"Damn it all, get the whips — I'll have the skin off everyone's backs," Lord B. said, but Captain Aitken shook his head.

"We've no time for floggings," he said. "We may all have the hair off our heads if we are not resourceful."

"There's that Frenchman, Le Page . . . I rather ruined his trousers," Lord B. said. "Perhaps he has baubles to spare."

"No sir, he's a Hudson's Bay man," the captain said. "They keep a strict inventory. Besides, he's already ransomed the women. I'm sure he's already distributed his presents. I hear he got six thousand fine peltries for them. That young man will go far."

"Can't we just go far ourselves?" Lord Berrybender inquired. "Charge past them and run for it — full steam ahead and all that!"

Again, Captain Aitken shook his head. "I have to think of the boat, sir — can't put her at risk," he said. "There's a thousand Indians in these villages. They're the river keepers. They expect their toll."

"I'm damned if I have an answer, then," Lord B. said, looking out his window. It was snowing still — the low ridges beyond the river had turned white. The sky whirled out snow and more snow.

"I've a thought, sir . . . clothes," Captain Aitken said. "The Indians do like finery. You and Lady Constance brought aboard substantial wardrobes, couldn't help noticing that. Fine garments, I have no doubt. Perhaps some of the jewelry is cheap enough that it could be spared."

Lord Berrybender was aghast and Venetia Kennet not pleased. She had already made a hasty selection of Lady Berrybender's jewelry — was the rest of it merely to be flung to painted savages?

"Give them my clothes, and Constance's gems?" Lord B. said, deeply shocked. So far as he could remember he had never parted with a single possession in his life, and here the captain was suggesting that he give his clothes to savages?

"They want me to give them my *clothes*, Gladwyn . . . speak up, man, you're my valet," His Lordship said.

"Though of course a grave loss, it may be the most sensible suggestion," Gladwyn said, with as much restraint as he could muster. Year after year he had taken care of Lord Berrybender's wardrobe. Though he didn't show it, his spirit soared at the thought of garish red Indians wearing those same wretched clothes.

Tasmin, once informed of the dilemma, stared down her father and managed the divestiture herself, assisted by Father Geoffrin, a man of unexpectedly strong opinions when it came to clothes.

"Terrible, terrible, awful garment," he said, casting aside one of Lady Constance's embroidered ball dresses. "Send it away!"

"*Atroce! Atroce!*" he shrieked, when Tasmin opened a drawer devoted entirely to Lady Constance's pantaloons — they were all in vivid colors.

"*Atroce,* maybe, but they might be our salvation," Tasmin pointed out. "Perhaps the Mandans can be persuaded that Mama's ugly pantaloons are garments of prodigious rarity and value."

Lord Berrybender, in a dark fury, wept, drank, and swore as the process of selection proceeded. Parting with the most insignificant garment went entirely against his grain.

"Take plenty of Tasmin's dresses . . . no, take *all* of them!" he raged. "Extravagant wench — always buying dresses. Now that she's married a yokel she'll have no need for respectable clothes."

"Do hush, Papa, you'll disturb Father Geoffrin's concentration," Tasmin said. "Don't you see that these clothes are all that's going to save us from the savages?"

"Humbug, don't believe it . . . Give it all away if you want . . . ruin me entirely," Lord B. said, clutching his one consolation, Gorska's excellent Belgian gun. He had already fired it off at a Mandan dog, killing the cur where it stood.

"Of course, one of the great attractions of Paris is the sewing shops," Father Geoffrin said. "I admit I could never stay out of them — it's the patterns that ravish one, you know. I'd much rather spend an afternoon in the sewing shops than worrying with my rosary or attempting to redeem prostitutes."

"What about this, Father Geoff?" Tasmin asked, holding up a vivid yellow blouse.

"Awful. How I do despise yellow," Father Geoffrin said, flinging the bright blouse on the take-away pile.

44

. . . and yet there had been an élévation, *impossible to conceal . . .*

Mademoiselle Pellenc in no way intended the thing to happen, but the fact was, Lord Berry-bender's voluminous vomiting quite drenched Monsieur Le Page's best trousers. It was Mademoiselle's view that the trousers were beyond cleaning: they must be thrown away and others secured. Mr. Catlin gallantly offered to lend Monsieur a pair, and in fact handed them over, his cabin being only two doors from Mademoiselle's.

"Should fit well enough," George said; he saw that the young Frenchman was deeply shocked by what had occurred. Though he must have seen some sights in his life as a trader, he had certainly not expected his noble host to vomit in his lap. His embarrassment was intense.

It was Mademoiselle's impatience that provoked the incident. She couldn't wait to get the reeking garment off the young Monsieur. Shy about finding himself in a lady's cabin, he was even more shy about undoing his buttons — in fact he proved so clumsy that Mademoiselle knelt down and assisted him. He wore his trousers tight — it was the fashion in Quebec. Mademoiselle had to peel them down his fine muscular legs. In an instant, once his legs were free, Mademoiselle rushed out and flung the smelly garment into the river; *les poissons* could nibble them if they liked.

It was when she returned to her room that the thing happened. Young Monsieur Le Page, blushing deeply, was struggling into the trousers Mr. Catlin had lent him; and yet there had been an *élévation,* impossible to conceal. The trousers quite refused to contain the young Monsieur's imposing staff. Moreover, he was gazing at Mademoiselle with a look of shocked tenderness, as he did his best to conceal this awkward sign of budding affection. In an instant Mademoiselle decided: she would marry Monsieur Le Page! Though the foul attentions of her captors had made her feel she would be unlikely ever to want a man again, she had not supposed her rescuer would be someone so sweet, so young, so blushing, so *agréable,* and yet at once so firmly made as this young Québecois who now stood in her bedroom, struggling to stretch his trousers over his prick.

"No, no, monsieur . . . let me," Mademoiselle said. He was but a boy — she herself was thirty-five, tied to a bunch of worthless English, beset by the garlicky Italian and the lustful Spaniard. Monsieur Simon Le Page was her hope. She hastily shut the door, went back to the trembling boy, and took him in hand — the conclusion, almost immediate, was quite copious — but for her skillful handling Monsieur would have messed another pair of pants.

"Monsieur, it is decided — I am yours," Mademoiselle said. "Where you go, I go too."

Simon Le Page was not quite sure *what* had been decided; but his heart swelled in his breast. Thoughts of the company he hoped to rise in were for the moment put aside. He would deny Mademoiselle nothing, they would have a snug log house in Three Rivers, children would come.

The next day — with ten of the *engagés*, who would be dropped off to trap the northern streams; with six thousand pelts, every one of which had survived Monsieur Le Page's exacting inspection; and Mademoiselle Pellenc, by this time busily bossing all the French, including the surly Malboeuf — the French party left the Mandan villages, themselves much brightened by many pairs of Lady Berrybender's colorful pantaloons — red, pink, blue, green, and lavender. The pantaloons had been a great hit with the Mandans, Rees, Hidatsas, Gros Ventres, and a sprinkling of wild Sioux. The Bad Eye had been given Lord Berrybender's great plaid cape, the one he usually wore when hunting stags in Scotland; and the lesser chiefs had been mollified with very proper umbrellas, a score of which Lord Berrybender had laid in before leaving Portsmouth.

Several of the party waved at them as they left. Only Lord Berrybender sulked.

"Never cared for losing servants — can't have too many servants," he said, as he sat with his claret and his fine Belgian gun.

45

"She does look disagreeable,"
Bobbety observed.

The steamer *Rocky Mount* steamed north, beyond
the Mandan encampments, on a bright, cold day
when the plains shone white with frost. Tasmin,
Bobbety, George Catlin, and Holger Sten stood
and watched — Lady Constance Berrybender's
bright pantaloons were on flagrant display among
the Mandan women. The Indians lined up to
stare at the Thunder Boat — even the Bad Eye
had dragged his great bulk, some of which was
covered now by Lord Berrybender's great plaid
cape, to the door of the skull lodge to listen as the
great water beast belched. Draga stood beside
him. She scorned the English clothes; what she
wanted was English scalps.

"She does look disagreeable," Bobbety observed.

"Not disagreeable, evil," Tasmin said. "I fear
she's ruined our sister Bess. I can hardly get her
to say a word."

"Yes, it's annoying," Bobbety said. "She does
not even care to hear my theories about the Me-
sozoic Age."

"Don't care to hear them myself," Tasmin
warned. "You're lucky I brought you Father

Geoff, who is interested in everything."

"Count on a Jesuit for a nimble mind," George said.

"He's only a faux Jesuit," Tasmin said. "Not much of a credit to his stern order. He seems to be one of those gentlemen who take a great interest in clothes."

On the deck below, Tim, the stable boy, was being flogged — the lashes firmly laid on, at Lord Berrybender's insistence, by Captain Aitken, who approached the task with some reluctance but a strong hand. George Aitken didn't believe the young lout was much at fault in the matter of the blankets and the muskets — the thoroughbreds, after all, were his responsibility — but he laid the cat on hard, anyway. The boy was certainly not worth much, and the captain had the remaining *engagés* to consider; they'd be into all sorts of mischief if they thought they could get off with a light whipping. Young Tim was hardly stoic; he was soon blubbering and wailing, but he was young and the stripes would soon heal.

Bess Berrybender, staring at the white, chill plains, heard the blubberings, but they aroused little sympathy for her former lover, Tim. She herself had hardly been stoic when Draga beat her. She had wailed and shrieked, and Mademoiselle had done the same, but no one in the Mandan camp came to their aid.

The liberties Bess had allowed Tim, in the time before her capture, seemed very distant memories. Though she was safe, warm, and comfortable again, she was gripped by a great passivity. Once much given to declamation, she now said nothing. When Bobbety tried to interest her in fossil fish she made no response. When Cook inquired about Fraulein Pfretzskaner, Bess only sobbed a little — she remembered the bloody hatchets.

The sly Mary had caught a baby raccoon and made it a pet. She came along with the little creature while Tim was blubbering, but Bess was not responsive to its furry antics.

"It is sad that you don't like my raccoon," Mary said. "I have named him Agamemnon."

"I enjoy nothing," Bess said. "I shall soon go in a convent and become a handmaiden of the Lord."

"If that is your aim you should have left with Mademoiselle," Mary said. "I have no doubt that there are convents in Quebec, since the French seem to require a great many nuns."

"I shall attempt to find an order enjoined to silence, so I shall never have to listen to noisy brats like you," Buffum answered.

Mary at once flung the small raccoon over the side — after a second, a splash was heard.

"If you don't even like my little pet, Agamemnon, why keep him?" Mary asked.

Bess didn't answer.

"You are rather a loss, good-bye," Mary said. She ran downstairs and persuaded one of the *engagés* to rescue her little coon, which was swimming desperately.

"Do you think my sister's eagerness to take the veil is genuine?" Tasmin asked Father Geoffrin. "Or might we expect her to become her old contentious self, someday?"

Father Geoff had been reading Crébillon — he had found the volume in Mademoiselle's stateroom, which was now his.

"Fornication seems constantly to be on this odd fellow's mind," he said, closing the book. "I have no opinion about your sister's faith, but if she does take the veil I recommend the Carmelites — they have such elegant vestments."

"There are times, Geoff, when you are less rewarding than even Mary's coon," Tasmin said. She was quite put out with the little priest — it occurred to her that if she had not encountered him and begun to babble about books, she would have cooled off, changed her mind, and gone back to her husband, Jim Snow, whom she had begun to miss quite severely.

As evening drew on — chill and dank — Bess bestirred herself and asked Cook for a little salve; she felt it would be only Christian if she applied some to Tim's bloody back.

"At least you weren't blistered by hot sticks," she told the apathetic stable boy. Tim, taking this as encouragement, grabbed Bess's hand and forced it against his groin — that being his usual, indeed his only, method of dalliance.

Bess drew back a fist and gave him a solid

punch — so solid that he looked shocked.

"I came to this dank hole merely to treat your wounds, as a Christian would, Master Tim," she said. "I will tolerate no more coarseness — I intend soon to become a bride of Christ."

"What? Be a nun? But we had such times afucking," Tim said.

"Those pleasures will be no more, not in the year of our Lord 1832," Bess said, as she left him.

46

. . . even in their pleasure
she was noisy . . .

Jim Snow did not miss Tasmin much, in the first
days after her departure. The truth was, her constant talk wore him out. She was forever talking,
asking, interfering, insisting, opposing, suggesting. Some nights she talked on and on, when
all Jim wanted to do was go to sleep. He had never
known such a woman — even in their pleasure she
was noisy, unlike his Indian wives. He had
cracked his bow and needed to make a new one,
which would be easier to do if he could give it his
whole attention and not have to continually be
answering questions. He didn't suppose Tasmin
would be gone long, or encounter much danger.
The night she had spent in the Oto cornfield had
done her no harm.

Tasmin was scarcely out of sight before the old
green parrot showed up. In the daytime the bird
would vanish, but every morning, when dawn
came, the old bird would return for an hour,
nodding by what coals still glowed in the campfire, like an old man by a hearth.

When two nights passed and Tasmin had not
returned, Jim grew doubtful. Perhaps he had un-
derestimated the danger — perhaps the Sioux

had come upon her. He walked a few miles up the river, following her tracks, and soon discovered that she *had* fallen in with someone, someone with very small feet who had been wearing sandals. It could hardly have been Charbonneau, whose footprints were a laughingstock among the trappers because of their great size.

"A buffalo could follow Sharbo," Dan Drew claimed. "I can barely track a moose, but I can track *him*."

There were no signs of conflict, which suggested to Jim that Tasmin had merely fallen in with someone from the boat, which by now was surely at the Mandan encampments. Probably she was back with her family, safe for a time. The steamer, he knew, could not afford to linger long at the Mandans, if George Aitken hoped to get it upriver to the Yellowstone before the thick ice formed.

Though Jim's new bow was finished, he had no sinews with which to wrap it or string it. For sinews he needed a buffalo — even an old one would do. He decided he had better go west, kill a buffalo, finish his bow, and then swing wide around the Mandans and catch up with Tasmin and the steamer somewhere near the Knife River. Then he could ask Charbonneau or one of the hunters to tell his wife that he had come for her.

That night he dreamed of her — in the dream he could even smell her sweet breath — and then woke, cold and disappointed, to see the old parrot, nodding by the coals.

In the afternoon it began to snow — a wind came up from the north and blew so hard that not much of the snow settled; instead, it whirled in clouds. One moment Jim could see far across the prairies, the next moment he could see only white. It was only by luck that he noticed the buffalo, twenty or thirty of them, their coats already carrying a thick blanket of snow. Moving with the flurries, Jim came within thirty yards of them and killed a bull and a calf; the bull he took for the sinews, the calf to eat. He found a little wood near a small frozen creek, enough to warm him through the blowy night. Not long before dawn the wind settled, the sky cleared, and the cold deepened. That morning there was no parrot by the fire. Jim drew the sinews, dried them, and finished wrapping his bow — he felt quite out of sorts with his wife, who could have been of help had she not gone storming off, for no reason. He intended to speak to her sternly about such impulsive behavior, the next time he was with her. A wife had the duty of obedience. Bow making could not be rushed. It required steadiness, a good eye, and a clear mind. Jim took his time with the wrapping.

He was moving northeast, toward the distant river, when he heard Indians singing — not many of them, five or six at most. A minute later their dogs caught his scent and began to bark. The song, faintly heard across the cold prairies, was no war song. It was a death song, a song meant to send a just-released on to the Sky House, to the company of other spirits. An old person, an elder of the little band, tired, his spirit fluttery, must have passed on. Growing up as a captive of the Osage, Jim had heard many such songs of passing. The song he was hearing now — repetitive, keening, sad — was, he felt sure, a song for a chief. And yet if a great chief of the Mandans had died the whole tribe would normally be there, wailing out this death song — not just these few singers. The dogs still barked — the singers knew he was near. Rather than turn west into the snowfields, Jim moved toward the sound.

The six old men who had been singing were just lifting a body onto a burial scaffold — a heavy body, too. They were struggling with it, but finally got it lodged securely on the poles of the scaffold. Three old women stood watching. Jim raised his hand in a sign of peace. The singers, out of breath from their lifting, paused for a moment and then resumed their singing. Jim recognized one of them, an old warrior named Step Toe — the old man often traded for tobacco with Dan Drew. The men with Step Toe were also old. Before many winters all of this little group would be on just such a scaffold themselves. Jim could make no sense of it. Why was this little group so far from their villages, burying an important chief?

To Jim's astonishment, the old Berrybender

parrot came flapping over his head, out of a clear cold sky, and landed on the corpse. No sooner had the bird landed than he said the same four words that he had said to Jim, at the earlier burial service, which had been for Tasmin's mother.

The Mandan mourners were shocked — they stopped singing at once and fell back from the scaffold.

For a brief moment, Jim felt his own hair rise. Was the bird some kind of harbinger, trained to speak over the dead? He expected that one of the Mandans would immediately kill it, but they didn't. Instead, they drew farther back, watching the parrot nervously. The parrot repeated the same mysterious words: *"Schweig, du blöder Trottel!"*

The Mandans retreated a few more steps, watching this strange talking bird warily. The parrot made no further comment — it bent and picked at a button on the corpse's coat, and when it did, Jim suddenly realized that the dead man was Big White, Charbonneau's escaped Mandan. Big White *was* a great chief, worthy of much ceremony — but why was he dead, far from his village, attended only by six old warriors and three old crones?

47

. . . a talking bird was walking back and forth . . .

Jim at once laid all his weapons on the snow-flecked, stubbly grass, in an attempt to reassure the Mandan mourners, who were terrified. Who could blame them? Their great chief Big White, absent for years, was now dead — and many miles from the village he was thought to be returning to. The Sin Killer had just appeared, out of a snow-storm, and a talking bird was walking back and forth on the corpse of Big White. It added up to a combination of events that might have shaken stouter hearts than this frail old bunch could muster. None of them looked capable of defending themselves from a foe of much ferocity.

Jim approached the Mandans slowly, indicating again, in sign, to Step Toe, that he meant them no harm. He stopped and waited, allowing the Mandans a minute to settle their nerves. Finally Step Toe came over — he was short and very thin.

"No tabac?" he asked. "We need tabac."

"No tabac," Jim said.

The old man looked disappointed.

"We have been to the springs," he said. "We like to go to the springs before the cold gets too

277

bad. I am not old myself but these others are old. The warm springs are good for their bones."

Jim knew the springs Step Toe was talking about — there were several bubbling, foul-smelling sulfur springs in the barren country five days' travel to the west. Many Indians used the springs, and some trappers liked them, but Jim himself found the smell so strong that he avoided them.

"We found Big White — he was already dead," Step Toe said. "He killed a Ponca — broke open his head with that big club of his. The Ponca is over there.

"There is not much game near the springs," he added. "We have been living on roots."

Jim saw that in fact the little band was starving. He at once gave them what was left of his buffalo meat and the old women immediately set to cooking it. Two of the old women and one of the old men were almost blind — they were the smoke starers, people whose vision had been weakened by too many years spent in small, smoky lodges. The parrot still paraded on the corpse of Big White — it occurred to Jim that the chief might have played with the old bird while both were on the boat.

The dead Ponca's head had indeed been broken open — there was ice on the clotted brain matter. Jim made a thorough search but did not find the old chief's famous war club.

Except for the fact of two corpses, there was little sign of struggle. Jim noticed the tracks of four horses — that was all.

"Was Big White shot?" Jim asked, after studying the horse tracks to no purpose. The Mandans were gulping down the half-raw buffalo meat. They all looked exhausted, and one old woman, blood on her chin, was already snoring loudly.

Step Toe held up a finger, jabbing with it three or four times.

"Somebody stuck him with a little knife," Step Toe said. "The wound was no wider than my finger — it went between his ribs and bit him bad."

"You didn't see the horsemen?"

"We saw no one," Step Toe said. "When we found Big White his spirit had gone, but he was still warm. At first we feared that someone might come and try to kill us too, but they didn't. I guess we were too worthless to bother with. Big White was a heavy man — it was all we could do to get him on that scaffold."

"Have you heard of a man called Malgres — a dark man from the south?" Jim asked.

Step Toe shook his head, but another of the old men, old Rabbit Skin, who had been half nodding, came awake at the mention of Malgres.

"I saw him once with some Poncas," Rabbit Skin said. "Some Poncas and the Twisted Hair."

"That's right — he works for the Twisted Hair," Jim said.

"A Frenchman was there when I saw them," the old man said. Being full had made him feel sleepy. He could barely remember the dark man, Malgres — he had been butchering a horse at the time, he seemed to recall.

"Malgres has a little thin knife," Jim indicated. "They say he's quick as a snake, when he strikes."

"I wonder if Big White really killed a grizzly bear with that club?" Step Toe said. "He was a great man, but he was always bragging. I knew him years ago, when I was younger."

48

Among excitable people, calm was the first requirement . . .

John Skraeling, known among the tribes as the Twisted Hair, from his habit of twisting his long gray mane into a knot so it wouldn't blow in his face on windy days, or spoil his aim if he was hunting, was annoyed when Draga told him that the steamboat had left the Mandan encampments three days earlier. All the river tribes were talking about the great Thunder Boat, with the rich English family on it. Skraeling had meant to be in the Mandan villages two weeks earlier — he, Guillaume, Malgres, and the two Poncas, one of whom was now dead — but the trouble between the Osage and the Pawnees had slowed them down. In any case, traveling with Guillaume — Willy, to the English — was never fast. Guillaume refused to be rushed; he was seldom willing to leave camp before noon. Malgres wanted to kill him because of his sluggish habits, but Skraeling forbade it.

"Don't you be cutting on Guillaume," he said. "We need someone who can talk to the Sioux. I can't, and you can't either."

"I don't want to talk to these filthy Indians," Malgres said — he himself was said to be part

281

Apache. Malgres was small, quick, hotheaded, and deadly. Skraeling tried to avoid long conversations with him; he had been looking for a safe way to be done with Malgres, but hadn't found one yet.

Georges Guillaume, the man Malgres wanted to kill, had been in the north country forty years, as hunter, trapper, trader, guide, slaver, spy. He spoke more native dialects than any man in the north, far more than Toussaint Charbonneau, Captain Clark's interpreter. Skraeling knew that Malgres's Santa Fe bravado would not help them much if they ran into forty or fifty Teton Sioux on a day when the Sioux were in a warring mood — as they usually were.

"The Bad Eye made me give two white women back," Draga said. "We had three but one attacked me and the warriors killed her. There are many women on that boat. It has only been gone three days. Some of the women would bring a good price."

"I'm more interested in that keelboat full of wine the men are talking about," Skraeling said. "That much wine would keep a fellow warm all winter. It's gonna get bad cold pretty soon."

John Skraeling hated the cold. Son of a Norwegian sailor and a Creole mother, he had been born to the humid warmth of Galveston. He himself had been a captive, taken by the Comanches when young; Comanche was the only native language he spoke. When he grew up the tribe let him go — very soon, with more and more settlers crowding into the Comancheria, Skraeling became a ransom specialist, buying back young captives for the frontier families or small settlements from which they had been snatched. He was paid for his work, but not much; it soon occurred to him that he could make a good deal more money if he snatched the children *and* rescued them. Generally the return would be made quickly — else the children might die, from the mere shock of captivity itself. Keep them three weeks and their families might consider them hopelessly tainted by contact with the Comanches; this was particularly true if the children were female. Comanche women became wives very young.

John Skraeling soon tired of the uncertainties that went with the trade in captives. He struck the old Spanish trail to Santa Fe and became a trader in everything *but* captives: pelts, silver, weapons, blankets, even spices. Six times he crossed from Saint Louis to Nuevo Mexico. He had been in Kansas when he heard about the great steamboat with the rich English family and its keelboat full of fine wine. With Malgres, Guillaume, and the Poncas, he had decided to follow it, mainly out of curiosity. A steamer on the shallow Missouri might encounter a lot of setbacks — there might be much to scavenge, if things went wrong.

But they had arrived late, and now the boat was north of them, with the bitter cold at hand.

"We could catch it," Draga said. "Take me

with you if you go. I'll see that you're warm."

Georges Guillaume sat comfortably by the fire, carefully scraping the rich yellow marrow out of a buffalo leg bone. He lifted an eyebrow at Draga's remark. Long ago, before she had begun to smell old, Draga had been his woman. What was the old slut suggesting? That she would build Skraeling's fires — or find him young women; or was she offering to be his woman herself? John Skraeling showed little interest in women anyway — why would he want a harsh, toothless old witch?

"Thank you," Skraeling said politely. "I'll let you know what I decide."

He had no intention of taking Draga with him, but he didn't want to offend her, either. Draga had the ear of the Bad Eye, a fact no trader could afford to ignore. In any case, as he had tried to explain to Malgres, courtesy and good manners did not go unnoticed in the Mandan encampments — modesty got one more than bluster or rage. Among excitable people, calm was the first requirement — the unfortunate encounter with Big White showed that clearly enough. Big White had actually been on the English boat — Skraeling had merely been waiting for Guillaume to catch up so Guillaume could ask the old man about the treasures on the steamer. But then one of the Poncas had foolishly insulted the old Mandan, an act of aggressive folly that immediately cost him his life. Then Malgres, whom Big White hardly noticed, struck with his knife before Skraeling could stop him, and the one man who could have given them valuable information about the treasure boat slumped down in the snow and died.

"Draga wants you to catch her some more white girls so she can beat them," Guillaume said to Skraeling. "She hates these white girls that the young men want."

Draga ignored him — she might lack the beauty of her youth, but she was not too old to please men. Almost every day, if she went to the shore to gather firewood, some young warrior would follow and seek to couple with her. Some she allowed, some she rejected. She knew, of course, that Skraeling didn't want her for himself. He was not a young man — in fact, he looked sick. Draga meant to watch him, observe where he squatted, see if there was blood in his excrement. Skraeling's cheeks were sunk in, and there was a rasp in his breath. Skraeling no longer wanted women, but he did still want money.

When he left the lodge to go visit the Bad Eye, Guillaume cracked another buffalo bone — he could not get enough of the rich marrow. Outside, the wind was howling — Guillaume was happy to be in a warm lodge, even if the old witch, Draga, was staring at him with hatred in her eyes.

"The Bad Eye made a terrible prophecy," Draga informed him.

"I don't want to hear it — I don't like bad

news," Guillaume said. "I need a new wife, Draga — nobody skinny. Can't you find me a young woman with some flesh on her bones?"

"Why should I find you wives?" Draga asked. Then she left the lodge — she wanted to hear what Skraeling said to the Bad Eye.

Guillaume threw a big piece of driftwood on the fire. His lodge was a good solid lodge of well-packed earth, warm even on the coldest days, though perhaps a little smoky. If Skraeling decided to chase the English boat, then let him do it with Malgres and the Ponca. Guillaume meant to stay in his warm lodge and eat buffalo marrow until the warm weather came. When Draga came back she found him sound asleep and snoring.

49

The sky to the north was bluish, like a gun barrel . . .

Tasmin woke to the snorting and snuffling of buffalo — many thousands of them crowded both banks of the river and covered the plains to the west as far as the eye could see. Those nearest the river had icicles hanging from their chins, and more icicles dangling from their shaggy sides, where melting snow had frozen hard. It was so cold that Tasmin's breath soon frosted up her windowpane.

To her annoyance Bobbety and Mary came bursting in, admitting air so frigid that to breathe it was like drawing fire into her lungs.

"My thermometer is quite smashed — the mercury kept sinking until the glass broke," Bobbety said. "That means it is very cold indeed."

"I believe I could have deduced that without a lecture from you, Bobbety," Tasmin said.

"The Piegan is rather annoyed because he can't paint himself today — his paints are frozen, and so are Holger Sten's, but Mr. Catlin had the forethought to trust his to Cook, who kept them in a warm place," Mary informed them.

"Even so he is not painting these numerous

287

buffalo — his fingers are too cold," Bobbety said.

For some days now Tasmin had been feeling the kind of restless frustration that she had felt on the day of the big hailstorm. Once again, just as she had resolved to go ashore and search for her husband, an unignorable impediment had been thrown up. Then it had been hail, now it was this terrible cold. The sky to the north was bluish, like a gun barrel; it offered no suggestion of warmth. Tasmin felt herself to be a hardy, healthy woman, but she was not so foolish as to suppose she could survive such cold. Besides, she was with child, her abdomen just showing its first slight curve. The Oto woman had been right to make her shirt loose. Vexed as she was at having to deal once again with the inanities of her family, frustrated as she was at not being with Jim, she knew there was nothing much she could do about it. Only that morning Captain Aitken, himself much disturbed by the sudden, brutal end to the fallish weather, had put it to Tasmin bluntly.

"You'd not last a night on shore," he said. "The Indians can stand it. Oh, sometimes they lose a toe or two. But they don't die. You'd die, Miss Tasmin."

"Captain, you must stop thinking of me as a Miss," Tasmin reminded him. "Cook can't seem to remember that fact, either. The one who remembers is Papa, and that's because he's lost a great fat dowry."

"Sorry," the captain said. He had a great deal more on his mind than forms of address. They were still more than one hundred miles, as the river flowed, from the snug trading post on the Yellowstone that was their destination, and yet the river *wouldn't* flow, if the cold didn't moderate. The edges of the river were crinkled with thick ice — it had happened in only one night.

Charbonneau came up to the bridge as the captain was talking with Tasmin.

"The Mandans said it was going to get bad cold," he said.

"I'm going to start running all night," George Aitken said. "I'll send some *engagés* in front of us, in a pirogue — they can feel out the snags and sandbars."

"But really, gentlemen, we can get out and walk, if we have to, can't we?" Tasmin asked.

"We can, but I don't know how many of us would make it — depends on the blizzards," Charbonneau said.

"We stayed a day too long at the Mandans'," the captain said. "Fixing that paddle was the devil of a bother. Little delays tell against you, when the season's failing."

"I'm sure my Jim is out there somewhere," Tasmin said, a little anxiously. "I hope he's not met with an accident. *He's* not likely to freeze, is he?"

Captain Aitken almost slipped and called Tasmin "miss" again — she looked so young and blooming. It was rather a mystery what sort of marriage she was intending to have with Jimmy Snow — a skilled young guide, certainly, but hardly the man to provide this smart young Englishwoman with a comfortable home life.

"Oh, Jimmy can handle weather," the captain said. "I'd be happy to see him myself, to tell you the truth. If the weather stays this cold we may ice in — Jimmy could be a big help if we have to tramp it."

Later, in her cabin, Tasmin locked herself in and withdrew into memory, as she had many times. She did her best to recall everything that had happened in her time with Jim. No book now interested her — she could think of nothing but her husband. She wanted intensely for him to come to her and remain her husband, and yet she could not decide, from a review of his behavior, whether such an appearance was at all likely. He had mentioned casually, in the midst of her pique, that he only expected to see his Ute wives every two or three years — what if he were intending to be similarly lax in regard to conjugal life with her? The thought of waiting years, months, even weeks to see him was intolerable! Didn't he miss her? It was a matter she had no way of judging.

In her life as a much-courted English beauty, Tasmin had rarely been prone to self-criticism. Guilt was an unknown emotion. She had taken Master Stiles away from her mother without a moment's qualm.

Now, in her chilly stateroom, surrounded by

the vast plains — bare except for the milling buffalo — Tasmin, long accustomed to blaming others for everything that went even slightly wrong, now turned her considerable skill at blaming herself. Why had she allowed the revelation of these distant Indian wives to upset her so? Why had she been so foolish as to leave a man who had been, on the whole, rather considerate of her, and who pleased her deeply? The obvious explanation was that she herself was an excessively spoiled piece of work. Her feelings of abandonment and loneliness were her own fault — Jim, after all, hadn't left her.

In her turmoil of spirit Tasmin struck out ruthlessly when any member of her family made the slightest demand. The pale, passive Buffum — already nunlike — she avoided. Bobbety she ignored, Mary she smacked; and she had nothing to do with her father, who in any case remained closeted with Vicky Kennet most of the time, nursing his stumps. George Catlin she froze out; the other specialists she rarely saw. The one person she took into her confidence, regarding her pregnancy, was Cook — no gossip, and gynecologically experienced as well — and Coal, Charbonneau's wife, made rounder and much jollier by the fact that she too was with child. The tundra swans had blessed her, Coal believed.

Coal and Tasmin had no language in common: what they had was a common state, the old, old state that came only to women. On sunny days Tasmin often went down and sat with Coal, comforted by her cheerfulness and impressed by her industry. Coal had insisted that her husband bring her rabbit skins — she had already made a warm pouch for her child, and assured Tasmin — in sign — that she would make her one too. Old Charbonneau was rather put out at being required to scour the plains for rabbits, but he did his duty and Coal worked the skins until they were supple and soft. Sometimes Tasmin helped a little, accepting Coal's instructions. Then she conceived the notion of making Jim a cap. Monsieur Charbonneau was required to secure two beaver skins from some Indians. Tasmin racked her brain over the question of head size. When her Jim did come she wanted his cap to be right, neither too small or too large. The final product looked rather Russian to her, but Tasmin was proud of it anyway and slept with it under her pillow at night. Somehow just having a fine cap waiting made her feel a little more hopeful that someday soon her Jimmy, her Raven Brave, would come back to his wife.

50

Insults, slights, teasings, rudeness she had borne in studied silence . . .

Venetia Kennet, five years now in service to the Berrybenders, had not once lowered herself to ask a favor of Lady Tasmin. Insults, slights, teasings, rudeness she had borne in studied silence, a haughty dignity her only refuge. Now and then she might lash out at Bess, slap Mary, curse one or another of the Ten; of course, she had always felt quite free to abuse the tutors, the *femme de chambre*, the kitchen help, the valet, and lesser riffraff on the boat. But Tasmin she let be — it was most unfair, of course, that Tasmin had been born noble and herself of common stock; but there it was, and Venetia felt that the best response she could make to this unanswerable injustice was to ask Tasmin for nothing — not even the loan of a book. This policy she had held to rigidly for the whole five years. On rare occasions, when Tasmin unbent and *offered* to loan her a book, Venetia Kennet had nobly, serenely, icily refused, and would have refused to the very portals of eternity had the family only remained in England, where life proceeded according to long-established rules.

But now the deep deep cold, so intense that

when Venetia went on deck even for a few minutes, the very roots of her teeth ached, was
forcing her to break this rule of rules in the interest of keeping alive her hopes of someday
being Lady Berrybender — which could only
occur if Albany Berrybender himself stayed
alive, and Lord B. was even then insisting, over
Captain Aitken's strong protests, that he *would*
go hunting immediately, taking Gladwyn, his
man, and Tim, the stable boy, who, between
them, would be expected to carry the guns.

"What, come thousands of miles to hunt buffalo and then not hunt them when they veritably
blanket the plains?" Lord B. asked. "Of course
I'll hunt them, despite this spot of weather."

When pressed to go with the hunting party,
Toussaint Charbonneau flatly refused.

"I've lost one Indian and I expect he's dead —
I'm sticking with the other two," Charbonneau
said. "It's a bit frosty for hunting, anyway."

Lord Berrybender was hardly pleased by
Charbonneau's refusal. He liked to suppose that
everybody on the boat worked for him and him
only. That a man would refuse to hunt with him
because Captain Clark had enjoined him to look
after two mangy savages hardly showed the
proper spirit, in Lord B.'s view. Charbonneau
might have a French name, but he exhibited a
very American sense of independence, a national
trait that Albany Berrybender had no use for at
all, since it led commoners to ignore the wishes
of their betters, as Charbonneau had just done.

It was Captain Aitken — worried for His Lordship's safety — who asked Venetia Kennet to see if Tasmin would attempt to talk sense to her father.

"He doesn't know what he's letting himself in for, Miss Kennet," Captain Aitken said. "He thinks because the sun's come out for a few minutes he won't freeze — but he *will* freeze, and so will his men."

Tasmin had been brushing the fine cap she had made for Jim Snow, enjoying the soft feel of the furs; she was not pleased to hear a pounding on her cabin door — very probably it was only Father Geoff, wanting to complain about the tedium of Walter Scott, whose *Kenilworth* he found lacking in both concision and wit. She opened the door with some reluctance and was astonished to see an obviously distressed Venetia Kennet standing there. Never in the years of their troubled acquaintance had Vicky Kennet pounded on her door.

"Goodness, Vicky! What is it?"

"It's His Lordship," Vicky said. "He proposes to go off hunting, despite this fearful cold. Captain Aitken thought he might listen to you — that you might try to dissuade him."

"Captain Aitken has an exaggerated view of my influence over Papa, I fear," Tasmin said. "I've never talked him out of doing anything he wanted to do, and no one else has either."

"I know — he is *so* willful," Vicky said, fearing that the case was hopeless.

"In my opinion a man as soaked with brandy as Father is very unlikely to freeze — but that doesn't mean the help won't," Tasmin said. "We can ill afford to lose many more servants — at least they can shoot guns if we find ourselves under attack."

She shrugged on one of the great gray capotes and followed Vicky Kennet to the lower deck, where a pirogue with two freezing *engagés* in it waited to ferry the hunting party to shore. Except for Lord Berrybender himself, the hunting party was in low spirits. Gladwyn and the lad Tim also had been issued the great gray coats, but both were shivering violently despite them. They looked like men about to ascend the scaffold. Yet Mary Berrybender, wearing only a thin sweater, stood by the almost naked Hairy Horn and neither seemed at all bothered by the extreme chill.

Tasmin wasted no time on niceties.

"Papa, do stop this folly," she said. "It's so cold it broke the bottom out of Bobbety's thermometer — it's obviously quite insane for you to go ashore."

"No business of yours, that I can see," Lord Berrybender said brusquely. "Anyway, the sun's out — things will soon be melting, I expect."

"No sir, no!" Captain Aitken pleaded. "The sun will be gone by the time you reach shore."

Lord Berrybender ignored him and turned toward the ladder, but Tasmin quickly blocked his access.

"Here's the count," she said. "You've already lost your wife, one child, a boatman, two Poles, our good Fraulein, and a smattering of toes and fingers. Now you stand ready to deprive us of Gladwyn and Tim, neither of whom is likely to survive such profound chill."

Lord Berrybender flushed red at her words — the impertinence! To the horror of the company he grabbed Tasmin by the hair and gave her a violent shaking; then he shoved her so hard that she spun across the deck and fell in the startled Piegan's lap. The man just saved her from a nasty fall.

"I *will* hunt, and I will hunt *now!*" Lord Berrybender shouted. "I don't think I've quite sunk to the point where I must carry my own weapons, either."

Without another word he descended into the pirogue and settled himself. He too wore one of the great gray coats. Gladwyn and Tim, offered no options, climbed slowly into the boat, being careful with the guns.

"Cold as it is you'll have to do the butchering quick," Charbonneau advised. "Otherwise the meat will freeze."

"I don't propose to butcher them — I just propose to kill them," Lord B. said. "Might take a tongue or two, if I'm in the mood."

With that he waved impatiently, and the pirogue made for the icy shore. The buffalo had moved off the river, but thousands were still in sight, a mile or two west.

"Best not to lose sight of the river, sir!" Captain Aitken shouted, cupping his hands. His voice echoed off the low bluffs to the west.

"Well, Vicky, so much for my influence," Tasmin said. "All I got was my hair pulled."

Father Geoff popped out of the galley, licking one of Cook's great spoons. Lately he had been spending a good deal of time with Cook, feeling that the shipboard cooking might profit from a little French expertise.

"What's the fuss?" he asked.

"No fuss, particularly — what's on that spoon?" Tasmin asked.

"Pudding," Father Geoffrin said.

As they watched, the sun disappeared. A dark blue bank of cloud, moving over them from the north, swallowed it so completely that no ray shone through. On the shore they could just see the three gray forms slipping and sliding on the ice. Soon the three men were dots against the shallow snow.

"I fear that's the end of Papa," Mary said. "I can't think why he is so unwise."

Captain Aitken, heartsick, said nothing. He stood at the rail, watching the deep cold cloud. Soon he heard the first distant pops from Old Gorska's Belgian gun.

51

He heard a kind of snuffle . . .

"Great sport! Great sport!" Lord Berrybender yelled, in high exuberance. "Never had such fine sport in my life. Keep loading, man. How many would you say are down, so far?"

"Tim would be the one to ask, Your Lordship," Gladwyn said, feeling that his hands might simply snap off, like twigs. He could not load properly with gloves on, and yet when he took his gloves off, his hands got so cold they would barely grasp a gun. Young Tim had already peeled half the skin off one hand by foolishly grasping one of the freezing gun barrels with an ungloved hand. Now, of course, the gun barrels were warm from Lord Berrybender's rapid fire, but that was no consolation to Tim, whose peeled palm burned like fire.

"Forty, I'd say, Your Lordship," Tim yelled. All around, within a radius of less than one hundred yards, great brown beasts lay sprawled, some dead, some still belching bright crimson blood into the snow.

"Good lad — do take a few tongues," Lord B. instructed. "Cook will be impatient if we neglect such a fine opportunity to bring back tongues."

As soon as Gladwyn handed him a rifle he turned and fired, this time killing a buffalo cow that was no more than thirty feet from where he stood. Instead of fleeing, as most animals did when under assault, the buffalo seemed quite indifferent to the shooting. Of course, the wind had risen, snow was beginning to blow a bit. Still, the odd thing was, the buffalo *did* seem to be massing together, milling around in a formless herd. One cow passed between himself and Gladwyn — another nearly stepped on Tim, who had not yet mastered the knack of neatly severing a buffalo's tongue from its bleeding mouth.

"I say, Your Lordship, they do seem to be crowding rather close," Gladwyn said, becoming alarmed. Buffalo were everywhere.

"The wind's keening so — I suppose they can scarcely hear the shots," Lord Berrybender said, as a great shaggy beast ambled past him, its coat snow-streaked, not ten feet away.

"I do rather wish they'd spread out," Lord Berrybender said. "It's rather more sporting if I have to do at least a bit of aiming."

He took a gun from Gladwyn — the man was shivering damnably — and shot the great shaggy bull, only to experience a startling change: the immediate disappearance of everything. Snow suddenly whirled around him so blindingly that when he held out the empty rifle to Gladwyn, not merely Gladwyn but the rifle and even his own arm disappeared into a swirl of white. He heard a kind of snuffle, then a buffalo just brushed him as it went past. Lord Berrybender felt it but could not see it. For a moment he thought he just glimpsed Gladwyn, but then the man vanished again. Lord Berrybender stood stock-still, his arm still extended, the empty rifle growing heavy in his hand. He expected, of course, that Gladwyn would take it and reload it, and yet he didn't. Lord Berrybender withdrew the gun and tried to pull up the big floppy hood of his capote, only to have the hood fill with snow before he could even pull it over his head. He pulled it over his head anyway — the snow melted and then froze again as it dribbled down his cheeks, forming an icicle just below his chin — it was the first time his chin had sprouted an icicle in his life.

Then he felt a hard bump and was sent sprawling — a buffalo had stumbled into him in the blinding whirl of snow. Lord Berrybender just managed to keep his grip on the rifle. When he tried to struggle up he found that someone else had a grip on the rifle too — the briefly lost Gladwyn it was! The two men were less than three feet apart, and yet could not see each other.

"Am I to reload, Your Lordship?" Gladwyn yelled, and then realized at once that the task was hopeless. He could scarcely see the Belgian gun, and could no longer manage the powder and shot. Fortunately he had clung grimly to a second rifle, which was loaded. This he handed to Lord Berrybender.

"Wrong gun! Wrong gun! Where's my Belgian?" Lord B. wanted to know. He had become extremely fond of Old Gorska's excellent gun.

Gladwyn was shaking so hard that he couldn't answer; in fact he had no idea what he'd done with the Belgian gun — though a moment later he realized it was squeezed between his shaking legs.

"Have to use this one, sir," he screamed, and Lord B. *did* use the second rifle, firing point-blank into the side of a great beast that had just loomed out of the snow, only feet away. The buffalo fell just in front of them, its shaggy coat steaming. Gladwyn could not resist — he thrust his freezing hands into the wounded animal's shaggy fur. Lord Berrybender, his own hands far from warm, did the same.

"Getting a bit thick, in fact," he said. "I believe I've killed forty-two buffalo, if Tim's count was right — perhaps the prudent thing would be to make for the boat."

Gladwyn's teeth were chattering so violently that he feared they might shatter. In the privacy of his modest quarters Gladwyn sometimes wrote verse; he thought he might just have a rhyme — "chatter, shatter" — if he could just hold it in mind until he could write it down.

"Where exactly is the boat, sir?" he asked.

Lord Berrybender, his hands warming as he pressed them against the buffalo, looked about and saw only white — uniform, monotonous white.

"I'm afraid I haven't the faintest notion," he

admitted. "Never much of a head for directions . . . got lost in my own deer park more than once. I expect Tim will know — just the kind of thing a stable boy *would* know."

"But where is Tim, Your Lordship?" Gladwyn asked.

"Gad, can't be far," Lord B. said. "He was just taking a tongue."

Suddenly a moment of absolute panic seized him. Where was Tim? More important, where was the Missouri River, the pirogue, the *engagés,* the steamer *Rocky Mount,* the languid but pliable Venetia Kennet?

"Tim, Tim, Tim!" Lord B. yelled, at the top of his voice. "Time to retreat, lad — come lead us home."

The howling, keening wind snatched his words and whirled them away so swiftly that even if Tim had been on the other side of the fallen buffalo he might not have heard them.

Tim, for his part, had lost not only the tongue he had just cut out of the buffalo, but the knife he had used to remove the tongue. Both dropped from his freezing fingers and were instantly lost. He was too cold even to yell — when he opened his mouth, cold filled it. By inadvertence he made the same discovery Gladwyn had made: the buffalo he knelt by was still breathing and still warm; also it was large enough to form a kind of barrier. Tim squeezed as close to it as he could get, even warming his icy cheeks in the thick fur. Though a moment before he felt certain that his would be a frigid doom, the fact that the animal he was pressed against still pulsed with the heat of life gave Tim a little hope. The buffalo would be his shelter and his stove. He thought of his three jolly brothers, all safely back in England, cheerfully shoveling out the Berrybender stables and making crude assaults on the milkmaids' virtue now and then. What a happy lot was theirs! Just faintly, once or twice, he thought he heard His Lordship calling, but Tim didn't answer; he knew he mustn't be tempted to leave his shaggy stove.

"The lazy rascal, where is he, now that he's needed?" Lord Berrybender complained. A great many buffalo were trampling and snuffling around them, on the whole rather welcome since they somewhat broke the chilling wind.

"Lost as us, I expect, Your Lordship," Gladwyn said, his teeth still chattering-shattering. "Lost as us."

"I wouldn't object to a spot of fire, if any wood could be found," Lord B. said. "Expect they'll send a party to get us, soon. Stout Captain Aitken knows his job — he won't desert us."

"Perhaps not, but how will he find us, sir — I mean with the atmosphere being so thick?" Gladwyn asked.

Lord Berrybender considered the comment, unhappily. The atmosphere was damnably thick — the sun that he had been counting on to melt things was absolutely gone; darkness was not far off. A shore party might stumble around for hours before lighting on them, crouched as they were behind a fallen buffalo.

"Kick around a bit, Gladwyn . . . there must be wood around here somewhere," His Lordship said. "Kick around, won't you? Be cheery to have a spot of fire."

52

She remembered the terrible wind that had keened and roared . . .

Despite the bitter cold, as the great inconstant wall of storm advanced toward them from the north, one by one the company aboard the steamer *Rocky Mount* left the warmth of cabin, galley, and bridge, to stand by the rail on the lower deck, watching the terrible storm come.

"Wotan is angry," Mary said. "He means to bury the whole world in snow."

"Don't know about that, but it's a fine blizzard, I guess," Charbonneau said. "The Bad Eye predicted it."

"Bosh, I don't hold with these red prophets," George Catlin said. "Why not predict a blizzard, since it's winter?"

"They say he can hear a snowflake form," Mary said. "They say he can hear the swan's breath."

"And now our own Papa has very likely gone to his death in this year of our Lord 1832," Buffum said.

"The spirit of the hunt was on him," Señor Yanez remarked, startling everybody. Señor Yanez rarely spoke.

"Yes, and the old brute's taken two innocents

with him," Tasmin said.

She remembered the terrible wind that had keened and roared, underneath the hail. Now the wind was keening again, and the snow wall had snuffed out the sun's light — there was only a ghostly glint on the snow.

Father Geoffrin shivered violently.

"So desolate, these plains — such melancholy," he said. "I often weep, and I don't know why. Snow is so much more a thing to be welcomed when it falls on cobblestones . . . or ancient walls . . . or lamplighters . . . or the shawls of prostitutes."

"Any chance we could find them, Charbonneau?" Captain Aitken asked. The light was almost gone, the snow wall advancing fast, and the black watery lead that would take them up the Missouri was narrowing by the hour. Still, he could not steam away and leave a noble patron. The loss of Lord Berrybender would mean the end of his career. His employers would not forgive such a calamity — none of them had been west of Cincinnati; they had rather rosy ideas about life on the wild Missouri.

"No chance, George," Charbonneau said. "The snow'll soon be blowing so thick you can't see the length of your arm. His Lordship *would* go."

"That he would — he nearly yanked my hair out when I tried to reason with him," Tasmin said.

Cook came out for a moment, took Father

Geoffrin by the sleeve, and led him back inside. She had begun to rely heavily on his advice in the matter of sauces and spices.

"It could not get this cold in Holland," Piet Van Wely announced. "The people would not stand for it — there would be protests and someone would lose his position."

"In Denmark also there are no such snows," Holger Sten declared. "Only where the Lapps live are there these snows — knowledge of the Lapps I do not claim."

Remembering, suddenly, Fraulein Pfretzskaner's terrible end, which could so easily have been her own, Buffum began to sob.

Venetia Kennet began to cry also. The thin, fading light filled her with the deepest melancholy, the darkest sorrow. His Lordship, her great hope, was gone, doubtless to be frozen — and now she found herself pregnant with his bastard. Cook had confirmed her status only that day. The pregnancy that had once been her hope was now her despair. The seed at last had sprouted, but the noble seeder was gone.

As Buffum sniffled and Venetia Kennet sobbed, a new sound reached them over the roar of snow — a high chant of some kind. They all turned and there was the Hairy Horn, calling out a high, eerie chant. He had thrown off his blanket — he faced the storm almost naked.

"The Hairy Horn wishes to end his life's journey soon," Mary said. "The melody he offers up now is his death song."

"Wouldn't pay too much attention to *that* claim," Charbonneau said. "He's said as much before and yet he's still eating a good portion of vittles, every day."

Venetia Kennet, too distressed to stand on ceremony, flung herself into Tasmin's arms and gasped out her secret.

"I am going to have a baby — you are not the only one, Tasmin," she said.

Tasmin gave the weeping cellist a consolatory pat or two. At least the woman was not without vigor, a desirable quality in the New World they were voyaging into.

"I wasn't the only one anyway, Vicky — there's our merry Coal," Tasmin said. "If you ask her she'll make your baby a snug fur pouch. Why, we can establish quite a nursery up on the Yellowstone — at least we can if we survive this desperate weather."

53

Getting the bear out proved a challenge . . .

Maelgwyn Evans liked to claim that he got through the bitter winters along the Knife River through the precaution of having taken six hundred pounds of wives: three Winnebagos and a Chippewa. Maelgwyn himself was skinny, but his lodge north of the river was well caulked, and the warm poundage of his four wives was proof against even the coldest night.

Of course, this stratagem only worked if he was *in* his lodge when the bitter weather struck. He and Jim Snow had gone three or four miles north, meaning to take a fat buffalo cow, before the blizzard hit. They easily killed a cow, took the liver and sweetmeats and a bit of flank, and were hurrying back to shelter when they saw the three men from the steamer come crunching ashore and start shooting into the buffalo herd, evidently oblivious to the fact that a high plains blizzard was swiftly advancing toward them.

"The one doing the shootin' is my wife's pa," Jim said. "The old one.

"She says he's stubborn," he added, watching the scene across the snowy plain.

"A man from the north, I expect," Maelgwyn said. "No one stubborner than a northman. Not practical minded, like us Welsh."

Jim eyed the hunting party, eyed the approaching storm, eyed the boat. He was calculating as to whether he had time to race over and try to get the hunting party to safety. He had had a chilly tramp north; once he knew that he was upriver from the steamer he rested for a day, allowing Maelgwyn's wives to feed him thick stews and rub him well with bear grease taken from a fat grizzly that Maelgwyn had killed in its den earlier in the fall. Getting the bear out proved a challenge, even for a Welshman with four stout wives.

"It was a wide bear in a narrow den," Maelgwyn said. Always eager to talk, he described the adventure at some length, while Jim dozed and got his rub. His Ute wives had the same habit; he could expect a good rub when he showed up. Tasmin had never rubbed him in that fashion, but of course he had yet to supply her with the fat of a hibernating bear. He wondered, as he dozed, if it was not more practical — as Maelgwyn claimed — just to have Indian wives, women well able to cure skins, pick berries, gather firewood, tan pelts.

"One of the benefits of life out here on the baldies is that not many English come this way," Maelgwyn said. "But now there's a steamer full of 'em. I don't know that I like it."

Maelgwyn was respected by all the beaver

men, north and south, because of the high quality of his pelts. Other trappers sometimes brought in more pelts, but Maelgwyn's were always prime — he secured the silkiest beaver, the fox pelt with the most shine, weasel tails, and pelts taken from wolves with their long winter hair. He traded no pelts with flaws — even John Skraeling, who didn't like the north, stopped at Maelgwyn's from time to time, taking his excellent furs back to Santa Fe.

"It's the wives," Maelgwyn claimed, modestly. "I've trained every one of them. I've my own little fur factory, here on the Knife."

Jim concluded that there was no way he could get to the foolish hunters before the storm engulfed them. Nobody, white or Indian, could do much in a whiteout. The only thing to do when a blizzard came was find a warm place and wait. He and Maelgwyn had to make haste themselves. The whirling snow was waist high when they got back to Maelgwyn's lodge.

"I expect those English will freeze," Jim said.

"It's likely, unless the buffalo save them," Maelgwyn said. "Buffalo crowd up in a storm. If the English can stay in the midst of them it'll knock some of the wind off. I was saved that way myself once, up on the Prairie du Chien — got in among two or three thousand buffalo. I had to keep moving, but I survived.

"If it clears by dawn, then the bad cold will hit," he added. "They have quite a few buffalo down. I expect we could find them by starlight, if the blow lets up."

"I don't know that old man, but he's my wife's pa," Jim said. "When the wind dies we might better try."

54

"Not a cork broken, not one"

The buffalo Tim crouched behind was cooling — it had died. Snow blew over the dead beast and over Tim. By chance his hand fell on the knife he had dropped earlier. Though he felt little hope, he grasped the knife with both hands and began to try to scratch out a little cave, beneath the carcass. He couldn't feel his feet, but still had some feeling in his hands. His ears stung like fire. He pressed his face against the dead buffalo and sucked in his breath as he worked. Slowly the trench deepened. He could just squeeze a little way beneath the hairy, inert body. He raked and raked, but then somehow lost the knife again. He tightened his coat around him and crowded in under the buffalo as best he could, shivering so violently that he thought his bones might snap. At moments he wondered if he had already died. He seemed to hear Lord Berrybender talking, going on about some great Spanish battle he had fought long ago. Tim heard him, then didn't hear him, then heard him again. Until the two men came in the starlit night and tried to get him to his feet, Tim had not been aware that the wind had died. He was at first not sure whether he was alive or in heaven, though surely his hands would not hurt so if it were the latter.

"Come on, you've got to walk," Jim told him. "It's not far to the river — we can't carry both of you."

"It hurts too much, I believe I am frozen," Tim said, very surprised to see Lord Berrybender staggering around, only a little distance away.

"Mustn't forget that Belgian gun," Lord Berrybender was saying. "Expensive, that fine Belgian — belonged to my hunter. Rather sentimental, my hunter. Lost his boy and killed himself."

"We can come back for the gun, sir," Maelgwyn said politely. "We have to get you shipboard and see to your feet, and the boy's."

Lord Berrybender just then noticed Tim, stumbling along supported by another stranger, a prairie fellow of some kind.

"Why, Tim . . . stout lad, stout lad," he said, feeling for a moment like weeping. The small fellow was hurrying him away, allowing him no time to gather his possessions.

"Might just grab that Belgian gun, Tim," Lord B. said. "Can't manage it myself, with my stump."

"Can't hold it, Your Lordship, hands won't work," Tim admitted.

"Nonsense, blow on your fingers, that'll do the trick," Lord Berrybender instructed. "Not disposed to lose that gun."

"You won't — I'll get it later," Jim said, annoyed at the selfish old fool.

"A savage could pick it up — thoroughly wasted on a savage," Lord B. began; but then he noticed that the two rescuers were looking at him in a not entirely friendly way. He could always send Charbonneau ashore to gather up the weaponry — or even Señor Yanez.

"But where's Gladwyn, sir?" Tim asked. "He usually carries the guns."

"Stout lad, you're right, of course," Lord B. said. "Gladwyn's job, quite clearly. But where is the fellow?"

"Gladwyn?" Maelgwyn asked. "That's a Welsh name, a bit like my own. Was the fellow Welsh?"

"Possibly Welsh — or was he a Cornishman? Fear I'm too cold to think clearly," Lord B. said. "Haven't got a spot of brandy on you, I don't suppose? Might clear my head."

Neither Jim nor Maelgwyn were encouraging on the matter of brandy.

"But mustn't we look for him, sir? Gladwyn, I mean," Tim blurted. It seemed to him a dreadful crime that the two of them were being saved while Gladwyn was being left.

There ahead of them, not half a mile away, sparkled the lights of the steamer *Rocky Mount*. It was by far the most welcome sight Tim had seen in his life. And yet no effort was being made to assist Gladwyn back to the warm haven of the boat.

"Gad, what became of the man?" Lord Berrybender wondered. "He *was* there, of course. We both rather clung to the buffalo — it was warm for a bit, before it died."

He looked behind him for a moment, as if a glimpse of the prairie where he and Tim had almost frozen might refresh his memory; then it came back to him!

"Why yes, I remember now," he said. "It was rather discouragingly cold. Then Gladwyn stood up and said he had someplace to go. Someplace to go. And off he marched."

"Where could he have had to go?" Maelgwyn asked. "There was no place to go."

"Yes, that's rather a puzzle," Lord Berrybender replied. "A good man in his way, Gladwyn. Never broke a cork, in all the years I had him. But up he stood. Said he had someplace to go and that he might be some time. So off he went. Unusual man. Never quite knew what made Gladwyn tick. Greatly skilled with the claret, though — greatly skilled. Not a cork broken, not one."

55

"Sons of Madoc, habeas corpus, kitchen maids in love with valets . . ."

Tintamarre's barking brought Tasmin out of a sound sleep, though it was scarcely dawn. The window in her stateroom was quite frosted over. Tintamarre had taken to sleeping in a corner by the galley, with the Charbonneaus. Now he was barking furiously.

When Tasmin opened her door she was greeted by air so cold that she was reluctant to go out, but when she did skip to the rail, just for a moment, to investigate the commotion, she saw, with an immediate deep flush, her husband, Jim Snow, attempting to boost her wobbly father high enough that the *engagés* could grasp him and pull him aboard. Not only was her father alive, but so was Tim, being assisted up the ladder by a small man in buckskins.

All sense of cold vanished: Tasmin knew her husband had come for her, just as she had hoped he would, and by some miracle, he had even saved her father. Without even waiting to put on her slippers, which she could never find when she was in a hurry, Tasmin raced downstairs.

Jim Snow had only just stepped on board, among the Charbonneaus, Cook, Captain Aitken, and the *engagés,* when Tasmin flung herself into his arms. To his extreme embarrassment she kissed him hard on the mouth — Jim quickly pushed her away and reached down to lift the shivering Tim into the boat. He gave Tasmin only a furious glance, a look that confused her. After such a long absence, was she not to be ardent? For a moment she felt on the verge of tears, so disappointed was she, but the small man in buckskins who had come aboard with Jim spoke to her in a kindly fashion.

"You'd be the wife, I expect," he said. "I'm Maelgwyn Evans."

"I'm the wife — not much wanted, I guess," Tasmin said.

"Ah, it's just his shyness," Maelgwyn said. "Bashful Jim is what we always called him."

Tasmin passed rapidly from hurt to indignation. Jim had turned away; he was helping her father hobble on to his stateroom.

"You are always too forward, Tassie," the wakeful Mary said. "Your Mr. Snow was in no mood for such a brazen display."

"Shut up, I was just glad to see him," Tasmin said.

Before she could even follow her husband a great cry went up from the kitchen. Eliza, Cook's buxom assistant, the one who was always breaking plates, came sobbing out of the galley and attempted to fling herself over the rail into the icy Missouri. Only quick action on the part of Maelgwyn Evans kept Eliza from fulfilling this desperate design. Maelgwyn caught a foot, just as Eliza was going over the rail — George Catlin, disheveled and confused, stumbled over and helped the small fellow pull the sobbing scullery maid back on board. The Hairy Horn, who, during the night, had concluded that his death song had been premature, was smoking his pipe as if nothing untoward was happening at all.

"What can it mean? Is the girl insane?" George Catlin asked.

"Not at all," Mary said. "Eliza was merely in love with Gladwyn, who is now lost and presumed frozen."

"But perhaps he *isn't* frozen," the rattled painter said. "It is very wrong to jump to conclusions where life and death are concerned. *Habeas corpus,* you know."

"If you don't shut up I'll certainly punch you," Tasmin told him. "I'm in no mood for pomposity just now."

"I'll go look for Mr. Gladwyn — he might be a countryman of mine," Maelgwyn said. "There's not too many of us Welsh, in this wild region."

"Many! I'm surprised there are any," George said.

"Oh yes, we were once quite a group — came over to seek the sons of Madoc, you know. There's a lost tribe here somewhere, but we can't seem to find it. We're rather dispersed now — I rarely see a Welshman. I'd be glad for a talk with this Gladwyn, if he ain't frozen to death. Always curious about my countrymen."

"Sons of Madoc, *habeas corpus,* kitchen maids in love with valets, old chieftains singing their death songs and then not dying . . . I'll soon be insane myself if I have to listen to much more of this talk," Tasmin informed them. She stared hard at the Hairy Horn, who had just accepted a large saucer of porridge from Cook, who went on cooking no matter what the frenzy.

"Don't frown so at the Hairy Horn, Tasmin," Mary pleaded.

"But *wasn't* it a death song he was howling last night?"

"It seems he was merely practicing," Mary replied. "His death is now postponed until the summer."

Just as she spoke there was a fluttering of feathers and a green bird landed on the railing. "*Schweig, du blöder Trottel!*" Prince Talleyrand remarked.

"If only Mademoiselle were here to welcome him," Mary said.

56

At this Tim began to blubber loudly.

"Damnable method! . . . damnable!" Lord Berrybender insisted loudly, between howls of pain. Jim Snow and Toussaint Charbonneau had cut his clothes off and were vigorously rubbing snow on his frostbitten limbs, while Captain Aitken and Maelgwyn Evans did the same for Tim, who yelled even more loudly than Lord B.

"Yes sir, but it's the *only* method that gives frozen flesh a chance," Captain Aitken reminded him, as he went firmly on with his rubbing. Careful attention had to be paid to even the smallest patch of frostbite: cheeks, ears, hands, feet, groin, toes all had to be checked.

"You *would* go ashore despite the chill, sir," Captain Aitken reminded His Lordship, whose groin area presented a particularly ticklish problem due to an evident leakage of urine, which had of course frozen hard on the noble lord's legs.

"Of course I went ashore, why not? Killed forty buffalo, too — only proper sport I've had on this wretched expedition," Lord B. insisted. "*Somebody* ought to be fetching those expensive guns instead of harassing me with this damned snow."

Then he howled more loudly as Charbonneau

began to address his yellowish legs.

Tasmin, Bobbety, Buffum, Mary, and Venetia Kennet all watched the proceedings impassively, from a corner of the stateroom.

"I had not expected to look on my own father's nakedness, not in this year of our Lord 1832," Buffum intoned, in her new nun's voice.

"Leave, then — who asked you to stay?" Tasmin said.

"Father *is* rather a horror," Bobbety said. "Very foolish of him to piss himself. If I am ever faced with an extreme of cold I will endeavor to empty my bladder immediately."

"Good for you," Tasmin said, painfully aware that her husband had scarcely glanced her way; he concentrated on rubbing snow on her father's cheeks and hands. Though she maintained an icy demeanor, inwardly Tasmin seethed. It was all very well to attempt to save her father's few remaining appendages, and the stable boy's too; but Jim *could* have spared her a look, even a smile — only he hadn't.

Venetia Kennet stared straight ahead — she meant to maintain her station as Lord Berrybender's loyal wife-to-be, but she didn't feel she had to follow the hospital work too closely. Her stomach, in fact, did not feel entirely settled; like Tasmin she was experiencing some queasiness in the mornings. She declined to look directly at Lord Berrybender's body, but it did occur to her to wonder whether he would be in possession of any toes and fingers at all, by the time she managed to coax him to the altar, an ambition she had by no means abandoned, despite the steady diminishment of appendages. Captain Aitken did not appear to be overly optimistic, when it came to fingers and toes.

"I expect the boy will lose two fingers, perhaps three, and about as many toes," he said. "There is also some doubt about his right ear."

At this Tim began to blubber loudly.

"Oh, don't let them saw on me, Bess — I can't endure it."

"Now, Tim, Captain Aitken must do as he thinks best," Buffum said, in cool tones.

"I fear His Lordship will lose two toes on his good foot — the leg itself is worrisome, for that matter," Charbonneau said.

"No, the leg is lost — the quicker we take it off, the better," Jim said flatly. This opinion shocked Vicky Kennet and so outraged Lord Berrybender that he immediately struggled off the bed.

"Nonsense, you shan't have my leg — be damned if I'll surrender my leg!" he said. "Who are you anyway, you young fool?"

"He's your son-in-law, Father — my husband, Jim Snow," Tasmin said.

"What? Son-in-law — and he wants to take off my leg, which is a perfectly good leg . . . perhaps rather numbed at the moment but a very adequate leg . . . carried me faithfully on many hunts," Lord B. protested. "The damn young butcher, why would he want to take my leg?"

"Because it's frozen," Charbonneau said, as matter-of-fact about the matter as Jim had been. "Apt to go putrid on you when it thaws. Last thing you'd want is a black leg — that'll kill you pretty quick."

"Get out, all of you! Take that blubbering stable boy and go!" Lord Berrybender demanded. "My Vicky can manage a touch of frostbite well enough . . . fortunately not squeamish, my Vicky. Nothing wrong with me that a fast bout with Vicky won't fix."

"Sir, vigorous rubbing is your best chance," Captain Aitken pointed out. "It won't save your toes but it just might save your leg."

"Vicky can rub me, then," Lord Berrybender insisted. "None better than my Vicky when it comes to rubbing."

"I do so dislike the word 'putrid,' " Vicky Kennet said in a somewhat strangled voice; suddenly her vision began to wobble. Lord Berrybender was ordering everybody out. There he sat, almost naked, his leg possibly putrid. The thought of a putrid appendage caused Vicky's queasiness to increase. She seemed to see the people in the room through an ever narrowing circle. Narrower and narrower the circle got until finally she could only see Lady Berrybender's old parrot, perched on the headboard of the bed where Lord Berrybender had received his rubbing. The circle shrunk to a pinpoint and then there was blackness, deep restful blackness.

"Quick, Jim, catch her . . . Vicky's fainting," Tasmin said.

Jim Snow spun and caught the collapsing cellist in his arms — in a moment he had deposited her on the bed from which the old lord had just risen. Lord Berrybender was far from pleased by this event. He didn't like seeing his Vicky in the arms of a young peasant, even if she was fainting. This same young peasant had somehow married his daughter, cream of the Berrybenders — and, were that not enough, the young upstart advised cutting off his leg. All in all it was too much — how inconvenient of Vicky to choose such a moment to faint.

"Mary, quick, run to Cook — the smelling salts!" Lord Berrybender commanded. "Why must this damn woman faint, just when I need her to be rubbing my leg?"

He stumbled back to the bed and began to slap Venetia Kennet's face — light slaps, to be sure.

"Wake up, Vicky . . . that's enough now . . . important job to do . . . no fudging, my girl," Lord B. said. "Get out, the rest of you."

One by one the company obeyed: Tim, still blubbering, Buffum, Bobbety, Captain Aitken, Maelgwyn, Charbonneau.

"Stop that, Father — Vicky's worn-out from worry," Tasmin said — her father was still fitfully swatting the unconscious girl. "Be generous for once. Allow her a little nap."

"None of your business what I allow her," Lord B. responded. "It's all your fault anyway, you disobedient wench."

Jim Snow whirled, grabbed Lord Berrybender by the shoulders, and shoved him so hard that he reeled across the room, smacked hard against the wall, and sat down. Tasmin saw the flinty look in her husband's eyes.

"You old devil, I ought to cut your stinkin' heart out," Jim said.

Lord Berrybender had not, in many years, received quite such a shock.

"What did the fellow say, Tassie?" Lord B. asked.

"He said he ought to cut your stinking heart out, and I expect he will unless you promptly correct your behavior."

"Cut my heart out — cut my leg off — and you married this butcher?" Lord Berrybender said, in rather subdued tones.

On the bed, Venetia Kennet was just beginning to stir.

"I married him, I'm very glad to say," Tasmin replied. "First man I've met who knows how to treat a selfish old brute such as yourself."

As they passed out the door she shyly took her husband's hand. This time Jim did not shove her away.

57

. . . dresses, hairbrushes, combs, mirrors . . .

"I'll say this, Jimmy — being married to you ain't like anything else," Tasmin said, once she had her husband in her bedroom. "Perhaps that's why I crave you so — I was always the one for novelty.

"I admit that I am somewhat untidy," she added. "But then I've always had a maid to pick up after me, and now I don't."

Tasmin's plan had been to coax Jim immediately into conjugal activity, but in fact the bed where such activity could be best pursued was at the moment a distressing litter: dresses, hairbrushes, combs, mirrors, several novels, slippers, an intimate garment or two, a spyglass, this and that. Jim seemed thunderstruck at the mere sight of so many things — her room, Tasmin realized, was the very opposite of his own spare existence.

Once inside the bedroom, with the door shut, Jim had permitted a kiss, but just as Tasmin was settling into it, hoping even sharper intimacies might follow, Jim pulled away and stationed himself at the window, as if to spy out the approach of enemies. Tasmin was quite vexed.

"Oh, Jimmy . . . why mightn't I kiss you? I've

waited so long!" she protested. "We're quite secure here — no one would dare disturb us."

"You don't know what you're talking about," Jim said. "You never do. What's that funny smell?"

"Oh, it's just Mama's scent — I took it under protection so Mademoiselle wouldn't be tempted to steal it," Tasmin admitted. She had taken to daubing a little on, now and then, to block the various stenches from the river.

"Makes my nose prickle," Jim said. "Can't you wash it off?"

"Good lord," Tasmin said, a bit exasperated. "You said yourself that Indian women anoint themselves with various greases. Why is my mother's scent so much more objectionable? You smell rather greasy yourself, but *I* don't care."

She rushed over and began to try to straighten her bed, or at least reduce the disorder on its surface; then, in her annoyance, she simply swept everything she could reach onto the floor — combs, books, brushes — a happy result of which was the rediscovery of a ruby brooch, once her mother's, that she had also chosen to protect from Mademoiselle Pellenc. She had looked for it for days, and there it was, beneath a small volume of Miss Edgeworth's edifying stories.

Jim Snow watched with frank curiosity, as if he were observing the activities of some new animal whose den he had just discovered. Tasmin felt herself growing distraught — she had never made a bed and found the process more complicated than she would have supposed. In fact she felt like crying because of the general resistance everything — sheets, objects, her husband — seemed to make to her efforts.

"I don't understand it, Jim — why can't you ever like *anything* I do?" she stammered — and then burst into tears. She had waited for this man through many lonely nights — all she craved was his sympathy, a touch, a look. That she couldn't just *have* it seemed too cruel.

Jim Snow was taken aback. He had been mild with Tasmin — why on earth was she crying? The fact was he didn't like being in small, close rooms. Except for his brief stay with Maelgwyn and an hour in Dan Drew's cave, he had not been indoors in several months. It meant adjusting his breathing and his looking: his habit was to study the distant horizons, where the first signs of danger were likely to appear, but the only way to do that, in Tasmin's room, was to stay by the window, which is where he stationed himself. Being on a boat crowded up with people, one of them a dangerous Piegan, made him feel tense, wary. He felt he ought to stay on the alert — and yet there was nothing in his caution that should have made Tasmin cry. He pulled a curtain across the glass and sat down by her on the bed, wiping her tears away with his finger.

"Sometimes it feels so easy, being with you,

Jimmy," Tasmin said. "But other times it feels so hard. I forget what to say. I don't want you to slap me again . . . it's very confusing."

"Now, I just slapped you the once, and that was for talking wrong," Jim said. "You've been flapping your mouth ever since we met, but you haven't talked wrong except that once."

"What did I say? I don't know what talking wrong means," Tasmin said, feeling that the whole thing was hopeless. "Couldn't you just explain yourself, rather than slap me?"

"Ever seen ferrets rut?" he asked. The question took Tasmin by surprise.

"Why no, I haven't, Jim — where would I see ferrets rut, and why would I want to?" she asked.

"You've got that musk smell on you," Jim said. He carefully sniffed the soft flesh of her neck — Tasmin was so surprised that she shivered.

"It's just Mama's scent," she said, hoping it was not going to be a reason for fresh reproaches.

Jim continued to sniff her neck.

"I expect you've been missing our ruts," he said, after a moment.

"I have . . . of course I have," she said, startled that he had put it so baldly. "I *have* been missing our ruts."

She turned to face him, then. The tension that had gripped him when he first came into her room — a kind of caged animal tension — had left him, but another, different kind of animality was in his look.

"Is that why women cry? Because they're missing their ruts?" he asked.

"It's one reason, I suppose," Tasmin said.

"Then hush up crying," Jim said. "We can have us a good long rut, right now."

"Oh, Jimmy, let's do," Tasmin said, blushing deeply at the thought that at last she would get what she craved.

58

"The white people will die like the grasshoppers die in the summer . . ."

White Hawk, the best hunter in the Sans Arc band, was pursuing six wolves when he came upon the small bloody white man. It was very cold — the wolf pelts, if he could take them, would be at their best, deep and soft. Wolves were hard to shoot, it was true, but White Hawk preferred hunting them to trapping beaver — with wolves, for one thing, it was not necessary to get one's feet wet, an important consideration when the cold was so bitter.

White Hawk had come across the wolf tracks only a little after dawn. He was hunting with Three Geese and a boy named Grasshopper. They saw the wolves some distance ahead — they were eating something. The three Sans Arc hunters had provided themselves with wolf skins for just such an eventuality. By pulling the wolf skins over them they might be able to crawl in rifle range, particularly since the wolves were making a meal and not paying too close attention.

On this occasion Three Geese refused to crawl — he was often finicky on a hunt, likely to pout if things weren't done his way.

"Suit yourself, stay with the horses, then," White Hawk said. He was rather fed up with Three Geese — nonetheless he and the boy, Grasshopper, hidden beneath their wolf skins, crawled close enough to the wolves to see that they were eating a just-born buffalo calf. Four of the wolves were skinny, but two of them were nice fat wolves, with excellent pelts. White Hawk had a good musket, supplied by his French friend Monsieur Sacq, but Grasshopper's gun was old and unreliable. The boy had tried to borrow Three Geese's musket, but the touchy warrior wouldn't lend it.

"I had better keep it, some bad people might be coming along," Three Geese said, an excuse that merely exposed what a stingy fellow he was, since no people at all were likely to be coming along, with the cold so bitter along the Knife River.

When they had crawled close enough, White Hawk killed his wolf neatly, but Grasshopper's gun misfired, causing him to say bitter words about Three Geese — he would have liked to have a nice wolf pelt to trade at the Mandan villages in the spring. It was while the boy was spilling out bitter words that the small bloody white man appeared, startling them both. Grasshopper wanted to shoot him at once, but White Hawk waved him off. He was interested in how the small man had got so bloody, a mystery that was soon solved. A dead buffalo cow lay not far away — probably the cow had died giving birth to the calf. The cow buffalo had not been dead very long. It looked as if the small white man had stumbled on the dying cow and had tried to warm himself by trying to squeeze into the place the calf had just come out of, which of course was a sensible thing to do if you had no fire on such a cold night. Finding the split-open cow, a large cow that had kept pumping warm blood, was probably what had saved the little white man.

The small bloody man did not seem hostile — he was very bloody and also very cold. White Hawk had no particular interest in him — he had his wolf to skin — and would have been happy enough just to let the man wander off and freeze; but then Three Geese came racing up and jumped to the wrong conclusion, which was that the buffalo cow had given birth to the small white man, along with the dead calf. It was typical of Three Geese's poor thinking that he could imagine such a thing. Three Geese often leapt to ridiculous conclusions, which he clung to stubbornly, sometimes for years.

Grasshopper, a boy of only fourteen years, became so confused that he didn't know what to believe. This did not surprise White Hawk — Three Geese could be very convincing when he jumped to a wrong conclusion.

"We must take him to the camp," Three Geese insisted. "I think the Bad Eye made a prophecy about this. I think he said that someday a buffalo would give birth to a white man."

"No, that was not the prophecy at all," White Hawk told him — he was working carefully with his skinning knife, so as not to mar his fine wolf pelt. The last thing he wanted was to argue with Three Geese about some old prophecy of the Bad Eye that Three Geese had got all scrambled in his memory.

"What *was* the prophecy, then, if you know so much?" Three Geese asked. Seeing the fine wolf pelt White Hawk had taken made him angry with himself — he should have crawled up and got a nice wolf pelt himself.

Grasshopper built a little fire, thinking they might as well cook a little of the dead buffalo. No sooner did the fire flame than the small white man came and huddled over it, shivering violently.

"What the Bad Eye said was that someday a white buffalo would be born," White Hawk explained, patiently. "When the white buffalo is born it will be a sign for all the tribes to band together and kill all the white people. The white buffalo will bring us all the power we need. The white people will die like the grasshoppers die in the summer, when we set the prairie on fire."

Three Geese refused to accept White Hawk's version of the prophecy, even though he dimly remembered that someone had talked about a white buffalo — it had been idle talk, very likely. He himself had seen millions of buffalo and none of them had been white. Of course, the tribes were always talking about killing all the white people; there were many councils on that subject, but the chiefs could never get together and decide on a time to do it, or a way to do it, either. Personally Three Geese thought there were just too many white people — an old witch of the Brulé band told him once that there was a great hole in the earth where white people swarmed by the millions, like hornets. The old witch woman of the Brulés said that no matter how many white people were killed, more would just come swarming out of the hole. But the old woman had been more or less crazy — most prophets, including the Bad Eye, were more or less crazy in Three Geese's view. Nonetheless he was not prepared to yield to the bossy White Hawk in the matter of this particular white man.

"He wouldn't be that bloody unless he came out of the buffalo," he declared.

Three Geese was so firm on that point that the boy, Grasshopper, began to have doubts himself. Perhaps the white man did come out of the buffalo. Grasshopper didn't know it for sure, but he was anxious not to get on the bad side of Three Geese by disagreeing with his opinion too openly. Three Geese was known to be vengeful — he held grudges against many of the Sans Arc people and other Sioux as well. Grasshopper didn't want Three Geese to get a grudge against him, so he tried to be respectful of his belief about the white man.

"We need to find somebody who can talk to this buffalo man," Three Geese insisted.

"Guillaume or Draga or somebody. We had better take him with us until we know what his story is."

"Oh, all right — leave me alone," White Hawk said.

Three Geese went over to the fire and tried to talk to the little white man in sign, but the white man had not the slightest ability to converse in sign — in Three Geese's opinion this fact alone proved his point. If the white man was at all normal he would know how to talk in sign.

"He must have come straight out of that buffalo," Three Geese insisted. "He cannot even talk in sign."

"All right . . . all right . . . ," White Hawk said. Why argue with a fool? He was not feeling particularly well, and even if he had been feeling better, would have had quite enough of arguing with Three Geese. He finished taking his fine pelt and ate a bite or two of buffalo liver that Grasshopper cooked for him, though his appetite was not strong.

By the time White Hawk and the others, with their small white captive, got back to the Sans Arc lodges, White Hawk had begun to feel hot and weak. He nearly fell when he got off his horse — his wives had to help him to his lodge. That night his fever soared and he began to have strange dreams — he dreamed of a white buffalo, and then of a white man who had buffalo horns coming out of his head. The medicine men came and gave him strong emetics, hoping to force the terrible fever out of him; but the medicine men failed. Gripped by a great illness, White Hawk died before dawn.

Privately Three Geese thought White Hawk died because he had scorned the prophecy about the buffalo man. Grasshopper became very worried; after all, he too had been doubtful of the prophecy. What if the big fever took him too? To give himself the best possible chance he told everybody that he agreed with Three Geese: the white man, still shivering, still bloody, had undoubtedly been born of a buffalo cow.

The women of the tribe cleaned the white man up, gave him some clothes of skins, and fixed him a small lodge, so he wouldn't be cold. They also gave him two twin captive girls, fat ones, just to make sure he stayed warm.

Soon people from other bands — Brulé, Miniconjou, Oglala — trickled into the Sans Arc camp, to hear the story and examine the miraculous being. News of the miracle soon reached Draga, who was very annoyed. She had no aversion to miracles, but if a miracle was needed she wanted to produce it herself, not have it happen in some remote camp of the Sans Arc.

"It's your fault," she informed the Bad Eye bitterly. "You talked about a white buffalo so much that it confused everyone. Now the Sans Arc think they have a Buffalo Man."

The Bad Eye immediately pulled the great cape the Englishman had given him over his head.

"I am going in a trance now," he said. "I'll listen to the spirits — they might know about this."

He didn't really know what to think about the strange news that the Sans Arc had themselves some kind of Buffalo Man, but he did know that when Draga used that deadly tone with him it was just as well to hurry up and get in a trance.

59

Three horsemen on unshod horses had recently passed . . .

Despite the deep cold, Maelgwyn Evans and Toussaint Charbonneau went ashore and dutifully gathered up Lord Berrybender's expensive guns. Then they made a bit of a search for Gladwyn — a search made with not much expectation that they would find the lost valet alive.

"I guess we ought to try and scratch him out some kind of grave, if we find him," Maelgwyn said. "It's a hard way to go, froze in a blizzard like that."

"The wolves may not have left enough to bury," Charbonneau said.

They had gone not more than half a mile from the circle of dead buffalo dropped by Lord Berrybender when they came upon a puzzling scene. Three horsemen on unshod horses had recently passed. There was a dead wolf, newly skinned; a dead buffalo cow, not skinned, but partially butchered; a dead buffalo calf, mostly eaten by wolves; and one of Gladwyn's shoes, covered with frozen blood. The shoe was close by the dead buffalo cow. A few live coals still glowed in the campfire.

"I guess he ain't dead, your Welshman,"

Charbonneau said. "He's just half barefooted."

"And besides that he's taken," Maelgwyn said.

"That beats being dead," Charbonneau replied.

"Maybe . . . it depends on who took him, and what kind of mood they're in," Maelgwyn said. "Some Indians can be pretty mean — he might escape the ice and get the fire."

"That's the chances a fellow takes — this Knife River country ain't for me," Charbonneau said. "It'll cheer up Eliza, though . . . she'll be glad to know that the fellow might be alive."

"Oh, you mean that girl who tried to jump overboard — the one I caught by the foot?" Maelgwyn asked.

"That's the gal, our clumsy Eliza — she's bad about bustin' the crockery," Charbonneau said. "And here we didn't even know she fancied the fellow till overboard she went."

60

"Who says our pleasures are languid?"

Once coaxed to bed, Jim Snow was not stingy with his attentions — Tasmin felt that her wait had been well worth it. They were at their conjugal occupations most of the morning, the satisfactions of which were intense; and yet all their sweet meltings and mergings did not quite reconcile Jim Snow to the closeness of the stateroom, or make him much less wary where possible enemies were concerned. His rifle was propped by the head of the bed, a circumstance that made Tasmin nervous. She was in the mood to let herself go and didn't want to have to be worrying about a rifle.

"What if it falls and goes off, like Papa's did?" she asked. "What if I buck around too wildly and knock it over?"

"Buck all you want — it won't shoot," Jim assured her. It was far too close in the stateroom — their bed was now a swamp of sweat. Jim wanted to open the window, or even the door, but people were always passing along the walkways — with the window open anyone would be sure to hear the sighings and squealings that went with a good long rut. As soon as they satisfied themselves for the day Jim meant to take Tasmin and get off the boat, back into the open air,

343

where he could breathe better; but they were not soon finished.

In one interlude Tasmin made Jim sit up in bed so she could trim his beard again. It was one of her favorite activities as a wife, trimming Jimmy's beard and snipping a vagrant lock or two of his hair.

"Where will we be when I drop our child, as you put it, Jimmy?" she asked.

Jim Snow shrugged. "We'll just be where we are — somewhere on the Yellowstone, probably, unless you're still in the mood to go to Santa Fe — and this ain't the best place to start from, or the best time of year to start."

"I just mean that I hope you'll be with me and not off on one of your rambles," she said. Though she still felt tremors of pleasure in her body, and was for the moment a happy wife, the thought of the child worried her. She did not want to be without him when it came.

"Don't be walking off like that, you hear?" he said, looking her directly in the eye. "I thought you'd soon come back or I would have chased you down."

As for where they would be when the baby came, what could he say? The baby was six months away, and they could all be in bad trouble within six hours, if the Sioux showed up in an ugly mood. Where they were when the baby came was not too important, as long as they were somewhere where game was plentiful.

"Get your warmest clothes and let's go," he

said. "I feel like I'm choking, from being in this close air."

"All right, Jimmy," Tasmin said. "But all this rutting's made me a little weak in the legs — I'm not sure I can tramp very far today."

She began to rake around in her tiny closet for anything that looked warm. Jim watched her pull out garment after garment, amazed at the supply of clothes his wife had. He felt sure he could get through his whole life with fewer clothes than she had just piled on the bed.

Tasmin stuffed a valise, then put on the loose shirt of skins the Oto woman had sewed for her — she was gathering up hairbrushes and combs and a book or two when there was a knock on the door. Jim immediately took his gun, but Tasmin peeked out the window and saw that it was only her sister Mary.

"It's only our brat," she said — "might as well let her in."

Mary, once in the room, stopped and sniffed.

"I smell lubricious secretions," she said; the look in her eye, as usual, was not entirely sane.

"What of it? — there are very likely to be such odors when husbands and wives have been about their natural work," Tasmin said.

Jim Snow had never seen anyone quite like this little English girl who used strange long words; he recalled that when he first saw her she seemed to be talking to a serpent — a white-mouthed moccasin, in fact.

"We have all been waiting patiently for you

and Mr. Snow to finish fornicating — a number of crises need attention," Mary said. "Are you through yet?"

"For the moment," Tasmin said. "Jim wishes to leave the boat — he finds the air rather close. What's this about crises?"

"Well, there's Father's amputation," Mary said. "He still opposes it but medical opinion is that the limb will soon rot. And then there's the ice — we're stuck fast now. Captain Aitken was very much hoping Mr. Snow would visit him on the bridge before he departs. You can come too, Tasmin."

"Of course I can come," Tasmin said. "I hope I don't need you to invite me."

"Fortunately Monsieur Charbonneau and Mr. Evans have found all Papa's guns," Mary said. "Papa was much reassured."

"What about that third man — did they find him?" Jim inquired.

"No, Gladwyn they did not find — merely one shoe, rather bloodstained."

"How odd," Tasmin said. "The rest of Gladwyn must be somewhere."

"Abducted by red savages of the Sans Arc band, that is the theory," Mary said. "Unfortunately the Piegan, Blue Thunder, left this morning, while you two were about your languid pleasures."

Tasmin gave her a thump on the head.

"Watch your tongue," she said. "Who says our pleasures are languid?"

"That's two out of three of Charbonneau's Indians gone," Jim observed.

"Yes, Monsieur Charbonneau is very upset — the Piegan disappeared while they were looking for the guns — Monsieur feels the failure keenly," Mary said.

61

"It's win all, lose all, in this game, Sharbo . . ."

Captain George Aitken, not entirely sober, had to face the fact of defeat. Upriver there was no longer an open flow: the ice had come. Already several buffalo were sniffing around where, only the day before, there had been rushing water. With the Yellowstone still more than one hundred miles away, the captain had to admit that the race had been lost, and the boat might be too, unless he was lucky. He knew that no excuse available to him — sandbars, mud banks, broken paddles, ice that formed earlier than had been expected — would move his employers to tolerance. Sandbars and ice were merely words to them; they had never stood where he stood, looking at the unforgiving line of cloud and a few cautious buffalo, already testing their icy bridge over the Missouri. All his employers would consider was the fact that the steamer *Rocky Mount* had not got where it was supposed to deliver its expensive human cargo. The failure would be reckoned his fault — indeed, he reckoned it so himself, although, tracing his way back day by day, he could not fault any of his hour-to-hour decisions.

"It's win all, lose all, in this game, Sharbo," he

said. "Win all, lose all. And we ain't winning."

Toussaint Charbonneau, upon discovering that the third of his charges — Blue Thunder, of the Piegan Blackfoot — had left the boat and vanished, immediately took to his cups. He felt himself beaten. Only the Hairy Horn, the one Indian he would have been glad to lose, remained on — indeed, could not be persuaded to leave — the boat. Captain William Clark was not going to like it.

Only two weeks before, steaming past two villages of the Omahas, Charbonneau had awakened in the dawn, stirred, as he always was on that stretch of the river, by the memory of his Bird, Sacagawea. There, on the shore, were the remains of the fur king Manuel Lisa's old fort, now fallen badly out of repair. It was in that same fort, twenty years before, that Sacagawea had been seized by a putrid fever; she had died just at dusk and had been buried that same night, outside the fort, as a precaution against the spread of the fever. Charbonneau could never float past her grave, as he had several times, without heaving a sigh and shedding a tear. He had been far from alone in mourning his Bird Woman. All the rough trappers vied to carry her to her grave; all acknowledged that she had been the finest woman in the fort. Even Manuel Lisa, who had seen more death on the Missouri River than any other man, came out of his quarters and stood in silence by Sacagawea's grave.

Every time he passed the spot where she lay it seemed to Charbonneau that Janey — as Captain Clark had called her — stretched out a hand to him, as if asking him to join her in easeful sleep — yet, somehow, his stubborn body kept living, despite many ills and discontents.

Now here he was, stuck in the ice north of the Knife River, more than a week's hard march from adequate shelter, with a bunch of English he didn't much like, having lost two of the three Indians that had been specifically entrusted to his care by Captain Clark. They were important Indians, honored guests of the nation, and losing them was no small thing — if the Piegan happened to get killed, as Big White had, it would surely affect relations with the Blackfeet, and relations with the Blackfeet were never easy. It seemed to Charbonneau that he could have managed better if only his Bird had lived. Coal was a fine healthy girl, but only a child, really. It was not to be expected that she could manage things as well as Sacagawea, who, after all, had carried their boy, little Pomp, all the way from the Mandan villages to the Western ocean and back, on their great trek with the captains, while managing to keep himself in good order and half the company besides.

When Tasmin and Jim, led by Mary and trailed by George Catlin, went up to the bridge they found that neither Captain Aitken nor Toussaint Charbonneau were in particularly good repair.

"We're stuck, Jimmy — stuck," Captain Aitken said. "I was too slow about the river, and now we're stuck."

He looked at Jim Snow and Lady Tasmin, blooming and blushing as if they had just awakened from a fine wedding night — the sight made George Aitken feel old.

"Why is that so bad, Captain?" Tasmin asked. "You have a snug boat, and there seem to be plenty of buffalo around, in case we run low on vittles. We brought lots of ice skates — our brats can go ice-skating now and then."

George Aitken scarcely knew how to reply. Lady Tasmin was in a state of high health and happiness — she had no inkling of the perils that awaited them in the frigid months ahead. Jim Snow, her young mate, seemed to offer altogether the best hope. If Jim would agree to guide a land party over to the Yellowstone they might get through the winter without much loss. There was a wagon and a buggy in the hold, and four horses. If they could only get a little break in the weather, a few days of warming, the situation might yet be saved.

Captain Aitken was about to ask Jimmy Snow to help them when pandemonium suddenly broke loose on the lower deck. There was a gunshot — then another gunshot. Then came a chorus of high screams, merging with low French curses and exclamations of despair from the *engagés*. Those on the bridge rushed to the rail and were astonished to see several *engagés*, evidently wild with terror, piling into one of the pirogues, which of course was immovably stuck in the ice.

"Quick, Sharbo, go see!" Captain Aitken ordered. "Is the Hairy Horn running amok?"

"Not the Hairy Horn — it's our papa, I expect," Mary said, darting fleetly down the stairs.

Charbonneau tried to follow, but got his feet tangled up and fell flat on his face.

"Get up, Sharbo, this won't do," the captain said, though he was none too steady himself.

"Very likely it *is* only Papa — he's always more or less amok," Tasmin said. "I think that's Vicky Kennet screaming — there's no telling what outrage the selfish old brute has committed."

"He must be shooting at the Frenchies . . . they all look pretty scared," Jim said.

"Perhaps Father Geoff could speak to him — priests are supposed to soothe unruly souls," George Catlin suggested.

"You're an optimist, George," Tasmin said. "Our fine priest is probably hiding under a bed — either that or he's in Mademoiselle's room, reading indecent literature.

"I expect you think we're all crazy, we English, don't you, Jim?" she asked, looking shyly at her husband. "These alarums are merely the stuff of day-to-day life, when the Berrybenders are assembled."

"We ought to be getting ashore," Jim said politely.

Tasmin was right — he *did* think the English were more or less crazy. His own main desire was simply to get away with Tasmin, to the emptiness and peace of the country, where it was easier to breathe and even easier to think.

"Ha, the great theft is revealed," Mary said, popping back up the stairs. "It's the claret. Papa sent Vicky to fetch him a bottle from the keelboat, whereupon it was discovered that there is no more claret. The *engagés* drank it all, every bottle."

"All? A thousand bottles?" Tasmin asked.

"All," Mary repeated.

"But why is Vicky screaming so, she's not an *engagé?*" Tasmin asked.

"No, but she's being blamed," Mary said. "Papa's chasing her with a horsewhip."

"I wouldn't mind if we left now, myself," Tasmin said. Jimmy had taken her hand, which she liked very much. Once again she felt like a wife, wanted. She did not intend to make the mistake of leaving her husband again.

"But Jim, we've the amputation to do, when His Lordship quiets down — and then we'll be needing a guide, to get this bunch to the fort," Captain Aitken pleaded.

Jim looked at Tasmin — it was mainly her family involved. George Aitken was in a bad spot — it would be hard to deny him a little help.

"Drat! Not for a minute of my life has Papa managed to do the convenient thing," Tasmin said. "What should we do, Jimmy?"

She gave his hand a squeeze, and to her delight he squeezed back.

"He's your pa, and he'll die if we don't get that leg off," Jim said. "I guess we better sharpen the saw."

62

Draga had brought some poison with her . . .

When the dark woman, Draga, came to the Sans Arc camp to attempt to discredit him and have him put to death, Gladwyn confounded her by speaking in Gaelic. In the whole time that he had been captive not a word of English had passed his lips; if the people thought he was just an ordinary Englishman, they would probably kill him.

In fact he knew little enough Gaelic — just a few songs and scraps of legend and rhyme, but to the Sans Arc it sounded like the babble of a Buffalo Man; it was enough to save him.

There were, unfortunately, a number of skeptics in the Sans Arc camp, older people mostly, who didn't believe for a minute that this skinny stranger had been born of a buffalo. But the Gaelic at least made them uncertain — no one had ever heard such strange speech. Three Geese, Gladwyn's main sponsor, considered the fact that the stranger spoke an unearthly language proof enough of his extraordinary origin.

"You see?" Three Geese said. "He is not speaking white man's language. That's buffalo he's speaking."

Old Cat Head, the most flagrant of the skeptics, was not convinced.

"I have never heard a buffalo speak like that," he pointed out. "I have never heard a buffalo say anything."

Cat Head didn't want to yield any ground to Three Geese, who had been much too full of himself since he brought the small white man to the village; but even *he* was rather startled by the strange language the white man babbled. At first Cat Head would have been happy just to hit the white man in the head with a good hatchet, but the strange babble caused him to waver. Even if the white man hadn't come out of the womb of a buffalo, he was still a peculiar man. Cat Head thought he might be some kind of holy fool — there was no point in acting rashly. Killing a holy fool could bring all sorts of calamities down on the people.

Draga did not welcome the presence of this Buffalo Man in the Sans Arc village. She knew he had come from the white men's big boat — the Thunder Boat, the Bad Eye called it — and she told the people as much, but to her annoyance, she was greeted with insults and sneers. The Sans Arc had always been independent and aloof. They scorned corn growers such as the Mandans; they were people of the buffalo and did not consider themselves subject to Draga's wishes, or the Bad Eye's either. Draga had brought some poison with her but the Sans Arc were not about to let her poison their holy fool. They never let her near the little man, lest she stab him or try to interfere with his food.

Draga had not expected to have much luck with the Sans Arc — like all the Sioux bands, they were difficult; but she had made the trip to the camp anyway, in order to bring the Bad Eye a report. Now that he was too fat to move around much he had begun to worry about messiahs and other prophets. It made him anxious to think that there was a Buffalo Man of some sort living with the standoffish Sans Arc. Any little threat caused him to build a new sweat lodge or go into a big trance. In two minutes Draga could easily have beaten the little white man to death with a stone, or even a big stick — but the Sans Arc maintained a good guard, so good that she was forced to go back to the skull lodge and report complete failure.

"A Sans Arc named Three Geese started all this," she said. "And that's not all."

"What else?" the Bad Eye asked. He hated bad news.

"They have given the white man two wives," she said.

"Is that all?" the Bad Eye asked. "Why should I care how many wives they give him?"

"These wives are twins," Draga continued. "They are called Big Stealer and Little Stealer, although they are the same size."

"Why are you bringing me all this terrible news?" the Bad Eye exclaimed. That the Buffalo Man should be married to twins was the worst possible news. Twins always had formidable powers — twins married to a Buffalo Man could lead to any number of calamities: wars, pestilence, flood. The old women were already talking about the likelihood of a great flood in the spring; there was too much snow upriver, they had heard. A terrible flood might even threaten the skull lodge — the Bad Eye might have to move himself to higher ground, which would be a lot of trouble.

"Maybe this Buffalo Man will just get sick and die, twins or no twins," he said.

"We won't be rid of him that easily," Draga said darkly.

Gladwyn was not quite sure what kind of special person he was supposed to be, but it was clear that the people who had taken him were determined to treat him well. They made him a warm tent and fed him tender buffalo liver and their fattest puppies. His bloody clothes were taken away and a suit of soft, warm skins was fashioned for him. He was not required to do any work at all. The most they required of him was that he come and sit outside his tent, by the campfire, when visitors came to see him. The boy Grasshopper was given a lance and made to stand guard so that no one could threaten him or get too close. He was always guarded; Three Geese saw to that. It was no secret that the Brulés and the Miniconjous were jealous of the fact that the Sans Arc had a Buffalo Man. There was danger that some envious warrior might just walk up and stab him out of pique. Grasshopper was told to lance anyone who made a suspicious move.

All Gladwyn had meant to do, when he stumbled away from Lord Berrybender in the terrible blizzard, was die somewhere out of range of the old man's hated voice. Lord Berrybender continued to give him orders even as they were freezing, orders about guns, orders about firewood. Gladwyn, His Lordship's man for many years, decided to die as his own man. He was about to curl up and let the blowing snow cover him forever when he had the great luck to stumble on to the buffalo cow just as she was laboring to get her calf out. Something had gone wrong in the birthing; the calf wouldn't quite come free, and when it finally did, with Gladwyn pulling and tugging at the warm calf, the cow's lifeblood came too, only slowly — so slowly that Gladwyn was able to use her warmth to keep alive. She was still alive when the six wolves came and began to eat her calf, though she died and was growing cold when the Indians came.

At first, when he was not sure what his captors meant to do with him, Gladwyn gave some thought to escape — but his half-formed plans were soon abandoned. He would probably just get lost and freeze after all, and even if he were very lucky and managed to get back to the boat, what would it gain him? He would once again be merely Lord Berrybender's man. When the theft of the claret was discovered, very likely he would be the one blamed.

Once in a while he did miss Eliza, Cook's fumble-fingered assistant, who readily offered her ample body to his embraces; but once the Sans Arc presented him with twin wives even Eliza soon faded from memory. It was true that the twins, Big Stealer and Little Stealer, bickered constantly, and sometimes grew so hot that they came to blows — but that was only to be expected of sisters. Him they never neglected. When he wasn't on show for envious visitors he lounged in his tent, naked amid warm robes. His efficient wives rubbed him with oils, attended quickly to his lusts, and even fed him with their fingers — tender morsels from the stew pot.

Gladwyn had no way of knowing how long his comfortable celebrity would last, but he didn't trouble himself by looking ahead. His lodge was warm, his wives competent, the prairies thick with buffalo. The tribe gave him a pipe and ample tobacco; his wives kept his pipe filled; Gladwyn smoked and rested. Blizzards blew, snow fell, geese probed in the Mandan corn, wolves howled, the hunting birds — eagle, hawk, owl — hung in the white sky or came dropping down on sage hen, quail, hare, or the incautious rat; the great bears slept in their dens, buffalo pawed the snow and grazed, while the Sans Arc hunters made many kills; slowly, in this way, the winter passed.